The Pricker Boy

The Pricker Boy

Reade Scott Whinnem

RANDOM HOUSE NEW YORK

Text copyright © 2009 by Reade Scott Whinnem
Jacket art copyright © 2009 by August Hall

All rights reserved. Published in the United States by Random House Children's
Books, a division of Random House, Inc., New York.

Random House and the colophon are registered trademarks of Random House, Inc.

Visit us on the Web! www.randomhouse.com/teens

Educators and librarians, for a variety of teaching tools, visit us at
www.randomhouse.com/teachers

Library of Congress Cataloging-in-Publication Data
Whinnem, Reade Scott.
The pricker boy / Reade Scott Whinnem. — 1st ed.
p. cm.
Summary: After finding a mysterious package in the spooky woods where they
have grown up, fourteen-year-old Stucks Cumberland and his friends are forced
to consider that their childhood bogeyman might be all too real.
ISBN 978-0-375-85719-5 (trade) — ISBN 978-0-375-95719-2 (lib. bdg.) —
ISBN 978-0-375-89299-8 (e-book)
[1. Emotional problems—Fiction. 2. Guilt—Fiction. 3. Interpersonal relations—
Fiction. 4. Forests and forestry—Fiction. 5. Horror stories.] I. Title.
PZ7.W57655Pr 2009
[Fic]—dc22
2008049340

Printed in the United States of America
10 9 8 7 6 5 4 3 2 1
First Edition

For all the lake kids,
wherever they may be

Contents

The Pricker Boy

1

Waking at Whale's Jaw

our years ago I was abandoned in the Metropolitan Museum of Art in New York City.

I have nightmares about a lot of things, but the scariest nightmares I have are about that day as a ten-year-old kid left alone in New York City. I relive those forty-five minutes in my sleep, except that in the dream version someone walks up to me and promises to help. It's always a friendly-looking stranger—sometimes a security guard, and sometimes an old woman with a grandmotherly face. The person takes me out of the museum and puts me in a car. We're miles away before it begins to dawn on me that this person is not who they said they were. It comes upon me the way things do in dreams, the way you just know that something has turned, something has gone wrong, something has never been right, only you couldn't see it at first.

The next thing I know it's nighttime, and the streets outside the car look like a war has just ended, like those black-and-white pictures of Germany near the end of World War II. Sometimes there are bodies in the streets, bodies of children, and other times those children are alive, but they have no parents or families or anyplace to call home. I beg the person to take me home, but they just smile and tell me that I don't deserve to go home. I don't deserve to ever go home again.

And there's truth to those nightmares—a little truth anyway. Anyone could have walked up to me, smiled gently, and offered me help. I would have been so relieved that I would have poured myself into their waiting hand. Anyone who looked even a little trustworthy could have led me anywhere.

It may seem obvious to you that I should've just found a security guard or a clerk and said that I was lost. It's obvious to me now, but it wasn't then. Back then I was too scared to do anything.

My best friend, Pete Morgan, was on that field trip too. We'd worked together on a science project and earned the highest grade of anyone in the entire fourth grade. That got us two seats on the field trip usually reserved just for the fifth graders.

There was only one thing at the Met that I wanted to see—the Arms and Armor exhibit. Just thinking about suits of armor gave me the chills. It still does today. It's something about the way they're frozen in place. Once there was a living man inside moving around and swinging his ax and making all that metal rise to violent life. When you get close to something like that, you get to thinking that just maybe there could be a man still hiding in there after all this time. Or maybe just his ghost. Maybe he can still move, and he's just waiting for the right moment to swing that giant battle-ax down through the protective glass case. Maybe while you're standing right there in front of it. Kinda thrilling, if you ask me.

That exhibit's all I talked about the whole two-hour bus ride down to the city. It felt so sweet to be away in New York City while all our friends were stuck back in school.

Around noon we gathered outside the museum to eat our brown-bag lunches, and afterward we had some time to go to the gift shop. I wandered to the back, and I guess I wasn't paying attention to the time. I didn't see anyone come to look for me, though Pete said that he did. When the parent chaperone counted heads, she got it wrong, and everyone took off. I was left alone looking at a book filled with pictures of swords and daggers and shining armor.

About ten minutes went by before I realized something was wrong. I walked all around the store but couldn't find a single person that I recognized. For a moment I thought it was some kind of joke. I thought they might be hiding from me to teach me a lesson. I rushed around the store as if I were playing a desperate game of hide-and-seek. Then I realized that I was alone, and that I was a long way from home. The one thing that I remember most clearly is panic.

It felt like someone had poured boiling water into my heart. I had no idea, no idea at all, what to do.

I was afraid that if I left the store, I might get lost forever, might never even be able to find my way back to the gift shop. I walked to the doorway and looked out into the Met's great marble hall, but I didn't see a familiar face anywhere.

The group finally came back. Our chaperone realized at some point that I wasn't there, and she turned the entire group of kids around. I was still standing in the gift-shop doorway when I saw Janis Terkle, a fifth grader everyone called Turtle because her neck was so short, coming toward me. When I saw her face, I didn't care how short her neck was, and I never made fun of her again after that day. That first recognized face meant that someone would lead me out of there, put me on a bus, and take me on the long ride home. That recognized face meant that I would see my mom and dad and little brother and grandmother and our house by the pond again. They had all been gone for those forty-five minutes. They had been gone for good.

I could tell that the other kids were ticked off. One of them barked at me for screwing up the whole afternoon. In the chaperone's voice I could hear relief salted with anger, but I couldn't hear her words exactly because I burst out crying. I didn't want the fifth graders to see me doing it, but I couldn't help myself.

I didn't get to see the Arms and Armor exhibit, and neither did the other kids. The teachers cut the afternoon short because of me. Some of the fifth-grade guys tossed me a sarcastic "Thanks, Stucks," or "Good going, Stucks," as they filed onto the bus.

On the whole ride back, Pete stayed right by my side. The chaperones made me sit up at the front of the bus, and Pete could've gone back there with the older kids, but he didn't. I wasn't saying much of anything, but he kept talking to me about the woods and fishing and all our friends coming back to their cottages for the summer. At one point I turned around and saw one of the older kids laughing and pretending to wipe tears away from his eyes. His name was Manny Fields. Pete saw Manny too. The next thing I knew, Pete was up and out of his seat and back the whole length of the bus and on top of Manny, driving fist after fist into his face, and then when Manny fell over, into the back of his head and between his shoulder blades. Pete broke Manny's nose and one of his own fingers. There was blood all over that seat in the back, and those older kids had to sit and look at Manny's blood the whole ride home.

Pete was suspended for the rest of the school year, but it didn't matter so much. It was late spring and school was about to get out anyway, and because I'd helped Pete with his work, his grades were high enough for him to pass for the year.

A few days later one of the fifth graders told me that Pete had given our chaperone the thumbs-up when she did her head count, even though he knew I was still inside the gift shop. Kenny Fortner told me. Kenny was a pretty good kid, and even though he was good friends with Manny, he wasn't the kind of kid who would lie.

Word got round quickly about how I cried. The other kids were pretty amused by it all, and I heard their laughing at lunch and in gym class and during quiet time when we were all supposed to be reading.

I don't like people laughing at me. Not for crying or anything else.

So that's when I decided to stop.

And I did. I never cry. It's been four years, and I haven't cried since. I won't cry, despite all the things that have happened lately, despite all the things that are going on right now. And there's nothing you could ever do to me, nothing you could ever say or show me or tell me that would make me let you see me cry.

Nothing. Try it. Try it right now. You'll see.

I'm dreaming about the Met as I wake up in the dirt, curled around the stones of the fire pit. I've walked in my sleep again. It's almost dawn, and I'm all the way across the dirt road, into the woods, and up by the fifteen-foot-high split granite boulder that we all call Whale's Jaw. When I wake up, Boris is there—faithful Boris, old Boris, who always seems to have one more summer left in him. He's growling.

I'm used to waking up in the yard. Even though I close my eyes in my room, I often open them in the bushes or down by the edge of the pond. Nine times out of ten, Boris is snoring next to me, his back pressed up against mine.

What I'm not used to is finding myself out in the woods, and I'm not used to Boris growling. His tail is straight, and his eyes are locked on the path that leads up to the stone wall about two dozen yards away at the top of the hill. I instinctively want to get up on the back of Whale's Jaw. It's always been home base for any game we ever played as kids, and that means it's safe. But I stick with Boris. I scratch his back and ask him what's wrong. I ask him what he smells. I try to calm him, but my nightmare of the city hasn't completely faded, and I just want to give in to my superstitions and climb the back of that rock as fast as I can.

Something small hits last summer's hard ashes in the middle of the fire pit. Something else, tiny and hard, hits the back of my skull. I look up just as Pete lobs a third pebble down from Whale's Jaw. It hits me just above my right eye.

"Oh man!" he laughs. "I'm sorry, dude! I didn't expect you to turn around." I can see by his eyes that he's been up all night. He looks like cigarette smoke and stale sleep.

I rub the spot where the pebble hit. "What's going on?" I ask him.

He laughs at me and shakes his head. "I saw you sleeping and figured I'd wake you up."

"What's up with Boris?" I ask. I stroke the dog between the ears. His growl rolls around in his belly. The hair on his back bristles.

"How the hell should I know?" Pete says. From the top of Whale's Jaw, it looks like you're perched on the snout of a breaching whale, and you get a decent view of the woods.

Pete stands and looks up the path that leads to the stone wall. "I don't see anything," Pete says. He tosses a pebble down at Boris. "Go get 'em, fleabag. Go up there and roust 'em out!"

Boris doesn't even look at Pete. "What is it, Boris?" I ask. Boris looks up at me, flaps his tail, and whines softly.

"Crazy dog," Pete declares. "What do you smell, crazy dog?"

Whatever is up the path, it's concealed in the thorns and brush just past the stone wall at the crest of the hill. Boris can smell it, and he doesn't like what he smells. I have seen him chase after just about everything. He'll gallop happily after a squirrel or rabbit, or romp fearless and stupid after a skunk. Boris isn't smart enough to be scared of any living thing that I know of, but something up the path is scaring him now.

"Probably just a chipmunk," Pete says. "That dog's a stink bomb, and he's dumb as a bag of hammers." He looks me over, smiles at the dirt on my arms and the pine needles in my hair. "Damn, you look like I feel. But at least you're wearing pajama bottoms. Remember that time you woke up in the yard in your underwear? Man, that was funny as hell."

"Yeah," I say, "but this is the first time that I've ever left the yard. I've never crossed the road before."

"Congratulations! You're getting better and better with each passing year!" Pete laughs. "You know, I do smell something. Can you smell it?"

"No."

"Soap or something. Too strong. Stinks." He takes a cigarette out of his pocket. He lights up, then waves the cigarette around until he's surrounded by the smoke. He breathes deep. "That's better." He smiles, then takes a drag.

The threat in the thorns must have moved on, because Boris stops growling. He grunts, slaps his tongue against his teeth, drops his ass down into the spot where I slept last night, and thumps his tail in the dirt. I pat his side and praise him for being a good dog.

"Does it freak you out waking up out here?" Pete asks. "Hey, if there *is* something out there, you think that hiding on top of this rock will save you?" Pete smirks and waits for my response, but I don't offer one. "What is it that Ronnie says about the thorns and the mist?" Pete lets the cigarette in his hand dangle limply when he says Ronnie's name. As he quotes Ronnie, he lisps, which isn't fair because Ronnie doesn't lisp. " 'On cold mornings, the fog rises from the center of Tanner Pond and makes its way up over the road and into the woods, drifting past Whale's Jaw and on up into the dark places near the Hawthorn Trees, only to find itself shredded to strands on the thorns of the backwoods.' " Pete holds his cigarette still so that a thin line of smoke actually does drift away toward the path up the hill. " 'The strands of mist wriggle like worms in a puddle before they just disappear altogether, dissolving into the ground and never finding their way back down to the pond.' " Pete chuckles. "What a wuss."

"Ronnie doesn't talk like that," I say, but I make sure to chuckle along with Pete when I say it so it doesn't really sound like I'm correcting him.

"He might as well talk like that," Pete replies.

"What are you doing out here anyway?" I guess I must sound like I'm accusing him of something, because he glares at me.

"It beats being at home." Then Pete uses some words that no one should ever use to describe their father, all the time sucking on his cigarette and squinting. "You should be happy with the parents you've got, Stucks. Be happy with your whole family. You Cumberlands may be crazy, and you may all have crazy nicknames for each other. Hell, sometimes I wonder if you even know what your real names are. But you're all okay. You won the lottery when you were born into that house."

Pete flicks cigarette ash down onto Whale's Jaw. "You know, Stucks, these woods are our woods. Yours and mine, year-round. No one else's. We made every path here, you and me, with our bare feet. We know every tree, know where the poison ivy is, know the names of every bug. Those summer kids, they've been around and all, and I used to think they were pretty good kids. But they don't know anything. They can't tell poison ivy from creeping Jennie. They're used to sidewalks and streetlights. They get scared out here as soon as the sun goes down. And all those stories . . . they're just stupid. Those townies, they're stupid. They believe anything that Ronnie says. They want to believe it. I'm never hanging around with those idiots again."

Pete takes another dramatic drag on his cigarette. He's trying too hard. He wants to look like he's smoking a cigarette more than he wants to smoke a cigarette. I'd probably be annoyed with him if he weren't my friend. I want to tell him to give it up, but it's tough to tell Pete to do anything.

"What about you? Are you an idiot? You think there's a bogeyman back there?" he asks me from his perch on Whale's Jaw.

"You tell me," I say.

"I've seen it all, Stucks. Seen more than Ronnie has seen anyway." Pete stares at me quietly for a full thirty seconds, long enough to make me squirm under the weight of his eyes. "And that pond . . ." Pete gestures with his cigarette toward the path that leads back to the houses and the water. "There's something nasty about that pond, for sure. That's what you need to watch out for. That pond's a tomb. There's zombies down the bottom just waiting to grab your ankles."

Now I know he's teasing. I laugh, and Pete laughs with me. "I should make up my own story," he chuckles. "The Tanner Pond Zombies! I could put Ronnie out of business!"

Boris looks at me and barks. He seems to have forgotten all about whatever was bothering him. "I'm going back home," I say to Pete. "You coming?"

"Nah." Pete snuffs out his cigarette on the top of the rock.

"Okay," I say. I don't know what else to say. I stand there awkwardly for a few moments. I feel like a stupid kid.

"So . . . I'll see you later, okay?" I offer. Pete waves me off. Boris and I take off down the path back to the house.

I don't know what to make of what Pete has told me. That happens a lot. Last summer he told me that it had gotten too noisy around, but I still don't understand what he meant by that. I rarely even hear a car, just birds and bugs and the wind. Pete said that all he could hear was noise, and that the only time he ever heard real quiet was when he swam out into the pond and floated on his back and let the water fill his ears. Even then, he said, the quiet never lasted very long.

Nana says that if you row out to the center of the pond on Memorial Day and drop a rock over the side, you'll hear it hit bottom on the day of the first frost. Of course, she winks when she says it. One thing's for sure: the pond is as deep as it is quiet. When we were little, we were warned not to swim out too far, but of course we pushed it, stretching the limit a little bit more each year.

But our parents never warned us about the thorns. They didn't have to. We know the rules back there, and we've always known never to test them. Pete was only half right when he said the woods belong to us. Part of them isn't ours. But we know the difference. We know where the line is. We know where not to go.

The truth about Tanner Pond and the thorns of the backwoods is a tricky thing to nail down. Ronnie Milkes says that from each and every thornbush a hundred branches grow, and a thousand thorns cover each branch.

He says that if you walk beyond the stone wall alone, you might feel the thorn branches twist like studded fingers around your ankles and wrists. You could try to scream, but you'd be on the other side of the line then. On the other side, the thorns only answer to one voice, and that voice is not yours.

But Pete says that's all bullshit made up by a summer townie.

So many people say so many different things. But there's one thing that most all of us agree on. Anyone who knows anything stays out of the woods beyond the Widow's Stone. Some say it's because of the thorns, others because of the poison ivy, and still others because of what may live back there.

Boris and I walk out of the woods and cross the dirt road to my house. I look briefly at the FOR SALE sign in front of Pete's house next door. So far, no one has come to look at the place. No one ever comes around here until the weather gets warm.

But this morning is the first real day of summer. And that means that people will be coming. The usual kids, in from the cities for the summer, coming in with their parents and cleaning up their cottages for the season. A lot of old friends are coming today. I give Boris a friendly slap on the back and leave him to nap in the morning sun.

2

The Boys in the Bushes

A large willow tree droops over the edge of the pond, its branches skimming the water's surface. A rope swing dangles from one of the tree's highest perches. The willow's roots cling desperately to a rounded clump of earth at the shoreline. Each summer, the tree seems to lean a little closer to the pond, like a shaggy-haired giant slowly laying its head down to rest.

My mother calls through the back window, "Stucks, keep an eye on Nana, please?"

"Yeah, Mom," I call back, taking Nana's arms as she tenderly steps over the roots in the path under the pines.

"Keep an eye on Nana! Keep an eye on Nana!" Nana sings to me as she steps to the edge of the pond. "Stucks is a good boy. He'll watch out for Nana." Nana throws her towel on the ground and stretches a black rubber swimming cap

14

over her hair. "Hello, Stanley," she says with a smile, waving at my little brother, the Cricket, with her left hand—the hand that has been missing its index finger since before I was born.

Some days Nana has no idea who the Cricket is. I guess he reminds her of Dad when he was young, which is why she calls him Stanley, which is Dad's first name. The Cricket doesn't mind being called Stanley. He doesn't mind being called anything except Stephen, which is his real name. He hates that name. Even the teachers at school pass the warning to each other from grade to grade: "Call him the Cricket, and if you can't bring yourself to call him the Cricket, call him Stanley. But you'll have your hands full if you call him Stephen."

Today, he has a metal bucket with him, and he's scooping up slime from the shallow water near the reeds. He brings it up to where I'm sitting in the grass and begins construction on a mud fortress. I stick my hand in to help him. The mud is cold. The pond hasn't given up its winter yet, and I tell the Cricket so. I draw my five fingers together in a point, bring them to my chin, and then pull them downward, drawing an imaginary icicle just like one that we once saw on the chin of a character in a Christmas cartoon. COLD.

The Cricket responds by placing his thumb to his temple and twisting the rest of his fist up and down. I KNOW.

"Nana, it may be too cold to go in," I warn.

"It's never too cold. Your grandfather and I once went

15

in at midnight on New Year's Eve." She sticks one foot into the water, and her face spreads into a wide grin. "We were buck naked, just like the Baby New Year. It was wonderful. If that darling man hadn't kicked the bucket, I'd make him go again this year!"

The Cricket dumps another handful of sludge onto the pile, and I watch as he walks down to the water's edge to gather more. He and I look a lot alike. His hair is slightly blonder, but apart from that he's a clone of me when I was his age. When I was about eight, the old folks used to tell me how cute I was, and now they say the same thing about the Cricket. Nana steps past him, pausing to gently pat him on the head before going out into the deeper water. When the water reaches her waist, she stops and drags her fingertips in circles across its surface. Her smile widens. "It's wonderful! Stanley, come join Nana in the water." The Cricket looks at me, and I raise my eyebrows. He lifts his fist and shakes it back and forth. I translate.

"It's still a bit cold for us, Nana." Up the hill, I can hear Mrs. Milkes start up the vacuum cleaner to remove the winter webs from their cottage. In the backyard, Mr. Milkes is hosing down the white patio furniture that no one ever sits in. They fuss over their cottage like insects. Or mice maybe. Gathering and dusting and cleaning and primping and trying to make their home as comfortable as possible. Or, more likely, they're trying to make their home as sterile as possible, comfort be damned.

"You should invite that Emily down for dinner. You should have a soda with her," Nana says from the water.

"Nana, please don't bring this up again," I plead, though I know it will do little good.

The Cricket's mouth curls into a grin. He traces his finger from his ear to his collarbone and flutters his fingers in my direction. A tiny giggle burps out of him.

This morning, after I came inside from talking to Pete out at Whale's Jaw, my friend Emily Haber stopped by. My mother had just laid out a plateful of wheat pancakes and turkey bacon, which she claims are just as good as white-flour pancakes and actual bacon. Emily sat down at our breakfast table, helped herself to a stack of pancakes, and started talking about all the work it was going to take to get their cottage ready, including crawling around underneath in the cobwebs to find the water shutoffs. I offered to help. Emily responded by turning the syrup bottle upside down and squeezing it until the last drop blurted out of the bottle. She looked down the bottle spout, and satisfied that the last drop had indeed made it to her plate, she placed the empty bottle back on the table.

The puddle of syrup coated the bottom pancake in the stack. My father reached over her and placed a fresh bottle on the table. I guess he figured she'd probably want more.

I told her I wouldn't mind crawling underneath the cottage, even with the spiders. That I actually kinda like spiders. When she didn't respond, I said it again. That made the Cricket burst out laughing. Nana threw him a scolding look and stared at Emily and me intently.

Emily said she'd be fine without my help. She said she had little interest in spiders, so she took no notice of them. She assured me that if she ever did "cultivate an interest," she would come back and we could "converse for hours about our favorite arachnids."

The teasing started after she left, and it hasn't let up. The Cricket keeps making our sign for Emily, tracing his finger from his ear to his collarbone, and fluttering his fingers. He pretends to swoon, then falls over himself, laughing and pointing at me. Nana keeps giving me dating suggestions that would be perfect if it were 1945. I try to ignore them both, but they're beginning to get under my skin.

The Cricket puts on his serious face. He's probably just gathering himself for another wave of mockery. Then I hear a soft meow from the bushes behind us, and some rustling.

"How long have you been there?" I bark toward the bushes.

I hear some more rustling, then a voice whispering, "Shoo, shoo, go back to the cottage." Above that rises the sound of a loud purr.

"Well?" I call, almost shouting. "How long have you been there?"

"Long enough," the voice responds.

"Right," I reply. I grab some mud from the Cricket's bucket and assist in the building of the great fortress. I wink at the Cricket, motion at the bushes with my thumb, and then wiggle my earlobe with my index finger. The Cricket smiles at me, lifts his fist, and nods it in agreement.

Ronnie Milkes jumps out of the bushes. "What did that mean?" he asks. His shirt catches on a branch, and he almost trips as he tries to untangle himself. A large orange calico cat follows him, purring and rubbing up against Ronnie's pant leg.

I smile as he stumbles, but I don't make eye contact with him. "You mean you don't know everything?"

Ronnie adjusts his shirt. His hair is neatly combed, held in place by a light coat of shiny gel. His pants are creased down the legs, and his shirt has a button-down collar. He stands near us, being careful not to get too close to the mud. "Darn cat," he says, then gives in, bends over, and scratches Morangie behind the ears. The cat meows and purrs louder.

"Don't you have a cottage to clean?" I ask him.

"My grandparents, uh, they don't let me help out," he mumbles. He squinches and unsquinches his nose several times as if something is itching it from the inside. "So, uh, fire tonight, huh?"

I pause just long enough for Ronnie to think that I'm not going to answer him. "Yeah, sometime after dinner," I admit, plucking a piece of rock from the Cricket's mud sculpture and tossing it into the pond.

"So, uh . . . what's the Cricket laughing at you for?" Ronnie asks.

"Do you have to know everything?" I snap at him.

"No," he mutters. I know he wants to change the tone in my voice, wants to get the summer going on a good foot, but he shouldn't have started things off by snooping in the bushes.

Nana splashes up to the edge of the water, singing, "Emily and Stucks, sittin' in a tree . . ."

"Nana!" I shout. "You're as bad as the Cricket!"

"What cricket? Where?" Nana asks, extending her hand to me.

"I mean Stanley," I explain, reaching to help her out of the water. She towels off, smiles with crooked teeth at Ronnie, and then walks up the path under the pines, singing, "Emily and Stucks, sittin' in a tree . . ."

Ronnie is smirking. The Cricket slaps a huge handful of oozing mud onto his sculpture. Brown gunk splashes toward Ronnie. A bit gets Morangie, but the old cat doesn't leap out of the way. She just glares at the Cricket, almost challenging him to do it again. Ronnie reaches down to brush off his pants.

"He didn't even get you," I tell him.

"Cricket, you are one goofy kid," Ronnie grumbles, and I am about to point out that at least he doesn't lurk around in people's bushes, when the Cricket lifts his fist, bends it at the wrist, and nods it in agreement with Ronnie. Ronnie repeats the Cricket's hand gesture back to him. "I don't know what this means," he tells him. He turns to me. "What's this all about?"

"He's just agreeing with you," I explain.

"So why not just say so?"

"It's our new thing. It's how we . . . talk," I explain.

"You two are bizarre," Ronnie protests. "You know how to talk. He's not deaf. And that's not even real sign language." The Cricket takes a handful of mud and plops it on his own head. He snorts at Ronnie and bares his teeth like an angry lion. He hasn't spoken a word in months. The Cricket's "speech" has become all pantomime, all cartoon buffoonery, all exaggerated, silly gestures. I told my parents it was because of a game we were playing. I told them we'd seen it in a Marx Brothers movie. We couldn't stop laughing at Harpo and Chico trying to talk to each other. I told them and I convinced them, and my parents are pretty hands-off kinds of people, preferring to "let the boys find their own way." I'm sure my mother, a true hippie with the dirt under her nails to prove it, read that phrase in a new-age parenting book somewhere. "Just so long as he's 'talking' to you," she said to me back in the spring.

When he feels like it, the Cricket'll start talking again. Until then, he and I have plenty of fun making up our own language. We build on it day by day. Like Mom said, we don't have to worry so long as he keeps talking to me. I won't worry.

But Ronnie doesn't need to know about family stuff that started in the winter.

"Will you teach me how to 'talk' like that?" Ronnie asks the Cricket, making quotation marks in the air with his fingers when he says the word "talk." The Cricket scowls as he looks back and forth at Ronnie's hands hanging in the air. He lifts his fist, bends it at the wrist, and shakes it back and forth, then pretends to open an invisible tin can with a can opener. NO CAN DO.

"I give up," Ronnie sighs. His nose is still itching. It's twitching and skipping around on his face like it's trying to fly away from his cheeks. He sneezes, and his nose settles down. "I think I've got a new story all worked out. I was thinking of telling it tonight at the fire." He reaches into his pocket and produces a white handkerchief. I catch sight of a patch of discolored skin on his right wrist, and an ugly memory twists my stomach. Ronnie wipes his nose. "I also got some fireworks this winter . . . ," he continues, then pauses. He sees me staring at the scar and tucks his arm down to his hip where I can't see it. His eyes flinch, and I look away.

"My grandparents and I, uh, went down south," he says, "and I got a whole brick of regular fireworks and some whistling bottle rockets. I got a lot of stuff. I could probably give you some, if you wanted. We have to be careful, though. I'm not supposed to light them off without my grandfather around."

I feel the urge to be nice to him, to let him know that he's okay. "I've still got some left over from last year," I offer. "Want to light off a few now? We could try to sink some rocks—"

Suddenly the hair on Morangie's back stands straight

up, and her back arches like a tiny camel's hump. Her teeth protrude from curling lips, and she lets out a hiss that sends Ronnie leaping toward the water. Boris steps out of the bushes, the wag in his tail starting just behind his neck and warbling outward until his whole rear end is wobbling back and forth. He's smiling—as close to smiling as a dog can get anyway. Smiling and drooling, drooling and smiling.

"Hey, boy," I say to him, and he starts walking toward me. He freezes, the wag stopping dead in the air. Boris's whole body becomes as stiff as a dart, and he points his quivering nose directly at Morangie.

I know exactly what he's thinking. He won't hurt Morangie, but he desperately wants to sniff her. He wants to inch closer and closer until he can stick his dribbling nose right up to her tail and suck in a good solid whiff. But I also know Morangie. Mrs. Milkes's cat has paid her dues in life, and she doesn't care how big the dog is. No one is going to stick their nose where no nose should be stuck.

It's over in about two seconds. Boris is too stupid to keep his distance, and Morangie catches him with every claw of her right front paw. Catches him a good one too, slicing hard enough to draw blood. Boris leaps back, tail between his legs, yelping in pain, and runs to my side. I pat the dog on his head. "It's okay, boy," I reassure him. "They say we learn something new every day."

Morangie could make a break for it, but she holds her ground, staring at Boris. She waits a second, then rushes forward, swiping again with her claws. Ronnie and I jump out of the way, scrambling down toward the water and almost taking out the Cricket's mud sculpture in the process. Boris runs for the road with his tail between his legs, Morangie screeching along after him.

"Stucks!" a voice calls to me from the house.

"What, Ma?"

"Is the Cricket with you?"

"Yeah, he's—"

I look around. He's gone. The bucket of mud is still there, but the Cricket is gone. "He was right here," I say to Ronnie. "Where could he have gone so fast?"

"Stucks?"

"Hold on, Ma! He was right here a minute ago."

Ronnie wipes his nose again, and I rip the handkerchief from him and chuck it into the water.

"Put that down and help me find him," I say.

I check the shoreline, being careful not to let my feet touch the water. He didn't go in the water, and if he had, it wouldn't be a problem. The Cricket can swim better than I can. That's how he got his nickname. He could kick so well in the water as a toddler that Dad said, "Boy, you swim just like a little cricket." And from that day on he was the Cricket. Just like when I was potty training and jackknifed into the toilet and got stuck. Up until that day my name had been Davey, but I've been Stucks ever since. Thanks, Dad.

"Cricket!" I yell again.

Ronnie starts checking among the pine trees. "He's just playing, right? Doesn't he do this all the time?"

Ronnie and I check around the house and then up the driveway. We enter the woods beyond the road and start walking the path.

"Ooh," Ronnie chuckles as we enter the woods. "A kid disappears. Just like Amanda Yearling."

I whirl on Ronnie and my hand comes up. He jumps back and covers himself. "Don't you ever do that," I say. "Don't ever compare him to—just don't." My hand is open as if I'm going to slap him. I don't want to hit him, but I don't know that I won't.

"Okay, Stucks," Ronnie says, stepping back. "I was just kidding. It's just a story."

I feel my hand in the air and it embarrasses me. I pull it away. "Okay. But . . . don't. Don't you ever try and put him in one of your stories."

"I'm sorry! I'm sorry!"

I nod, which is the closest thing to an apology that I can give him.

We walk to the spot where the first paths split off. "Check out those and meet me at Whale's Jaw. If you find him, shout to me."

"Isn't he just playing?"

"What's your point, Ronnie?" I say.

"Nothing. It's just . . . you seem really mad."

"Are you telling me how to treat my brother?" I glare at him. He holds up his hands in defeat, then starts down one of the side paths.

"Cricket!" he calls, his voice calm and gentle. "Hey,

Cricket, if you come out I'll give you a whole pack of bottle rockets! I'll even help you light them!"

I don't waste my time calling out. The Cricket's never going to call back, regardless of what bribes we offer. The game, the hiding, is always more fun than anything anyone has to offer. I run past the old fort and the twin climbing trees. The ground under my feet is damp and pretty cold, and it makes me think of winter and ice and the skin of snow that had covered everything for months. But underneath the canopy of trees the air is humid. I can feel it when I draw breath. Finally, Whale's Jaw looms in front of me. I trot up to it, allowing my hand to drift across its rough surface. I pass beyond the granite slabs, step around the fire pit. All around me I can feel the woods. I know the roots and stones that'll trip you if you're not paying attention, know the hole on the far side of Whale's Jaw where the chipmunks live, know the poison ivy that grows along the left side of the stone wall at the top of the hill. I can feel all the years that we've played out here layered one on top of another.

But today more than anything I can feel that stone wall and the border that it marks between the woods that we know and the woods that we never cross over into. It's not good to go back there alone. I should wait for Ronnie, but I can't. The Cricket doesn't always understand borders, and I have to make sure that he hasn't gone back there.

I walk up the ridge toward the marker at the break in the stone wall. We call that marker the Widow's Stone, though I don't remember why. It's a tall stone, like a square post stuck in the ground that rests flush against the right side of the break in the wall. The top is flat and broad enough to stretch your hand upon. We used to dare each other to go up there alone and slap the top of it when we were the Cricket's age.

I'm almost at the Widow's Stone when I hear Ronnie's voice.

"There he is!" he calls from behind me. I take four steps backward and turn around. There, sitting on top of Whale's Jaw, is the Cricket. He claps his hands, points up the path at me, and laughs silently into his open palm, slapping his knee with his other hand. I march down the path. Goose pimples rise on my back. I rub my thumb across the pads of the fingers of my right hand. STUCKS. I curl my two index fingers together and tug. ANGRY AT. I curl the three middle fingers of my right hand toward the palm and wiggle my thumb and pinkie. CRICKET.

The Cricket pouts, lifts his fist, bends it at the wrist, and cocks it back and forth. I immediately lift mine and nod it up and down. I fold my arms, glaring at him. Out of the corner of my eye, I catch sight of Ronnie. "He didn't mean anything," Ronnie says quietly.

"I don't like him out here alone!" I snap back, but I can feel my anger dissipating. I can never stay angry at the Cricket very long. I shake my head. I lift my fist, shake it back and forth, and then hook my index fingers and tug. NO . . . NOT ANGRY. I cross my arms and line up the

27

pinkies of both hands side by side. BROTHERS. I open my right hand and wiggle the middle finger toward my chest. COME TO ME.

The Cricket smiles, then skitters down the back of Whale's Jaw. He leaps to the ground next to me, grabs my arm, and leans back, swinging off it from side to side. He makes a fist and taps it over his heart while making a sucking sound out of the side of his mouth.

"You're forgiven," I say aloud, and he covers my mouth to stop me talking.

Ronnie has walked up the path near the ridge. He looks like an ostrich wiggling its skinny neck to grab a glimpse of what lies beyond the Widow's Stone.

"Ronnie?" I call.

He hops back down the path. "Still gives me the shivers," he says, shaking his head back and forth.

The three of us leave the woods together.

3

Old Stories

*R*onnie is sitting opposite me across the fire pit. The flames are level with his chin, and the waves of heat make his face appear to wriggle. He leans forward in his chair, taking a self-indulgent pause before he finishes his story. "Something new was out in the cornfields," he says. "Now there were two scarecrows instead of just one. One was made of the farmer's discarded clothes; the salesman had seen that one on his previous visit. But the other sent a cold shiver down his spine and caused him to hurry on down the road to the next house. 'For a second there,' he thought to himself, 'I could have sworn that was the old lady herself!' "

Nobody speaks for a moment. Ronnie's face goes limp and he stares into the fire. He's putting on a cool front, but it's obvious that he's waiting for our praise. It's obvious to me anyway.

I let him have his moment briefly before jumping in. "So, anybody want to go up to Thorwall's farm tonight and pinch some corn?" I say.

"I don't eat corn," Emily says, more to herself than anyone else.

"So did you like it?" Ronnie asks, almost whimpering, but it's a fake. He knows all his stories are good. He's never missed with any of them. I want to call him an arrogant ass, but I have to give credit where it's due.

"Another good one, Ronnie," I admit. "You tell a good story." The Cricket is sitting on the ground next to my chair. He has a beach towel wrapped around his shoulders. He places his thumb to his chin and then slaps his open palm against his rump. GOOD TAIL.

"I don't know what that means, Cricket, but I'll assume you liked it," Ronnie says.

I pick up a long stick and start moving the orange coals around, giving the darker coals air to breathe. The smoke from the embers is saturating my clothes, and the heat cups my face like a skintight mask. We're not really supposed to have a fire out here, but our parents can't see all the way to Whale's Jaw from the cottages. Besides, we hike out buckets of water, just in case. No big deal.

Our friend Vivek Patel comes up the path from the road. We haven't seen him since last September, but instead of saying hello, he just shakes his head. "You people again." He sighs. He stands there stiffly, not a crease of a smile. "Every spring I hope and I pray for a better summer, but then along comes June and it's just you guys again. It's a repeating nightmare that I live in—"

"Oh, please shut up," my cousin Robin laughs.

He lifts his eyes to the star-pocked sky. "What have I done, Lord, to displease you so?"

Vivek's parents are college professors who spend the summer reading and writing. Their cottage is always quiet, and they pretty much let Vivek take care of himself. Somewhere in that mix he learned to be a complete wiseass, and he's pretty good at it. He gets us laughing most of the time. Most of the time.

I grab him a lawn chair and he takes a seat, saying hello to us all by passing his hand over the group in one wide wave. "You missed a great Ronnie Milkes story, destined to become a classic," I say. "You should have gotten here twenty minutes ago."

"Ronnie's stories always become classics," Vivek says gravely as he wipes the winter grunge off the seat of the chair. "He tells them three hundred times over. From my cottage I can hear his grandfather say, 'Maw, this would be such a nice place to summer if we could just get that boy to shut up.' "

"Aw, I like the stories," Robin says.

I cringe every time Robin opens her mouth. *Aw, I like the stories.* Who says that? A complete pain in the ass I suppose, a pain in the ass who comes and hangs around your

31

house all summer long. Every summer my Uncle Bill and Aunt Ellie pawn her off on us for at least a month, and sometimes right up until Labor Day. Tonight her hands are still wrinkly from helping my parents with the dishes. Late last summer I made the mistake of not smiling when my mother told me to do the dinner dishes, and she said, "Why can't you be more like Robin?" She regretted it the instant it was out of her mouth. It was two days before I spoke to Mom again.

There is a long awkward silence between us. "So . . . ," Vivek says. "So . . ."

No one responds. I look at all of them, but no one is making eye contact. The only one willing to look at me is the Cricket. I ruffle his hair.

Vivek lowers his voice almost to a whisper. "I saw that their house is up for sale."

No one jumps in to fill the silence that follows, so Vivek stumbles along further. "I just, you know, saw it on the drive in, and thought it was . . . I guess I was surprised. I mean, they've lived here since . . . forever. Didn't Pete's grandfather build that place?"

"You know what, Vivek?" I say. "How about you stop talking about something that you know nothing about?"

"Oh what, so we're not going to talk about Pete all summer long?" he asks me.

I raise my voice, raise it loud enough to carry out into the woods. "Okay. Go ahead, Vivek. Tell me what you really think of Pete."

"Hey, don't do that! I didn't mean to—"

Emily cuts in. "How about another story?" she asks Ronnie. "I always liked the one with the old lady on the steps. Or the one about the dog."

Robin has been staring into the woods, but now she turns back to us. "A dog? There's no story with a dog."

Vivek is watching me over the fire. I glare back. He shakes his head and turns to Ronnie. "Perhaps it was an invisible dog," he offers. "That's why Robin doesn't remember it." It's a weak joke, but at least he's trying to smooth things over.

"There's no dog story," Robin says.

"Yes, there is one," Emily states. She twists a long thin branch off a nearby maple and begins peeling the bark off.

"We just don't know what *kind* of dog," Vivek says, faking suspicion. "Ronnie, why won't you ever tell us what kind of dog it is? It could be a slobbering dog, a fat dog, a three-legged dog, a dog possessed by the spirit of a Salem witch who was burned at the stake."

Robin smiles. "Stop being silly," she says. Next to me the Cricket has covered his mouth to stifle his laughter.

"No, seriously. A possessed German shepherd is one thing, but a possessed Mexican hairless really isn't that scary at all. I'm dumb and I don't have much of an imagination. Tell me what I'm supposed to picture in my head!"

Ronnie ignores him. "I know the one Emily's talking about, but I don't want to waste them all in one night.

Besides, it's the first fire of the summer, so there's one I have to tell."

"It's getting late for one of us, though," I say as I stand up. "I have to take the Cricket in for bed." The Cricket responds by screwing his face up into a scowl and throwing a slapstick punch in my direction. He crawls quickly over to Robin's chair. "Come on," I plead, but he holds tight to Robin's leg. I make the sign with my thumb and pinkie, then with my index finger draw a crescent moon in the air. CRICKET BED.

The Cricket holds up his fist and shakes it back and forth. He hides his head under his towel. Robin puts her hand on his shoulder. "Let him stay for the story. Your parents won't care."

I hold back a few choice words, but only because my friends are here. "It's time for bed; it's not for you to decide—"

"Cousin," she says firmly, "he'll be fine for a few more minutes. So go sit yourself down and listen to Ronnie's story."

Sometimes Robin acts more like a grandmother than Nana does. I sit back down and start to poke at the fire again. The Cricket lifts the towel and smiles at me like a mouse that's just escaped the claws of the cat. I stick out my tongue at him, and he ducks back under his towel.

Ronnie pauses, staring intently at the nearly full moon before turning his attention back to us. "I swear I did not make this one up. It's the story of *him*." Ronnie takes another deliberate, drawn-out pause. "It's the story of the Pricker Boy."

"Oh, *him*!" Vivek says. "I thought you meant Neil Armstrong. Now there's a story!"

Robin pulls the towel off the Cricket's head. "Are you ready to be really scared?" Normally, the Cricket would scowl at anyone who talked to him in such a condescending way, but because it's Robin and she's a girl and she's letting him stay up, he just acts shy and smiles back.

"How could he not have heard this before?" Vivek asks. "Ronnie tells it twice a day. Ladies and gentlemen, Ronnie Milkes will be having shows starting at seven and nine p.m. Tickets are on sale at the booth."

"I don't have to tell it if you guys are sick of it," Ronnie says. He sighs and settles back in his chair.

"Oh, Ronnie, now don't be that way," Vivek chides him. "You tell your little Pricker Boy story, and then I'll tell all about Neil Armstrong. He walked on the moon, you know. Neil, that is, not the Pricker Boy. Unless you've changed your story."

For all I care, Vivek can take shots at Ronnie all night long. I don't really want to hear the story.

Actually, that's a lie. I do want to hear this year's version. I want to find the little pieces of the story that Ronnie has added in over the winter. I want to try and spot the stones that he's flipped over, and then watch the bugs come out.

"Please tell it," Robin says, reaching out and touching his arm. "Vivek is just teasing you. Please tell it." She rubs

Ronnie's forearm, and being touched by a girl is all it takes to satisfy his ego.

"Okay. But you have to understand. This story is different. It's not made up. This one is true. I researched it myself, saw a lot of the old newspaper clippings. This one is for real. So if anyone is going to get too scared, now is the time to leave." Ronnie looks directly at the Cricket as he says this, and the Cricket responds by baring his teeth at him.

Just like he has hundreds of times before, Ronnie starts the story of the Pricker Boy. The first line has never changed. "He was a real kid once, just like any of us. He lived about a hundred years ago. There were no cottages on Tanner Pond back then. Only woods. His father was a trapper who took animals in these woods and then skinned them and sold their hides and meat. The boy's mother had died many years before. He had never known her."

As Ronnie speaks, I move the coals around with my fire stick, trying to get the best airflow through the logs. The fire begins to swell and glow, lapping at the dry wood.

"They ate the things that his father trapped, like muskrats and squirrels and opossum. The kid's clothes were made from the hides that his father said were too ratty to sell. The other kids would make fun. The boy would skip school to avoid their teasing, only to be beaten by his father later in the day for skipping."

I stab the poker into the coals. A burst of sparks rides the updraft. I watch them rise up through the branches and wink away when they hit the cool air twenty feet up. I can hear the night bugs in the woods around us, and I wonder for a moment why night bugs always sound like they're farther away than they actually are.

Ronnie leans forward so that the flames light his face. "The boy often felt like an animal in a trap. He was dim-witted, but he was eager to please. It was easy for the other kids to play him for a fool. They would coax him out onto the thin ice of a stream during winter, or convince him to play a trick on the teacher for which he would surely get caught. Too late, he would notice their snares. He would struggle to free himself, but finally he would give up and timidly await the consequences of his foolishness."

That's new. Ronnie didn't use that part last year, that stuff about the boy being trapped like one of his father's animals. I like it. It's something that I never would have thought of. I get up and grab two more logs, throwing them both on top of the fire. The flames tear into them as Ronnie continues. "One day before school a group of kids cornered him. They told him that his mother was really alive. They said that his father kept her locked in one of his traps out in the woods. They said that he beat her and fed her raw meat every day. They said, 'She begs to see you, but your father just laughs and beats her more.' They told the boy that if he could find her by the pond, he might be able to save her and they could run away together."

That's new too, and I see Robin flinch at the thought of the woman locked up and beaten like an animal. I hope she's thinking that the Cricket should have gone to bed like

I said. But through the flames I can see the look on the Cricket's face, and he's not scared. He and I have watched a lot of old horror movies together, so spooky stories don't easily scare him. He's just happy to be up past bedtime, sitting by the fire with the big kids.

"The boy ran off into the woods. Near the Hawthorn Trees that stand beyond the Widow's Stone, he found his father. Hoping that his father would eventually lead him to his mother, the boy crawled through the brush and followed his father as he moved from trap to trap. Unaware that he was being watched, the father went about his work and returned home at the end of the day.

"But the boy didn't come home that night. The father became worried, and he asked in town after his son. The teacher said that the boy had once again not shown up for school. The father got angry and returned home, thinking, 'Fine, let him spend the night alone in the woods. It will serve him right.' None of the schoolchildren said a word, afraid of what might happen to them."

Robin shifts in her chair. I can see her eyeing the height of the fire, but she won't say anything. She wanted the Cricket to stay up with her, and he's staying up. She's chosen her battle for the night and won. She isn't about to challenge me again.

Somewhere far away I hear thunder roll. Ronnie loves the thunder. He smiles a bit, like he thinks that God Himself is sending the storm to be the sound track to his masterpiece.

"That night was bitter, bitter cold. When morning came, the father became frightened and asked the local constables for help. The children in town still said nothing, fearing that they would get into trouble. The father did not go into the woods that day, but stayed at home waiting for the boy. Any animal that had gotten caught in his traps the night before would have to suffer for another day."

"Watch those flames," Emily warns, though she isn't even looking at the fire. She has almost stripped the bark completely off her branch.

"It's cool," I say.

"I'm feeling like a rack of ribs over here," Vivek says, waving his hand at the fire.

I don't know why, but I grab another log and throw it on. I see Robin shake her head, but she says nothing. Ronnie looks ticked off at being interrupted, and before we can say more he starts in again. "The next night was so cold that by morning a thin layer of ice had covered the pond. Still the boy did not return. The third night was colder yet, and several farmers in town lost livestock in the freeze. That night, the father had a terrifying nightmare of his boy caught in a trap and struggling to free himself as he slowly froze to death. He awoke in the morning and took off into the woods, desperate to check each and every trap before nightfall."

Robin pulls the Cricket closer to her, probably more for her sake than for his. She glances nervously out through the pines. I adjust a few of the lower logs, and more oxygen pours through the heart of the fire. "The trapper did not find his son. But he did find something, and he never enjoyed a decent night's sleep again."

More thunder, and then before it dies away, a second sound. Something groans in the darkness behind me. I see Ronnie's eyes flash wide. Robin jumps up. Even Vivek looks startled. Emily just turns her head toward the noise and furrows her brow.

"What the hell is that?" Vivek asks. Robin wraps her arms tightly around the Cricket, though he doesn't seem worried in the least. Something moves in the woods. I can hear its feet shuffling in the leaves. I recognize the sound.

Boris steps out of the shadows. He walks up to me and bumps into my chair. "Good boy," I say. "You know how to time your entrance." Boris drops down next to my chair, and I rub his ears.

"Great timing," Ronnie admits as everyone settles back in. He goes back to the story before the mood lightens. "Near the Widow's Stone, underneath the thorns of a pricker bush, the trapper discovered one of his larger traps, the kind that a full-grown man could barely open using both arms and all his strength. It had been sprung by something. The teeth of the trap were bloody, and bits of fur had been left behind. But the bits of fur had been dried, treated, and sewn together—sewn together by the father's own hand.

"It wasn't the fur that scared him most of all. It was the thorns. The thick branches of the thornbush wove in and out of the bloodied teeth of the trap as if they had been growing over the metal for decades."

In the distance something flashes. It is a good five seconds before the thunder rolls behind it. There's plenty of time for Ronnie to finish his story before the rain gets to us.

Emily looks up briefly, and our eyes meet. She smiles quickly but turns back to her task before I can smile back. I feel stupid, though I don't know why.

"The boy was never found. Local people began to tell stories. They said that he had simply faded into the woods, and that the woods had decided to protect him. His skin hardened like bark, and he grew thorns over every inch of his body.

"Children started disappearing into the woods by Tanner Pond. Even the adults began to fear that he was still out there, waiting in the thornbushes to take his revenge on them. The thorns were his friends. They could wrap their branches around an intruder and wait for the Pricker Boy to come. Then with prickly arms he would pull his prey deeper into the brush, leaving the sliced bodies behind, but leaching the soul and dragging it back to a stone pit deep in the woods, past a nest of boulders even larger than Whale's Jaw. Those twisted, suffering souls down in that cold, awful pit are the trinkets that tally his revenge . . . the pennies that mark his treasure . . . and the minions that pledge him worship."

I clear my throat. Ronnie stops, stares at me, and waits.

I shrug and ask, "What?" Then I remember. It was at this point in the story last year that Pete had started laughing at Ronnie. *"You still believe that crap?"* he had laughed. *"Okay, Scooby Doo, I'm really scared."* That night, Ronnie had refused to finish the story.

I throw Ronnie an apologetic wave, and he leans back in his chair to continue. As he backs away from the flame, his face is filled in with black shadows deep enough to hide even his buggy eyes. "There are people who would laugh at this story," Ronnie admits. "There are people who would say that it's not true. But I know for a fact that he has killed at least two kids. The first was Amanda Yearling, a young girl about seven years old."

I try to focus on the story, but it starts drifting away. It's here and at the same time it's not, like the way the bugs can be close around us in the darkness while still pretending to be far away. Like how thunder seems so distant from the lightning, but really they're together all the time.

"The constables searched the woods for days before finding her floating facedown in a shallow creek. Her body was covered from head to toe with scratches. The second victim was Willie Wilson, who disappeared about twenty years later. His scraped and bruised body was found at the base of a tall tree, his head split open like a pumpkin.

"They said that Amanda had gotten lost in the woods and had died of exposure, and that Willie had fallen through the branches from the top of the tree. But Amanda grew up around here. She knew the woods well enough. And Willie's friends said that they were playing together in the woods and that Willie had just stepped away for a second when he disappeared. He hadn't been climbing any trees."

I can hear the fire breathing, breathing and growing and moving about in the pit like a newborn calf trying to find its legs. Ronnie raises his voice to shout over it. My body is still there with my friends, but my mind is closer to the thunder and the bugs and the embers. For a moment I think that they can talk to each other, that the water in the clouds and the fire on the ground are whispering something about us to the bugs hidden under the rocks and the leaves. They're saying something bad, and I need to know what it is.

Ronnie continues. "There is one salvation. If you hear him, if he begins to come for you—and he'll come fast; he can move through the thorns as easily as you or I can run down the path to the pond—if he gets your scent and chases after you, you have to run back to the Widow's Stone. He can't follow you past the Widow's Stone. But he won't forget your scent. And he won't rest until he finds you."

I know he says those words, because I know the story and I know how it ends, but those words are nowhere near me. I'm inside the fire, I'm out at the bottom of the pond, swimming for the surface with no air left in my lungs. The flames are roaring in my ears and I can see Pete reaching down into the water for me. I'm swimming toward him, but my feet are burning and I can't tell if I'm moving toward the surface or heading deeper, toward the bottom. *"You claim that crap is true?"* Pete is saying to me, laughing out loud. And then I'm shouting back at him, just like I did a year ago when he laughed at Ronnie. I don't know why I felt any sympathy for Ronnie then. Maybe I was still angry with Pete for what he had done to Ronnie's wrist.

"Okay, Pete," I scream through the water. *"If it's all crap, why don't you go back there right now? Go back there in the dark and leave your pocketknife in the Hawthorns. If there's nothing to be afraid of, then you should have no problem walking alone past the Widow's Stone, back through the prickers all the way to the Hawthorns."*

Pete stares at me from the water's surface. Never in his life did he expect me to take Ronnie's side over his. I keep swimming, but I can't tell if I'm swimming to save myself or to get the chance to take a swing at him. Pete reaches into his pocket and pulls out his knife. He points it at me through the water, just like he pointed it at me across the flames last summer.

Ronnie holds up his arm, now golden in the firelight, and points his skinny finger up toward the Widow's Stone and the woods beyond. "One thing's for sure," he says, concluding the story the same way he has for years, "anyone who knows anything stays out of the woods beyond the Widow's Stone."

4

Song of Bees and Dragons

Something clicks in my head, the tugging at my memory stops, and I am back with my friends. I realize just how high the fire has risen. Suddenly the wind shifts, and the flames flap higher. I jump up and pull some of the larger logs to the side of the pit. The flames start to subside.

Robin stands up, pulling the Cricket up with her. "I'm going to take him to bed. I'll be right back." The Cricket offers no protest; he's already half-asleep.

Emily places a hand on Ronnie's arm. "Nice job, Ronnie. I was almost frightened this time."

"You didn't seem to be listening," Ronnie complains.

She looks her cleaned branch over from top to bottom. " 'They said that he beat her and fed her raw meat every day.' That was brand new. You never used that line before tonight."

Emily's blond hair is pulled back in a ponytail, and she is wearing no makeup. Simple clothes, just jeans and a hooded sweatshirt. Nothing frilly. Nothing fancy. Nothing painted or primped. She reaches into the pouch of her sweatshirt, pulls out a marshmallow, and puts it on the end of the stick she has stripped the bark from. How long that marshmallow has been in her pocket is anybody's guess.

Vivek watches the marshmallow longingly, but he knows better. We long ago gave up waiting for Emily to offer us snacks from her pouches and pockets.

"You always claim that it's true," she says, positioning her marshmallow near the flames. "Is it, Ronnie? Tell me the truth. Finally now. Is it true?"

Ronnie gives her his best poker face, but behind that face he is savoring the power that comes with having a secret to hide. "You ask me that every year," Ronnie says, "and every year I tell you the same thing."

Vivek rubs his chin and, mimicking his father's thoughtful pose and thick Indian accent, says, "I think this will require some analysis." We all burst out laughing. We always do when Vivek imitates his father.

Vivek continues, still imitating his father's clinical, scientist's voice. "Every year, the text of the story changes a little here and there. It's strange for a *true* story to evolve so. It's very . . . um . . . pupatory."

"Pupatory?" Emily asks.

46

"You know, like a butterfly. It pupates. Goes from a butterfly to a caterpillar."

"You mean from a caterpillar to a butterfly," Emily laughs. "But there's no such word as 'pupatory.' "

"There should be!" Vivek says. "If there were, I wouldn't sound so stupid right now, would I?"

Ronnie laughs, but I find it less funny. "What I don't understand," I say, looking directly at Ronnie, "is why you always leave one part out." Ronnie squints curiously at me across the fire. "His color, Ronnie. You're a great storyteller, but you never mention what color he is."

Ronnie shrugs. "I guess I never really thought about it. I'm not sure what color he—"

"He's gray," I say, deliberately challenging him. "His skin is gray like the bark of trees in winter. And thorns cover every inch of him. Everywhere. His face, his hands, his ears . . . everything."

Vivek continues using his father's voice. "And now Stucks Cumberland offers the thesis—"

"Cut it out," I interrupt him. "I'm serious."

Emily's marshmallow is turning black. She looks at me. "And how, exactly, would you know that? Ronnie did all the 'research' into the story."

What she means is, *Why are you trying to take Ronnie's story away from him?*

I lean forward in my chair. "Because, Emily, I'm the only one who's seen him."

Even Ronnie appears shocked by what I've said, but he soon recovers and tries to pick up the thread that I've left dangling. "Yeah! Yeah, I remember that. We were just kids. That was years ago! You were scared to pieces!"

"Really?" Emily asks. Her marshmallow catches fire, but she doesn't care. She's more interested in defending Ronnie.

"And what exactly did you see?" Vivek asks. His face can't hide a slight smirk. He still thinks I'm pulling his leg. He's waiting for me to burst into a smile and say, "I can't believe you fell for that."

"Full body," I say coolly. "In the woods near here. I was about six or seven at the time. Ronnie was there, but he didn't see him."

"I remember!" Ronnie says. "We were building that fort down where the wild grapes make that canopy! We could see the rock wall that connects to the Widow's Stone. You said he came right up to the edge of it!"

"Day or night?" Emily asks.

"Day!" Ronnie blurts out.

"No," I correct him. Ronnie is only playing along in the hopes of mining more credibility for the story, and I'm not going to let him in. "It was dusk. We were just about to head home for the night."

"What was he doing?" Emily asks. She throws the burning marshmallow, branch and all, into the fire pit.

I shrug. "He was just standing there. Watching us. I could see him clearly. It wasn't a flash in the trees, some animal ducking out of sight. When I looked at him, he didn't even look away. He just kept staring at me. He must have looked at me for half a minute, then he walked back into the woods."

Ronnie's brow wrinkles. "You're serious."

Robin comes back from the house, pausing for a moment when she sees everyone staring at me. "Everybody all right?" she asks.

Vivek's face breaks into a grin. "Come on, bud. You were a little kid. You saw a deer or something. You saw antlers or whatever. I mean, you never told us this before."

"Well, perhaps . . . ," Emily starts, then pauses. "Listen, I know this is just a story that Ronnie's been telling since we were little kids, but you might find this interesting. I remember this one night. I heard something following me home in the woods along the road. It stopped when I stopped, walked when I walked. It wasn't my imagination, I know that." She looks around at all of us, then shrugs, "But then again, I was ten at the time." She reaches into the pouch of her sweatshirt, pulls out another marshmallow, and tosses it into her mouth.

Boris groans next to me, and I reach down to scratch behind his ears. I feel the first faint drops of rain strike my arm.

"Wait a minute," Robin asks. "Are we still talking about the Pricker Boy?"

"Come on," Vivek says. "This is kid stuff. You don't actually believe this!"

"I know there's something," I say. "I woke up here this morning. Boris was with me. He'd smelled something up the path that leads to the Widow's Stone. He was standing there growling, his tail straight out, his fur all spiked up."

"This morning?" Emily asks.

"You were half-asleep! There's nothing up there, Stucks," Vivek says.

"Okay," I say, and then pause. Everyone around the fire knows what's coming next. "Whoever believes that there's nothing up there in the woods can go," I say flatly. "You know what to do."

Vivek laughs. "Oh, good one!" He points at me and Ronnie. "You guys planned this! To make the story scarier. 'Cause we're older now and don't believe this crap."

Ronnie shrinks back in his chair and wraps his hand around his scarred wrist.

"Come on," Vivek says. "Please. We're not kids anymore, Stucks."

I throw my hands out. "Fine. We're not kids, and it's just a story. So prove to us how grown-up we are, Vivek. Here." I pull a stone from the edge of the fire pit, grab my fire poker, and using the charred end, mark an X on the rock. I toss it gently toward his feet. "You know what to do."

Vivek stares at the rock. "Come on, Stucks."

Robin chimes in. "Vivek, you don't have to go anywhere. This is silly."

"She's right. No one has to go anywhere," I say. "You

50

can claim it's all crap and not back it up. . . ." I wink at Vivek, and I see his pride flare.

Robin's voice chirps like a flustered chickadee's. "No, Stucks! He doesn't have to prove anything to you. Vivek, ignore him. He usually saves this side of his personality just for the family."

Ronnie jumps in. "Listen, this is just a story. Just a story, okay? Let's relax and talk about . . . I dunno. But I didn't tell it to get people mad at each other. Let's relax here."

"Just a story?" I can't help but raise my voice a bit. "I thought you said it was true!"

"Stucks, calm down!" Robin chirps again.

"Stucks, relax," Vivek adds.

A long silence follows. A warm wind rolls through the trees, and lightning flashes near the far shore. "Maybe when we were kids we all had a good scare over this," I say. "Watch out! Hug your teddy bear, 'cause here comes the spooky story! But what about those kids, Amanda and Willie? What really happened to them? Emily says something followed her home one night. What was that? Explain these things to me, someone, please!

"I believe that there's something back there. Something bad. Something that may have even hunted us at times. Something I have seen, whether you believe me or not. Even Boris here has seen it. The hair on his back stood straight up. Boris is the dumbest dog on the planet!" Boris flops over sideways, bumping my lawn chair, and whinnies like a

51

horse. I scratch his belly. "If Boris is smart enough to know there's something back there, what does that tell you?"

They all stare at me. Ronnie has given up altogether, relinquishing the reins of his most prized story to me. "And here's what else I think. I think that each of you believes in it too. If you've outgrown it, then prove it. Prove that you're not still afraid. Any one of you. Take that rock and go up into the woods past the Widow's Stone and back to the Hawthorns. Go alone in the dark and leave the rock. In the morning we'll all go up together to find the rock, and I'll admit that you were right."

"I'd go," Emily says. "But I'm not going to do it just to prove something to you."

Thunder begins to rumble on the other side of the pond, and Boris groans nervously. "Well, Vivek?" I ask. "You started all this."

Vivek begins to stutter. "Look, I—I . . . I just got here. It's the first day of summer! Why be mean to me? I'm just . . . hey, why me?"

I glare at him through the flames. "We're older now and don't believe this crap. Isn't that what you said, Vivek? So show me how much you've grown up."

Vivek leans forward and picks up the stone. "It's not fair. It's just a story." He turns and disappears into the darkness with the stone, mumbling, "Why me?" over and over again as he goes.

Robin shakes her head at me across the fire.

"I don't want to hear it, Cousin," I say. I get up and

reach for one of the buckets. Earlier in the day, the Cricket made several trips with his small metal bucket to fill up these large white ones, while I sat on the shore watching him. Only now do I smell the soft odor of algae and fish scales. I don't know why I never noticed the stink and the muck of the pond before. I think the water is more orange this year—in fact, I don't remember it ever being orange before. Not so you'd notice. Maybe there was an extra load of leaves last fall and the tannins have soured, brought the rot up from the bottom.

I drop the bucket and step down the path, away from the orange flames. Boris wobbles to his feet and follows me.

The cooler air feels good on my cheeks. I look up for the stars, but tall clouds swell in the sky, crackling with energy. I breathe. I just breathe. I stand there for a second, or maybe it's a minute, or it could be five. I honestly don't know.

The next thing I hear is Robin calling out for me. The rain starts pouring down on top of us, making my bucket of water pretty redundant. I run back up the path with Boris. Vivek is standing there in the rain, as white as a sheet and still holding the stone in his hand. Huge drops of water splash into the fire, causing it to squeal. The fire pit hisses like the open mouth of a dragon, spitting clouds of steam.

"What's wrong?" I ask.

"Guys, there's something up there. Something on the rock in the center of the Hawthorns," Vivek says.

I hope he's joking, but he looks terrified.

"I saw something there, and I reached out to touch it

53

just to make sure. Then I turned right around." He drops the stone by the edge of the fire pit.

"What was it?" Robin asks.

"It felt like a dead animal. Like a rat or something."

"A dead rat?" I ask with a nervous laugh.

"I didn't pick it up and look at it!" he shouts at me over the thunder. "But that's what it felt like. A dead animal, all wrapped up in rope or something. That's the only way I know to describe it."

Lightning flashes across the sky. We all look at each other, trying to figure out what to do next. Part of me thinks we shouldn't go look until morning, but another part knows that it simply will not wait. Besides, if we all stick together, we'll be fine. We'll be terrified, but we'll be fine. The thorns only claim people when they're alone.

"I want to see it," I say. "I'll go if we all go together."

"To the Hawthorns?" Ronnie screams. "At night? But it's raining! My grandpa will want me to come home—"

"Don't be such a baby, Ronnie!"

He surrenders. "Okay, I'll go. If everyone else goes."

Everyone moves except Robin. "You're not serious!" she says.

"How else are we going to know what it is?" Emily says.

"I don't want to know!" Robin says. "This is scaring me. Seriously!"

"Be scared then, but you're coming anyway," Emily says, grabbing her hand and pulling her along with us.

I lead the way, taking a few quick steps up the path. I stop, and Ronnie bumps into me from behind.

Lightning flashes again, illuminating the trees and the rocks all slick with wetness. Behind the Widow's Stone, his gray skin shiny and darkened by the rain, I can see the Pricker Boy waiting. I slip and fall to the ground. My friends immediately reach down to help me to my feet. I brush off my hands on my jeans as quickly as I can, the earth feeling leprous on my palms.

The lightning flickers again. This time, the apparition is gone.

"You okay?" Ronnie asks.

I don't answer him. I turn around and put my arms out, sweeping my friends back down the way we came. I move them all quickly past Whale's Jaw, past the dying fire, past where Pete and I built that old fort, past the twin climbing trees and all the way out into the road, all the while carrying the feeling that something is watching from behind.

"The morning," I say once we get back to the road. "The morning will be soon enough."

We split off then. Vivek and Emily walk home together. Robin and I deliver Ronnie to his screaming grandparents before going back to our own house. Even after we get inside, I can feel that thing, feel it reappearing at the Widow's Stone and watching us on the path. I can feel it there, though I can't be sure myself of what I've actually seen.

5

Turning Stones

When I open my eyes, all I see are thorns, millions of their branches twisting away in the darkness. The leaves are dripping, and the lightning is still flashing nearby. Everything is slick—slick from the rain. It takes me a moment to realize that I am standing next to the Widow's Stone, on the exact spot I saw the Pricker Boy standing earlier this evening. I can feel the mud beneath my bare feet. My heels are sinking into it, and I can feel worms, tiny worms crawling in between my toes. I jump away and bolt down the path toward Whale's Jaw. Before I get two yards, I slip in the mud and fall to the ground.

I feel him before I see him. I don't even have to turn around to know he's there. I try to get up, but the mud is greasy, and my hands and feet keep slipping. I turn to look at him. He is standing at the break in the wall, staring down at me. Every wet thorn on his skin gleams. He doesn't make a move toward me. The wind dies away. I struggle to my feet.

He nods at me, and my fear fades away. He has no plans to hurt me. His lips aren't moving, and he isn't talking, but I know he wants something. He'll leave me alone if I will only bring the others, Ronnie and Emily and Robin and Vivek. I nod. I don't know why. I can't explain my actions. I just nod.

His eyes twinkle. He wants one more. He wants the Cricket. I shake my head and stumble away. I slip once again down into the mud. I scream at him, but no sound comes out of my mouth. I try to stand, but I fall in the mud, sliding down toward Whale's Jaw. I can hear the Pricker Boy on the path behind me, sure-footed, the thorns of his feet acting as cleats in the mud. For every yard I can struggle along, he moves three. I am almost to Whale's Jaw when his hand grips my ankle. I feel the prickers on his palm sink into my skin. He drags me up the hill, past the Widow's Stone and down the path into the thorns.

The woods around me come alive. Something is wriggling around my legs. My skin is tearing. Branches from the pricker bushes are reaching out and wrapping themselves around me, securing me to the ground. Beneath me, the earth breaks open, and I fall into a narrow, muddy crack. The thornbushes pull me down deeper. Above me, I see the Pricker Boy's body change. His torso remains the same, but his lower body elongates like a centipede's. Dozens of orange legs extend out of him. The legs circle the rim of the hole and start kicking dirt on top of me. He begins screaming, screaming and giggling at the same time. Mud fills my mouth, closes off my ears. He turns to look at me, and just before my eyes are buried I see his face, all gray and covered with thorns. Two pincers suddenly jut out of his cheeks. He laughs. His legs scrape at the ground and cover me over.

I open my eyes again, but this time it's to morning sun. I'm lying in Nana's garden. I hear a voice say, "Good morning."

I struggle against the sleep, but I can't answer, can't even move, can't react to a voice that could belong to anybody. My eyelids slowly close again. I know that I'm really awake, but the dream is still there. It still feels real in my half-awake brain. I force my eyes open again, and through their fog I see the leaves of Nana's artemis plant. I have a vague memory of Ronnie and me as little kids helping her weed the garden. She used to talk to the artemis when she pruned it, calling it her 'Old Uncle Henry' and telling it about the dreams she'd had the night before.

"Are you all right?" the voice asks.

I draw three deep breaths. "Bad dreams," I croak.

Emily sits cross-legged right next to me. "Sleepwalking *and* nightmares? What do you have against a good night's rest?"

I feel black dirt stuck to the side of my face. I try to wipe it off, but it smears on my hand. Boris flaps his tail and proceeds to lick my face clean. "What time is it?" I ask. Boris and I had bunked next to Nana's lilac bush, a relatively harmless spot, considering where I just dreamed I'd been.

"A little after dawn," Emily says. "Have you ever watched someone's eyes flickering when they dream?"

"If you knew I was having a nightmare, why didn't you wake me up?"

"I did," she says. She's still wearing her pajamas, but hers aren't covered with dirt. I'm a mess of twigs and leaves. I blink at her. Seeing the face of a friend calms me, makes the dream unravel and float away much quicker. I run my hand through my hair to try to achieve some kind of composure, but it only elicits a wince and a shake of the head from Emily. She reaches over and plucks pieces of Old Uncle Henry from my hair. The affection surprises me, but as she squints at the leaves, I realize that she just wants to examine them more closely. "I didn't sleep much either," she tells me. "Not that I was really afraid, though. The night seemed restless. It felt like I had to stay awake for my family's sake, because they were all sleeping and needed someone to listen for them. Then the sun came up, and everything just melted. Everything was okay again. It does seem silly now, doesn't it, now that the daylight is back?"

I shrug.

"Strange how the mind works in the dark. We should pay attention tonight, just as dusk comes, to see how our perceptions change."

I have no idea what she's talking about.

"Maybe Vivek didn't see anything at all," she adds, "but there's only one way to find out, and I'm interested."

"Only one way to find out," I say, and stand up. "Just give me a minute to get changed."

"Changed?" She looks down at her own pajamas. "Do I look changed?" She grabs my arm and pulls me up the driveway, calling Boris along behind her.

The woods are still soaking wet, and Whale's Jaw smells of damp moss and leaves. Boris pauses at the base of the rock and looks at me dumbly.

"Go on, old boy, go get it," I order him. He whimpers, flaps his tail in the dirt, but does not move. "Chicken."

"We'll go together," Emily says. She takes Boris by the collar and gives a little tug, and the dog reluctantly follows along with us.

The Cricket and I are down by the water. He's searching for crayfish. He turns over one rock after another, reaching down and plucking the shellfish out of the water before they can scoot away. For fifteen minutes I can see Ronnie watching us from his bedroom window. The Cricket has three crayfish in his bucket by the time Ronnie leaves his grandparents' air-conditioned tomb and makes his way down to the water. The purr of Morangie gives him away again as he tries to sneak up on us.

"I saw you and Emily this morning." He smirks. The cat jumps around his feet, rubbing her face against his leg.

"Really, Ronnie?" I say. "Well, aren't you clever?"

"I wasn't spying," he says, almost apologetically.

"No, you just like to stand at your window and stare at people for hours on end."

"If my grandparents were up, I would've asked to go outside!" he protests.

"You're a creep, Ronnie. Deal with it."

He hesitates a minute, pokes his nose into the bucket to count the crayfish. Morangie meows, hoping to catch his attention. "So?"

"So what?"

"So you found it. What was it?"

Poor Ronnie. He always loves to have the secrets, but it causes him such pain to have one kept from him.

"Noon today, we all meet at Whale's Jaw. I'll bring the package. But I'm not talking about it until all of us are together."

"Just tell me," he says, almost pleading.

"When we're all together. The package is a message, and it's a message for all of us. We'll look at it together, and we'll talk about what to do about it together." Ronnie stands there for a minute before turning around and heading back toward his cottage. Morangie runs after him. Ronnie will try Emily next, but she won't tell. I try to ignore the fact that it feels good to torture Ronnie like this.

Robin is the last to arrive, and I think that Ronnie and Vivek are about ready to kill her by the time she shows up. It's nice to see someone else irritated by my goody-goody cousin for once.

"So what is it?" Ronnie asks when she finally gets here.

"Emily and I got up early this morning—" I start.

"Just tell us!" Ronnie blurts.

"Listen to Ronnie getting all forceful here!" Vivek says. "It was all a joke, Ronnie! We were putting you on! There was nothing up there!"

From the hurt look on Ronnie's face I can see that he believes Vivek, and why shouldn't he? It wouldn't be the first time we teamed up to make Ronnie look like a fool.

I open my bag and reach down inside. The thing has dried some since the morning, but it's still slippery to the touch, and the feel of it makes me want to gag. "After Emily and I looked at it, I wrapped the package back up exactly as we found it. I wanted you guys to see exactly what we saw," I explain.

I take the package out of my knapsack and place it on the back of Whale's Jaw. It's some kind of animal skins sewn together, rolled into a bundle, and wrapped up tightly with string. Vivek winces when he sees it up close.

"It stinks," Ronnie says, pulling his face back.

"Wet fur usually does. I think it's rabbit fur, but I'm not sure," Emily says.

Ronnie steps forward again and looks at it closely. "Yeah, I think you're right," he declares.

I loosen the string, and the package falls open. Everyone else just stares, not quite believing what they see. "Oh my God," Robin whispers.

A number of objects fall out of the bundle. They are wet from the rain but otherwise in very good shape. Very good shape indeed, considering that some of them have spent years out in the woods.

"That's my book," Ronnie says, picking it up. "That's my H. P. Lovecraft book. I gave that up years ago."

Vivek reaches over and picks something off the pile. "These are my old baseball cards," he marvels. "These are the ones that we used . . ." He looks at me.

I smile. "When you were having trouble in math. I used the players' stats to teach you percentages."

"It worked too."

Robin reaches in next, selecting a flattened roll of papers secured with a rubber band. "It can't be," she says. "Oh, Ronnie, look at this!" she squeals. "Look!" She unrolls the paper. "These are the comics we made when we were little. Remember? You wrote the stories, and I drew the pictures!" Ronnie looks over her shoulder at them and smiles.

"This one's my locket," Emily says. She picks it up and wipes it on her shirt.

"But all these things were lost, right?" Vivek asks. "Didn't we lose all these things?"

"We didn't exactly lose them," Emily says. "We gave them up doing widow's walks."

Robin remembers and immediately drops her hand-drawn comics on the rabbit skin. "All of these things were left on widow's walks?" she asks, her voice shaking a little.

The widow's walk was a kids' game from years ago. The rules were simple. There were certain bad omens in the woods. One was accidentally cutting yourself and drawing blood. Another was throwing up. Or seeing a salamander with red spots. Or if you were "it" more than five times in one game. If anything like that happened to you while you were out in the woods, it meant that the Pricker Boy was watching you, that he had your scent. The only way to ward him off was to do a widow's walk.

You took something of value, walked past the Widow's Stone and onto the path through the thorns, and placed that thing on a large stone that sits in the middle of the Hawthorns. The others, the watchers—at least one—stood at the Widow's Stone and waited for you. As terrifying as the walk was, you knew that the Pricker Boy couldn't get you so long as you had your friends with you. Of course, you also had to trust that your watchers wouldn't run away and leave you out there alone by the Hawthorns. Over the years we had given up all kinds of objects: packs of gum, toy surprises from cereal boxes, handfuls of firecrackers, scratch-and-sniff stickers, plastic army guys. Each one of them was an offering to the Pricker Boy. *I will give up this special thing if you will only forget about me.* Usually the rest of the group decided what would be left in the Hawthorns.

"Ronnie Milkes, you have to go back to the Hawthorns and leave seven jawbreakers and a pinch of your grandfather's pipe tobacco."

"I can't steal my grandpa's pipe tobacco!"

"If you don't, the Pricker Boy will get you."

"The widow's walk," Vivek says. "It was a good thrill. You know, when we were *ten.*"

Ronnie shakes his head and steps back. He looks up into the woods beyond Whale's Jaw. "This isn't so. This can't be so." He turns and looks directly at me. "This can't be so. You know, Stucks? This can't be." He places his book on the rabbit skin and steps away as if it's diseased.

"Oh come on, Ronnie," Emily says. "The book is still yours. It belongs to you." To prove her point, she fixes her locket around her neck. "See? I'm still alive here."

Ronnie looks at her and shakes his head. "This is wrong." He stares at the locket as if he desperately wants Emily to take it off and place it on the rabbit skin.

I reach into the pile and pull out a pocketknife.

"That's Pete's knife," Ronnie says, turning his face away. Vivek pulls the knife from my hands and examines it closely. The words PETE MORGAN are carved into the plastic on the side. Pete carved them using my pocketknife, as I had marked the side of my own with the very knife that Vivek now holds in his hands.

"So let me get this straight," Vivek says. "When we were kids, we used to leave things on the offering stone in the Hawthorns so that the Pricker Boy would leave us alone, and *now that we're getting way too old for that,* he's started leaving stuff for us?" He waits for a response, but no one jumps in. "Maybe he wants to play hide-and-seek with us! Or ring-around-the-rosy? Remember ring-around-the-rosy?"

"You were scared last night," Emily says. "If we're too old for this, then what were you afraid of?"

I look Vivek straight in the eye. "We might be too old for stories, but this package is here. Someone or something left it for us to find."

Ronnie picks his book back up again. He looks the binding over, checks the pages. Apart from the rain of last night, there doesn't appear to be any damage to it at all. He opens the book and begins flipping through the pages. He shakes his head back and forth, still not believing what he is seeing.

"I loved this book," Ronnie says. "How could it be out in the woods for all those years and still look like this? Vivek's baseball cards should have disintegrated long ago." He lets out a little gasp. He pulls out a four-leaf clover, pressed flat and dried in the pages of the book. He smiles weakly and holds it up for Emily to see. "You gave me this, remember? You found it and gave it to me, that day that . . ."

Emily smiles at him and nods. We all remember that day. It was one of those days when Ronnie had gotten on

66

someone's nerves, and we all turned on him the way little kids do. We started ignoring him, and he went home crying. That day we decided to establish the Bad Ronnie Club, a club that anyone could belong to so long as their name wasn't Ronnie and they promised never to speak to anyone named Ronnie. At some point that afternoon, Emily found a four-leaf clover in the woods. She marveled over it for a few minutes before plucking it. She stood and turned her back on the Bad Ronnie Club and brought the clover to him. The club dissolved by dinnertime.

Ronnie carefully places the clover back in the book and closes the pages.

"Whose was this?" Emily asks. She hold up a ring. "Stucks?"

I reach out and take it from her. On the outside of the ring, two etched bands weave round each other. There's no inscription. I rub it with my fingers to take some of the age off. It might be gold. For all I know it could be brass or copper.

"Anyone remember a ring?" I ask.

Ronnie shrugs. "I don't think so."

Vivek smiles. "In my ears sometimes, when Emily talks too much."

"I think I had a ring," Robin says. She scrunches up her nose trying to remember. "I might have left it. I remember I got it at the Eastern States Expo. No, wait. I still have that ring. I think."

"So that doesn't really help us, does it?" I say.

She glares at me, but thankfully she ends her story about the ring and her big adventure at the Eastern States Expo.

"Anyone?" I ask. No one has any ideas. "Come on— someone has to know who this belongs to. We didn't do a widow's walk unless we were giving up something important. Last chance." When no one says anything, I flick the ring into the air with my thumb, catch it again, and slide it into my pocket.

Vivek asks, "So what about you, Stucks? What did the evil Santa of the forest leave you?"

I reach into the pile and pull out a small statue. "It's the Empire State Building," I tell them. "I got it on a trip to New York City in the fourth grade." I don't tell them that Pete had bought it for himself at the gift shop, and that when he saw how upset I was he gave it to me.

I toss the statue back on the pile.

"So what now?" Robin asks desperately. "Something isn't right here. What do we do?"

Vivek nods his head and furrows his brow. "I think the polite thing to do is to go and say thank you. We go find his little gingerbread house and knock on the door and say, 'Hey, you know what? You're okay after all, bud. Let's have tea.'"

"It's not a gingerbread house," Ronnie mutters. "It's a pit. He lives in a stone pit."

Emily rubs the locket with her thumb. "That's not a bad idea. We go say thank you. . . ."

"I was kidding," Vivek says. "Hey! I was kidding! Remember me? I'm the guy who kids!"

Emily ignores him. "Fear . . ."

I can almost see the wheels turning in her head. I don't have to say anything, just sit back and let her do the work.

"We face the fear," Emily says. "We're all afraid." She points at the package. "This is unsettling—interesting, sure—but unsettling nonetheless. The best way to get it out of the way is to face it."

Robin looks at Emily as if she's lost her mind. "Are you saying we should go back there? Into the woods beyond the Widow's Stone? Where? To a, uh, a gingerbread house? What would we be looking for?"

"A stone pit," Ronnie mutters again, but this time it's not to correct her, it's to answer her. "Deep in the woods, past boulders larger than Whale's Jaw."

"A stone pit deep in the woods past boulders larger than Whale's Jaw," Emily repeats, confirming our destination.

"So, Vivek," I say. "Will you go, or do you just want to make silly jokes?"

"I can do both!" he says, smiling. Then he takes a breath and drops the smile. "Bud, if you all want to romp through the woods, then I'll romp through the woods with you. Just so long as we all go together."

"I'm not going," Robin says flatly.

Vivek throws his arm over her shoulder. "Would you

rather play ring-around-the-rosy? Wanna play ring-around-the-rosy with me, baby?" He wiggles his eyebrows and winks at her.

"Jerk," she replies, then pushes him away.

Vivek claps Ronnie on the back. "What about you, bud? Ring-around-the-rosy or a stroll through the forest of damnation?"

Ronnie shakes him off but doesn't answer. He hangs his head down, darting his eyes back and forth because he knows that we're all watching him.

"Look, Ronnie," Vivek adds, "it's creepy either way. Ring-around-the-rosy was written about the bubonic plague. People would carry posies in their pockets to hide the smell of their pus-laden sores."

"That's not entirely true," Emily says. "In actuality, the song has many interpretations. For instance—"

Vivek wags his finger at her. "Oh no you don't. As much as I love your encyclopedia stories, Emily, that's not the point here. What I'm saying is that if we're going to freak ourselves out, we might as well do it like big kids, not babies." He gently places his hand on Ronnie's shoulder. "We do it as friends. No practical jokes. No hiding or leaving someone behind. No tricks."

"Okay," Ronnie says. "I'll go."

Vivek squeezes Ronnie's shoulder, then turns to Robin. "What about you, hoochie mama?"

"No."

"If you don't go, I don't go. . . . But then I'll call you 'Robin the Spoilsport' for the rest of the summer."

Robin sighs and nods her head. "I hate you, Vivek."

"Naw." He smiles. "You just don't like me. Right now, anyway."

"Vivek is right, though," I add. "For now, just in case, we keep to the old stories. We pretend that all the stories are true. Amanda Yearling and Willie Wilson died because they were in the woods alone, right? So we're going to stick together. We don't separate for any reason. We go in together, and we come out together. Understood?"

Everyone nods.

"Let's go!" Vivek shouts. "All for one and one for all, especially me!" They all turn and start up the path.

"No," I say.

Emily turns to me, confused.

"I need a day. I have something to do." They all stare at me. "Isn't it . . . I think that it's going to rain. Isn't it supposed to rain this afternoon?"

Emily shakes her head no.

"Look, I just need a day, okay? We'll go in the morning."

She shrugs and walks back down the path. "Okay, Stucks. We go in the morning."

6

A Witch at the Dinner Table

"No," Pete says.

He and I are following the edge of the pond where the shore hooks around the cove. Pete's wearing his jean jacket, even though it's a little too muggy to be wearing a jacket. I suppose that makes sense. He wears that jacket even when it's too cold for something so light, so it's only logical for him to wear it when the weather gets too warm.

"Why?" I ask him. "I don't get it. Why don't you just come with us? I asked them to wait so you could come."

"I told you, I'm never hanging out with those kids again."

I'm following along behind him, placing my feet exactly where he places his. I know the rocks along the shore as well as he does, well enough not to stumble, but if I just follow his exact steps then I don't even have to think about it. "We don't have to make a big deal out of it," I tell him. "You just come along."

Pete steps across the pile of rocks in the shallow water in front of Hank Paulding's place. Hank collects rocks each fall, claiming that one day he's going to build a stone dock twenty-five feet out into the pond. "Rocks don't rot!" he once told me. Pete and I told him that when he finally gathered enough rocks we'd help him make his dock. Hank's never going to get enough rocks to build a dock, but our offer was sincere. If by some miracle he ever did get around to doing it, we'd jump into the water to build with him.

One of Hank's rocks wobbles under Pete's foot and then mine, but we're ready for it and compensate by leaning out slightly over the water. "You think that Ronnie'll be happy to see me?"

"I'll take care of Ronnie," I say.

We reach Pete's backyard and walk up to the house. We sit under the overhang that serves as their back porch.

"What's the point?" Pete says, putting his feet up on the woodpile and lighting a cigarette. "This place'll sell before the summer's half over. I'll be gone. It's a waste of time. I don't want to see them, they don't want to see me, so there's no point in starting something that was finished a year ago."

"Come on, please!"

"No."

"As a favor to me? I don't want you to go without at least . . . hell, I don't want you to go at all. It'll suck around here in the wintertime without you to hang out with."

Pete doesn't say anything.

"Please," I ask.

"Have you forgotten the English language? Do you know what the word 'no' means?"

I don't respond.

"Look at me!" he shouts. "What does 'no' mean, Stucks? What does it mean?"

" 'No' means 'no,' " I say meekly.

We sit quietly for a while. Pete doesn't even smoke his cigarette. He just lets it dangle between his fingers. We watch the pond. Emily was right. It isn't raining, but it is overcast. The water is still and gray. Gray above and gray below.

"How about you come with me?" he asks. "I'm heading out tonight, catching a ride with Craig and Dean. There's a party down in the sandpit behind Thorwall's far cornfield. Dean's picking up a keg."

"I dunno."

"You don't have to drink. It wouldn't hurt you, but you don't have to."

"How would we get home?"

"Craig. Or if we had to we could walk it, cut through the woods. It would take a while, but that might be cool too. It's not like your parents would notice. You get home at dawn, flop down in the bushes somewhere. They wouldn't know shit about it."

"Dean doesn't like me," I say. Dean scares me, but I don't tell Pete that.

"Forget about Dean," Pete says, waving his hand. Ashes fall onto his jeans, and he brushes them off. "I can handle Dean. He's a lot harder to handle than Ronnie, that's for damn sure, but I'll handle him."

"I dunno," I say. I don't want to go, but I want to go. I want to hang out with Pete again, but I'd rather we do it in the woods with the others, not at a drunken kegger with people screaming and falling all over each other. "I'll think about it."

"No you won't," he says. "You'll hang out with the kids in the woods and go looking for the bogeyman."

I stand up. "Dinner's on the table. You coming?"

"That wouldn't go over so well. My mother doesn't want me over there. She doesn't even want you stepping foot in our yard, so you better duck under the pines if you don't want to hear her screeching."

"Come with me. She'll never know."

Pete snuffs out his cigarette. "You just don't get it, do you? Nobody wants me around! Nobody but you!" He stands up and pushes me gently back toward the pines. I don't say anything else. I know I've already pressed my luck. "I don't care about any of them. I don't want to see them, and if you don't stop nipping at my heels like a puppy, I won't want to see you either." I step backward and stumble over their lawn mower. Pete grabs my arm as I fall, lifts me back onto my feet.

"Go home," he says. I duck underneath the pines and head through to my house.

"What are we eating?" I ask.

The Cricket had been eating happily, and watching him act silly has cheered me up a bit. When I question what is on my plate, he pulls back his fork and eyes it suspiciously. He holds the forkful of dinner up to his ear, listening to it carefully, then cautiously placing it back on his plate as if it were explosive. Silently moving his lips, he pretends to question his glass of milk about its curious neighbor. They converse in mime, but when the milk offers no real answers he turns to his buttered bread with a broad smile and an imaginary notepad, ready to record the facts. My mother is trying not to laugh.

"It's called American chop suey," my father says. Upon hearing the name, the Cricket lets a karate chop fall on the table. From now on, that will be the sign for Dad's cooking, I have no doubt.

My father can be a great cook. When he plans well, he can create gourmet meals that you never want to see end. But it's a different story when it comes to improvisation. Whenever the fridge becomes overloaded with leftovers, my mother will ask my father to do the cooking, and the result is always a hodgepodge of the various styles my mother has been experimenting with all week. It's not unusual to find yourself eating fish-curry goulash, or green scrambled eggs, or the ever popular soup. If it's soup, you never look at what your spoon brings up, ever.

Inspired by the Cricket's goofiness, I decide to press my father. "Couldn't Mom have cooked tonight?" I ask. My mother smiles, and Robin looks uncomfortable.

"Stucks, there is an artistry to what I do," my father retorts. "One day, when you are grown-up and paying your own grocery bills and are no longer a burden on your mother and me, we will have to change our phone number because you will constantly be calling me for recipes just such as this."

I take another forkful. It isn't bad, really, whatever it is. It's just fun to give my father the business.

"What do you think, Nana?" I ask.

"I don't know what you're talking about," she says bashfully, her eyes focusing on me through a haze. "I was having my own conversation . . . with me."

The Cricket is sitting next to Nana. He is eyeing her left hand. I can tell that he is about to reach out and touch the finger stub, which has fascinated him since he was a baby. He puts down his fork and reaches slowly forward.

Nana lunges at him, releasing a squeal and grabbing at him with the hand. Horrified, the Cricket leaps back, blank terror in his eyes. He hops out of his chair, then starts giggling. Nana chuckles—no, in fact she cackles—and as the Cricket sits back down, she reaches over and rubs the top of his head with her four-fingered hand.

"Oh, Stanley," she says. "Oh, Stanley, you do make me laugh."

The Cricket blushes, pulls Nana's hand from on top of his head, and looks closely at her fingers. He runs his hand over the four that are there, touches her wedding ring, and then lingers on the spot where the stub is. The finger is intact up to the first knuckle, and Nana is still able to wiggle it back and forth.

"You think I'm a witch, don't you, Stanley?" Nana says, wiggling the stub for him. "Stanley thinks I'm a witch." She reaches over with her right hand and rubs his head again. "And I am. I am a witch, Stanley."

The Cricket's eyes grow wide. I can't tell if his amazement is pantomime or sincere wonder.

"But it's okay, because I'm a good witch. I'm the best witch ever." She winks at the Cricket. "And I put a spell on you, Stanley. A good spell, to keep you safe." She pulls her hands away and resumes her meal. The Cricket smiles and picks up his fork. Nana looks up and down the table. "Where's Peter?" she asks.

Pete used to take three or four meals a week with us. My parents always made sure that we had enough food to include him. He hasn't sat with us for a while, and every so often Nana notices the absence and remembers that he should be here.

I stop eating and wait for one of my parents to answer. My father reaches over and touches Nana's hand. "Remember, Mom? I explained about Pete."

"I don't remember," Nana confesses.

"He's not my friend anymore, Nana," I say. A simplification to be sure, but a much shorter story than the truth.

"Perhaps that's for the best," she says. "For now, anyway. But wait for him. When he calls, he may need you to get back, Stucks."

My mother catches my father's eye, then looks over at me. My father shrugs. "Are you planning on doing any fishing this summer, Stucks?" he asks awkwardly.

Before I can answer, Nana continues. "Something's turned in Peter. I saw what he did to young Ronnie. It was cruel. The demon's come to him, for sure."

My father tries to cut her off. "Mom? I think we should—"

Nana ignores him, instead looks directly at me. "But heed these words. Alone one might get lost. But don't underestimate what the unity of friends can bring to bear against the demon." She points at all of us around the circle of the table, then at the center. "You'd best listen, Stucks. Don't underestimate it. It's always right here."

I feel myself flush. I pray my parents don't ask her what she's talking about. "Well, let's not leave the conversation at that," my mother says, laughing nervously.

An awkward silence rolls over us, and desperate for a way to fill it, my mother continues her line of thought.

"Robin, remember last summer? Pete was very kind to you."

Robin cringes. "Yeah," is all she says.

"What are you talking about?" I ask. I don't remember Pete doing much of anything last summer that could be considered kind.

"Nothing," Robin says.

"Tell me."

Robin allows her fork to wander over her chop suey. "Last summer, I really thought that my parents were going to get divorced."

"I remember," I say quietly. I may not like Robin all that much, but that doesn't mean that I wanted Uncle Bill and Aunt Ellie to split up.

"Well, before I left for the summer, my mother said to me that if they had one more fight, she was going to leave him for good. Then a few weeks after I got here, I called them, and I heard it start, right over the phone. My mom started laughing, and she said to me, 'Well, honey, this is it.'"

Robin pauses for a moment, and I notice that Nana and the Cricket aren't paying attention. She has started teasing him with a noodle, trying to stick it in his ear.

"When I got off the phone, I went down to the water, and then Pete found me. He didn't say much, just that things weren't great with his own parents. But he was really sweet and patient and spent the whole afternoon with me, listening."

Nana gets the noodle in the Cricket's ear. He laughs, then sits up straight. He growls like Frankenstein. He reaches up with a supposedly undead hand and pulls the bit of noodle brain from his ear. He looks at it, growls at it, then eats it.

Robin continues. "I know about his bad side, but when he was good, no one was better. I miss him."

"Oh please. You spend two months out of the year here, if that. He's my best friend year-round. Don't go getting all dramatic on me."

"That's it, isn't it?" she snaps. "I'm not good enough for you and your pond and your woods because I'm only here in the summer."

"You only come when it's warm," I say dismissively. "Try coming when the wind whips over the ice and cuts through your coat even when you're all the way out at Whale's Jaw."

"So I'm not as strong as big bad Stucks? Maybe I shouldn't even go tomorrow then."

"I don't want you to go anyway."

Robin shakes her head. "You're such a jerk."

My mother and father exchange a look. Another awkward silence settles on the table, and this time I'm the one to break it. "Are Mr. and Mrs. Morgan going to get divorced?" I ask.

My father clears his throat. "We don't talk with the Morgans about their personal problems. We're not their therapists."

"I know, but I was just wondering—"

My mother interrupts me. "Let's change the subject."

"I think we've tried that a few times," I say. "Without much luck."

Now it's my mother's voice that gets sharp, which is a rare thing that always throws me off guard. "Well, then you start us off. You're planning a trip out into the woods tomorrow. Looking to get a good case of poison ivy?"

"Yeah, sure, Mom," I say, turning my eyes to my plate and ignoring the satisfied smile on Robin's face.

"Just be careful. You know what poison ivy looks like. Remember when you were little and you got into some? You had it on your arms and your legs and your stomach, even your—"

"Yeah, Mom, we get the point."

My father chimes in. "You're a bit too old to have your mother putting calamine on your bottom."

Robin laughs so hard that she coughs out a bit of chop suey.

"How you got it there I'll never know," my mother says.

"Could we please stop talking about poison ivy and calamine and my bare ass?"

"Calamine is crap," Nana tells the Cricket. "I can make him a mint balm that would do the trick. And, he'd smell all minty and fresh, which would be nice for the rest of us." The Cricket can barely hold in his laughter.

Luckily, my dad comes to my rescue. "I remember my

82

first case of poison ivy. Remember, Ma? I didn't know what the plant looked like. Bill told me that the leaves would give me magical powers, so I let him rub a little on my back. Little did I know that he was spelling out the word 'nitwit' in broad letters across my shoulder blades. Ma, why didn't Bill get in trouble for that?"

"Because it was funny," Nana replies.

"I guess it was."

"And it taught you good lessons. Watch out for poison ivy. And watch out for Bill, I suppose."

"How old were you?" I ask.

"Oh, I don't know. Let's see. . . . Bill was probably nine, so that would make me seven."

"My father did that to a seven-year-old?" Robin asks. "That's so cruel!"

"You don't understand boys," my father tells her. "They're rough-and-tumble. They just do things like that. You'll understand someday when you have boys of your own. Boys like running around and playing games and exploring the woods." My father smiles as if the wondrous days of his youth are flooding back to him. But I see my mother and Robin bristle. He doesn't realize that he just stepped smack-dab into a tar pit that will gum him up for the remainder of the evening.

"Uncle Stan!" Robin barks. "Girls like to do those things too!"

"Sometimes I just cannot believe that I married this man," my mother says, her hand slapping her forehead.

"I was just saying . . . ," Dad starts, desperately searching for an explanation to retreat to. "I was just saying that boys, generally speaking now, not all boys mind you, I mean, not all girls don't, but more boys like the woods than girls do. Just generally."

"Right," my mother says. "Girls, you see, like to play with dolls and have tea parties."

"Well, more so than boys, yes," my father says sheepishly.

"Uncle Stan!" Robin says.

I smile. I love my family's hunger for debate. This argument could carry us safely through the end of the meal and across dessert, and surely my father will still be trying to defend himself as the dishes are drying in the rack.

Nana blinks her eyes and looks up and down the table. "Where's the Morgan boy?" she asks again.

7
Blood on the Ground

We all stand together for a moment next to the Widow's Stone, the sentinel that marks the boundary between our land and the land that belongs to our spiked bogeyman. Before us, nets of intertwining thorns stretch off into the distance, broken only by the occasional stone wall or lonely tree. Our first destination, the Hawthorns, looms ahead. Their dying branches reach up toward the sky with open, brittle fingers. Their roots tangle in the dirt with those of the pricker bushes. Between us and the Hawthorns, a ragged path cuts through the brush.

Emily takes the lead. As she goes, she plucks at the long thorn branches that loop across the path, passing them back to the next person, who in turn passes them to the next. I look around at the thorns. They really do seem endless.

The Hawthorns are like three old women, frail and

barely breathing. Ancient and silent, the trees have never borne many leaves, but they sprout just enough to stay alive each spring. Parts of them are rotted, just waiting for the next hurricane to come along and shake the dead pieces to the ground. Other parts are clearly alive, flowing sap, but slowly, as if asleep. Each tree is covered with three-inch spikes. The Hawthorns sit about twenty feet from each other, and if you were to draw lines between them they would form a perfect triangle. In the middle of the triangle sits a granite boulder, about waist high with a flat top.

Vivek touches a spike on one of the trees, then immediately jerks his hand away. "Sharp as they look," he says, shaking his hand in the air.

"Hawthorns are sometimes called witch trees," Ronnie states. "In folklore, it was believed that hawthorns were witches that had turned themselves into trees. And . . . uh . . ."

"Yes?" I prod him, already knowing the rest.

"Well, according to what I've heard . . ."

Emily breaks in. "According to legend, if you find several of them growing together, it's best to stay far, far away. It's said that only carnivorous insects will fertilize the flowers, and because of that, the flowers smell of death and murder." She reaches out and plucks a clump of small red berries from the branches. "The fruit are called thorn apples and are believed to be poisonous. In one story, a mother applied the juice of the apples to her nipples to kill an unwanted baby."

"That's ghastly," Robin says. "Are you making this up? Because if you are, you can stop now."

"She's not making it up," I say. "And if you knew a flower from a fungus, you might know about hawthorns too."

Vivek bursts out laughing. " 'A flower from a fungus?' You sound like you were raised in Munchkinland."

Emily clears her throat. "The fruit and the sap of the tree were supposedly used in witches' potions. The tree is also very unlucky. You should never, ever bring a sprig or flower of the hawthorn into your home. To do so will bring death to a family member. And the trees are said to attract fairies. Those fairies get very upset if the tree is harmed in any way and will bring sickness to the house of the offender." She studies the hawthorn berries in her hand for a minute, then absently tosses the pieces to the ground. Ronnie stares down at them fearfully.

Vivek is walking around the boulder inside the triangle. He gasps. "Oh boy! Something scary! I mean, something scarier than Emily!" He jumps back from the stone.

I move around to where he is standing, and what I see makes me feel icy cold inside. Two words have been scratched into the back side of the stone: I'M SORRY.

"I don't like talking stones," Vivek whimpers.

Ronnie crouches down next to the boulder. He reaches his hand toward the letters but quickly pulls it back before his fingers reach the stone. His other hand closes around his wrist, covering his scar. "Looks like it was carved by a rock or a piece of metal. Who would have done this? And why?"

87

"That's what I want to find out," I say.

"Is this some joke?" Robin asks, directing her words right at me. "If so, then you're sicker than I thought."

I shake my head. "Oh for crying out loud."

"Well, look, Stucks, who did that? Who wrote that? This might be your idea of fun, but I don't like being scared. I—"

"The universe doesn't revolve around you, Robin!" Her face goes a little pale, and I resist the urge to add, "I told you that you couldn't hack it out here."

"All I'm saying—"

"Is that you're a baby! So go back to the house! I don't care."

"Nobody's going back," Emily says calmly. She steps between us, facing me. "We agreed to do this together, remember?"

"Stucks, you make me want to puke," Robin says.

"I'll hold your hair back for you!" Vivek shouts. We all laugh. Even me, even Robin. The color comes back into her face. "Onward," Emily says. She steps toward the path on the other side of the Hawthorns. She picks through the thorny branches carefully, handing them back to Vivek, who hands them to my cousin, who then hands them to me. I hand them off to Ronnie.

I hear Ronnie curse. I look behind. One of the thorn branches has caught Ronnie's left arm, dragging a ragged cut. Tiny bits of blood form, and one drop falls and hits the ground. He looks up at me.

"Not me," he says. "Why did I have to be the first one cut?" He covers his cut with his free hand, then scuffs with his shoe at the spot on the ground where he had seen the blood fall. "I don't want it to be me, not my blood." His foot works furiously, trying to dilute the spot of blood with leaves and dirt.

"Don't you start," I say. "We're all together. Nothing's going to happen to you. And look." I show him a scratch on my own arm. "I got cut too. We'll all get cut a dozen times before we're out of here. Don't sweat it."

"But that's my blood on the ground," he pleads.

"So he'll get you first," I say. I'm joking. Kind of. Part of me wants to see the expression on his face, and he doesn't disappoint.

"Me first? But I don't wanna be first."

He's so pathetic I have to fight the urge to laugh. But I've tortured him enough. "Okay, we do it like we did as kids. If you think he's after you, then you leave, I dunno, your favorite comb in the Hawthorns. And then he goes away. Widow's walk. Simple, right?"

Ronnie nods. "Okay. But I don't like this, Stucks. I don't like the way my story is turning out."

The farther we get from the Hawthorns, the thicker the thorns get. As they get thicker, they have more opportunity to do their work. Emily and I are wearing jeans, so we're more protected than the others. Ronnie is wearing long pants, but he can't keep them clean, and he'll catch hell from his grandfather when he gets home. Robin and Vivek are wearing shorts. They both get cut quite a bit.

We're all having a tough time, but Robin thinks that she's having the worst of it, I can tell. I see her sweating. I'm sweating too, but she's sweating more. I think it's stinging her eyes. She's the only one who winces when her skin gets hit by a thorn. And she keeps looking around as if she expects something to dive out of the woods at her. I look around too, but not because she's looking around. I just want to see what there is to see. I'm not scared.

We've been walking for about a half hour when the path begins to slope downward. When it levels off, the ground becomes muddy. Pools of still water dot our path. As we approach the puddles, slippery things—things that will one day be frogs when their legs form—flip and skitter to hide in the moist leaves.

The path begins to rise again, but not before it is blocked by a large, still puddle. It is only eight feet across, but it stretches into the thorns on either side of the path like a long, dark worm. I look down into it to see how deep it is, but the water is as black as oil, and all I see is the reflection of the tops of the trees and the sky above.

"I'm not stepping into that," Ronnie says. "No way."

"Yes, you will," I say.

"It's disgusting. You don't even know what might be in there—leeches or snails or worms. No way."

My hand snaps forward and grabs him by the wrist. I

yank him toward the puddle. The action is so quick that I even startle myself.

"Hey!" Vivek shouts.

But it's already too late. Ronnie's foot has sunk shin-deep into the muck. Emily grabs me and pulls me away from him. My heart is thumping quickly.

"What are you doing?" she whispers to me, then steps forward into the puddle alongside Ronnie. She takes his wrist. He pulls away. It occurs to me that I grabbed the scarred one.

"Why did you do that?" Ronnie asks me. Sniffling, he makes his way across the puddle. Emily stays with him until he reaches the other side. Ronnie's pants are covered with black mud halfway to his knees.

Emily slogs back through the puddle. She helps Vivek and Robin through, then comes out again on my side. Her jeans, like Ronnie's pants, are thick with slime. I move forward toward the water, but she places her hand on my chest. "That's not going to happen again," she says quietly.

"It got him across, didn't it?" I say. I try to push past her, but her hold on me is surprisingly strong.

"That's not going to happen again," she repeats, looking me directly in the eye.

"You're in charge now?"

"If I have to be," she says, then releases me.

As I turn away from her and step into the puddle, I swear that I smell cigarette smoke from somewhere nearby.

* * *

"I think we've been going through poison ivy," Robin says.

"Cousin, you wouldn't know poison ivy if your own name was written on the leaves," I tell her.

"Okay, Mr. Woodsman, how about I pick some and use it to write the word 'ignoramus' on your back? Then we'll see if it's poison ivy or not, huh?" She begins searching the ground for vines and mumbling something about following in her father's footsteps.

"Can you even spell 'ignoramus'?" I ask her.

"She could probably miss a letter or two and still get her point across," Vivek offers.

"Has anybody thought that maybe it's time we went home?" Ronnie says timidly, avoiding eye contact with me. "I missed lunch, and I didn't tell my grandpa that I would miss lunch, and when he sees me like this I'll be lucky if he lets me out of the house again all summer."

"We haven't seen any 'boulders larger than Whale's Jaw,' " Emily states.

"See?" Ronnie says to the rest of us.

"I'm not agreeing with you, Ronnie. I'm saying that, geologically speaking—"

Vivek stops her. "Emily? Dumb-guy language, please."

"You're not as dumb as you pretend to be," Emily responds. "But I'll play along. Whale's Jaw was dropped in these woods over ten thousand years ago by a receding glacier. It's called a glacial erratic. And we've been looking for more glacial erratics—boulders larger than Whale's Jaw—since we left."

92

"Whether you believe it or not, I'm too dumb to look for glacial erratics," Vivek says. "I've just been looking for 'big rocks.' "

"The point is that it's strange, very strange, that we haven't seen any. Whale's Jaw wouldn't be out here all on its own. And according to Ronnie, the Pricker Boy's stone pit is marked by other erratics. But so far there are none."

"Still, it's getting late," Ronnie says.

"I'll go back with you, Ronnie," Robin offers, trying to be oh-so-pleasant, though I think it's just an excuse.

"We're not going to split up now," Emily says. "We'll take a vote."

Robin sighs. "I'll admit it. I want to go back." She wipes sweat from her brow and swats at a mosquito that's buzzing by her ear.

"I was hoping we'd see something by now," Vivek says. "Clouds of bloodsucking bats. The Creature from the Black Lagoon. Godzilla. Ronnie's grandfather in a black cape. Something scary. I'd hate to turn back now without something to show for it."

"We could just come back tomorrow," Robin offers.

"If we come back tomorrow, we'll have to fight through all that again," I say. "We need to keep going."

All eyes turn to Emily. She reaches into her pocket and pulls out a handful of red pistachios. She begins cracking them and tossing them into her mouth. Very quickly her fingertips begin to turn red. "Well," she starts, and then pauses, looking up at the trees and tossing pistachio shells into the bushes. "I'm still interested. If for nothing else than to find an explanation for what we haven't found."

"Sometimes you talk like a mental patient," Vivek says.

"I suppose so," she responds.

"Okay," Robin says. "But I need to . . . visit the bushes."

"Let me go with you," Emily says. They strike off toward a weak break in the brush. The three of us guys stand together awkwardly for a few minutes. Ronnie opens his mouth to say something to Vivek but then decides against it. I don't think he wants to look at me. He stares at the path that Emily and Robin have just gone down.

"Are you trying to look at the girls while they go wee-wee?" Vivek asks him.

Ronnie's face goes red. "Nuh-no!" he stammers. "I wouldn't . . . of course not!"

"You little perv!"

"Stop it!" he shouts, his voice wavering. "Don't you start picking on me too!"

Vivek chuckles. "I'm just trying to make you laugh, bud. You look a little tense."

Ronnie smiles as if the joke has suddenly dawned on him. A moment later we hear Robin screaming.

Without hesitating, all three of us lunge into the brush. I can hear Robin calling out to us. I can't hear her well, but she sounds desperate, as if she and Emily are in danger.

We're all stomping through the brush toward them, and I feel a bit of a thrill. I guess that the other guys feel the

94

thrill too. We're guys. It may seem old-fashioned, and my mother would kill me if I ever admitted it to her, but every guy gets a little rush of adrenaline when he has the opportunity to run to the aid of a damsel in distress.

"You guys gotta see this!" Robin yells. Suddenly she and Emily don't sound like they're in trouble at all. In fact, if my cousin thinks it's cool, it's probably not something that you need to rush to see.

Then I see the first one, just off to my left. A boulder as big as a tractor trailer. Then another, even larger one just beyond it, and still another on the right. It's almost as if we're running through a shallow valley made of stone.

We find the girls. Robin can't stand still. She hops up to us. "Can you believe it?"

"Look!" Vivek shouts. "A glacial erratic! I mean, a big rock!"

Emily is staring straight up the side of a thirty-foot-tall rock face. She calmly reaches forward with her finger and pokes it as if she's testing to see if it's real. Satisfied that it's solid, she starts to eat her pistachios again.

"See?" I shout. "I told you! I told you it was real!" I punch Ronnie lightly on the shoulder. He winces and rubs the punch away.

The rock's at least twenty-five feet long, and it seems top-heavy. Looking up at it makes me dizzy, makes me feel like the whole thing is about to fall over on top of us. This place is like a dream. Giant stone monuments form walls all around us. We're under tall, slender pine trees, so there's not much brush. The trunks look like thin supports holding up a solid ceiling of intertwined pine branches.

And the strangest thing of all . . . it feels peaceful. My first thought is that I'd love to camp right here under the protective pine roof, right up next to this wall of stone. I'd love to wake to the sun speckling the orange pine needles on the ground. I can't explain it. Here I am deep into the Pricker Boy's territory, and I've found a place so calm and quiet that I'd rather sleep here than in any other place in the world, even my own bed in my own home.

I'm not tired, but still I could curl up right now at the base of one of these trees. If I did, I can almost believe, really believe, that the pine needles would give way slightly, as if they were covering not the hard ground but layers of soft blankets.

I shake my head clear of thoughts of peace and sleep.

Off to the left side, a wide path hooks around between this stone and another, smaller one. Ronnie walks over toward the path. "That almost looks like . . . it's wide enough to be a road between the boulders." He runs up to see what's behind the stone. "Oh no." He stumbles backward. I catch him before he falls on the rocks, then walk up to see what he's discovered. I feel the others come up behind me.

My father has been telling us for years about an abandoned house that he and my Uncle Bill had once found way out in the woods. He said that the place had been empty for ages. The walls were covered with black mold both inside and out. Inside, you had to watch the floor-boards because if you stepped onto the wrong ones, you'd fall right through into the basement. It was full of rickety furniture and shattered glass and decaying mattresses and plates and pots and pans. They used to spend hours out there poking around. He found a broken pocket watch one time, and Uncle Bill found three silver-dollar coins.

One day, they found some papers in a desk with the name "Hora" on it. From then on, they called it the Hora House. When Dad told us about it, we didn't hear him correctly, so we called it the Horror House. He corrected us, but we called it the Horror House anyway.

One summer day when I was about eight, my father disappeared into the woods. He was gone for three or four hours. When he came back, he told us that he had gone off in search of the Hora House. He had wanted to take us back there and show it to us. He thought we'd think it was cool. And it would have been. I'd have gone back into the woods with my dad. Sure, it was heading into Pricker Boy domain, but I was littler and I figured it'd be okay if I was with my dad. I mean . . . he's Dad. When you're a little kid, what more do you need to chase the monsters away than your dad?

But he couldn't find it. He said he searched for hours but came up with nothing. I remember him being really down about it. Like there was a piece of his childhood that he wanted to share with us, but it had evaporated over the years. Like it never really existed at all.

But it does exist, and I know because I'm staring down at it right now. The Hora House is right in front of me.

Or what's left of it, which is not much. Most of the wood rotted away long ago. The only things still standing are a tall stone chimney on the right side and a small portion of the far wall. In front of us is a hole cut sharply into the ground. It looks like a giant knife blade reached down and sliced out the earth. The basement walls are built of flat stones laid without any mortar. Laid well, I guess, considering they're still holding up long after the wood above them has rotted away. A single white birch tree grows straight up from the bottom of the cellar.

My heart pounds, but I don't think it's from fear. This is a discovery, our first real discovery, considering we already knew about the Hawthorn Trees and the offering stone. I jump down a slight, stony incline until I'm level with the house.

"Ronnie?" I ask. "I seem to remember you mentioning this in the story a few years back. You haven't brought it up in a while. Why don't you tell us again?"

"I can't," he says. "Not right now." He wipes his hand across his brow, and I can see his fingers shaking. He's had this place woven into the story for years. Sometimes he includes it, and sometimes he doesn't. But I'm not sure he ever really believed in it. Now he's face to face with it, and he can't deny it.

"I think now is the perfect time," I insist.

He keeps to the edges of the boulders and doesn't walk

up to the foundation. I don't think he can. "Okay," he mumbles. "This is the Horror House. I mean, uh, it's really called the Hora House. I heard about it from Stucks, who heard about it from his dad. I went to the town hall and the library and looked up a little about it. I found out that . . . uh, Stucks? Can't I tell it at the next fire?"

"Come on, Ronnie," I laugh. I want him to say it, if for no other reason than to try to freak out my cousin, who has probably heard about the place from her own dad.

"Well, the Hora House was built in the 1940s by Daniel Hora, who was a guy from New York who'd made it big in the . . . in the . . ."

"Hat business," I say. I don't know if it was hats, but I don't want Ronnie to get stuck.

"Yeah, hat business," Ronnie continues. "He wanted a cottage way off in the country, so he had one built deep in the woods. That's where this path comes from. It's what's left of the road he had cut through the woods to reach the house. . . . It's just the way I'd always imagined it to be."

Emily keeps circling around the foundation, peering down into the bottom.

"He had a wife, and one weekend they wanted to get away. But he got held up at the . . . uh . . ."

"Hat shop," I say.

"Yeah, so he sent his wife on ahead to meet a car at the train station. He showed up later that night, long after dark. As he approached the house, he heard laughter from inside."

Robin goes pale. This was worth it all, all the bugs and the sweat and the blood, worth it all just to see that look on her face.

"Turns out that in the few hours she was left alone, the wife had gone completely insane. Completely. Spent the rest of her life in an institution, babbling about a monster that appeared out of the mist. Claimed that hollow-eyed little children danced in circles around the cottage while she went crazy inside. Daniel Hora never came back to the cottage. And when people asked him, he told them that the earth in these woods was cursed and that no one should ever walk there again." Ronnie turns away, unable to look at the house anymore.

"And now," I add, "the foundation of the Hora House forms a stone pit."

"Like the Pricker Boy's stone pit?" Vivek asks. "Uh, um, but you've got a bit of a time-line problem there."

"What's that?"

"Well, the Pricker Boy was 'born' around when? A hundred years ago, so Ronnie says. But then hat man built his cottage in the 1940s, right?"

"So?" I ask him.

"So you're making it fit because you want it to. The Pricker Boy couldn't have lived in a stone pit that wouldn't be dug for another fifty years or so."

"Maybe the pit was here, and Hora dug his foundation around the pit."

"Or maybe Ronnie can create magical places with his

mind! This is crazy. You hear a little of this and that and Ronnie writes his story around it, and then we find this place and you both try to make it all fit together. Just to scare us." He stares at Ronnie and me. Emily passes by on her third trip around the foundation and smiles at Vivek.

"Okay, maybe Emily isn't scared, but she's as bonkers as a drunken bedbug. Look at me—I'm scared enough to puke. Look at Robin, bud. She's your blood. Doesn't that mean something to you? You just found a piece of your father's and her father's history, a second-generation discovery, and you're using it to scare her silly. This could be really cool . . . but it isn't."

Robin folds her arms in front of her chest, gripping her elbows tightly. Despite the heat, she appears terribly cold. I'll admit it, I'm enjoying her fright until, out of the corner of my eye, I see Emily leap down inside the foundation.

And immediately, without reason, I am as terrified as both Ronnie and Robin.

Her feet hit the half-rotted leaves in the basement of the Hora House, and things that have been sleeping down there for years and years now wake up and begin to spin around her ankles. Emily can't see them, but I can.

She starts poking around the walls of the foundation. She trips over an old bottle and picks it up, holding it up to the sunlight. One of the things comes up with her wrist and wraps around her forearm before dripping back toward the ground. She pokes at a few old bedsprings. All the while, those things are waking up and swirling, rising around her, flapping like mad birds. They are angry things, tiny things, young things that have been asleep for so very long and don't like being woken from their nap.

"Get out," I say.

Emily looks up at me. "Excuse me?"

"Get out. Now."

"But this is interesting," Emily says, completely unaware of what is twirling around her torso.

"You have to . . . you have to get out. Climb, now! It isn't safe!"

"We should go," Robin says. "Please! This doesn't feel right!" I'm amazed that we're actually agreeing about something, and I wonder for an instant if she can see what I see.

"But how often do you get the chance to—" Emily protests.

"Get out now!" I scream, and Emily climbs out of the cellar.

She looks me up and down as if I'm some kind of specimen wiggling in a dish. "Are you okay?" she asks.

I look down into the cellar. Whatever lives down there begins to settle in again.

"We should get on with this," I tell them, and I begin to head back. I don't look over my shoulder. As soon as I feel the Hora House disappearing into the trees behind me, as soon as that nest of boulders is no longer visible, I feel better, like I've once again woken up from a terrible night vision.

My heart calms down. My head is clear. I've learned enough for today. I'm ready to go home.

8

Disappearance

As soon as the weather was warm enough for us to sit
in a boat without freezing our asses off, Pete and I
would get up early and gather our gear and sneak through
the woods to Ed Giles's cottage. Ed Giles is a loudmouthed
retiree who winters down in the Florida Keys. He spends
the whole summer asking us year-rounders how the winter was, just so he can tell us how warm the water is in the
Keys at Christmastime. Overall, he isn't a bad guy, though.

We'd grab the hull of Ed's Sunfish and take it down to
the pond. Ed wouldn't be up to his place for a few months
yet, and we figured that he wouldn't mind if we borrowed
his sailboat for a few hours. Actually, we didn't care
whether he minded or not. What was important was that
he wouldn't know.

We couldn't get at the sail or the rudder, so we always

nabbed two canoe paddles from under his cottage. We'd slip into the water and paddle quietly down past our houses and into the cove, where our parents couldn't spot us. Once in the cove, we'd let the Sunfish drift, guiding it with only the lightest paddle strokes, moving so slowly that we would barely ripple the smooth water.

Pete usually chose our fishing spot. I still don't know what led him to pick one place over another, but whatever spot he chose for us to cast into was sure to bring fish. The ones he reeled in were always bigger than mine, and to this day I don't know why he was a better fisherman than I was. He'd even let me use his rod, reel, and bait, and he'd use mine. He still got bigger fish. Bass for him, crappie for me.

One April morning a couple years ago, we were out on the water just after dawn. Pete brought a couple hot dogs, and I grabbed some worms from Nana's compost pile. We coasted into the cove, baited our hooks, and cast out into the pond. The early morning sunlight made the bugs flying over the water light up golden. Sunset is nice on Tanner Pond, but there's nothing like sunrise. The water at sunset isn't usually calm, and even if it is, you can sense people up and moving around and talking, even if they don't come out of their cottages. In the early morning, though, most everyone is still asleep, and the water and the light and the fish are only there for the privileged few. Those fishing and those reading, and not many others.

Except Hank Paulding. On that particular day, Hank was up too. He's a year-rounder, like us, a harmless guy who hasn't quite reached middle age, but he's missed his window of opportunity for getting married, and he behaves accordingly. Pete and I once left ten bars of soap on his doorstep as a joke. I guess it was a little mean. But it was funny too.

Hank came down to the pond, stepped out onto his wobbly rock pile, and called out to us across the water. Pete held up his finger. "Quiet, Hank," Pete called back, keeping his voice as low as possible.

"Oh yeah, fish," Hank replied, still too loud. For some reason Hank has never learned that sound carries over water. On a morning like that one we would have been able to hear two people having a normal conversation from clear across the cove. Secrets don't stay secrets if you let them get too close to the water.

"What you boys fishin' for?" Hank asked us.

"Fish," Pete said.

"Pike?" Hank asked. "Bass? Bream?"

"Fish!" Pete said.

Hank looked at the water as if he were trying to spot fish and shoo them over our way.

"I'll tell you how to catch trouts!" Hank said.

Pete nodded. "Okay, later." He tried to wave Hank off, but it worked about as well as it usually worked with Hank.

"You use corn!" Hank said.

Pete looked at me as if Hank was crazy. Hank was crazy, so I don't know why Pete looked so surprised.

"See, all these trouts is stocked. They stock them

around Saint Patrick's Day. And you know what they feed those trouts in their trout farms? Pellets! Pellets that look just like corn." Hank looked at us as if he'd just shared secret military launch codes. "Those fish think corn is what they've been eating all along! You fish with corn, and you'll catch tons of trouts, believe me!"

Pete picked up his oar and started pulling at the soft water. We glided away from Hank. I turned around and waved to him as we left. Hank was a nut, but he wasn't a bad nut, and I didn't want him to think we were just trying to get away from him, even though we were.

"Might as well drop dynamite down on them," Pete said once we found a new fishing spot. "It's not fair to the fish. It's wrong."

My line wiggled. I reeled in. I pulled in a little one about six or seven inches long, which was about usual for me. "Pumpkinseed," I said.

"Bluegill," Pete said. "See that blue spot just behind the gill? That's how you know it's a—say it with me—"

"A bluegill," we said together.

"Pumpkinseeds have orange on them. Orange, you know? Like a . . ."

"A pumpkin," I said. I could never tell them apart. I'd see a pumpkinseed with what looked like a blue spot on him and call him a bluegill. I'd see a bluegill with a slight flash of red on him and call him a pumpkinseed. They're all crappie and I should've just called them that.

I reached down to take it off the hook. "Easy," Pete said.

"I know," I said. Actually, I didn't care much about being gentle. I was going to grab that fish as tight as I could and hope that one of its dorsal spikes didn't stab my palm.

"No, no," Pete said, taking the fish from me. "You grab him like that and you'll scrape off the slime. Then he'll get sick, and he'll be floating in a few days. Might as well whack him on a rock. And you twist the hook like this; otherwise, you'll tear his mouth open and he won't be able to eat."

"Might as well whack him on a rock," I said.

Pete laughed. "Yeah." He dropped the bluegill over the side of the boat. It flipped and vanished.

I baited my hook with a worm and cast out again. "I hope I catch one of them trouts," I said, and we laughed. I caught a few more crappie, and Pete picked up one decent-sized bass. We didn't talk much. The pond was so calm, and with everyone still asleep, the only sound was the whizzing of our reels when we cast out.

"My dad hits me sometimes." Pete said it so quietly that I barely heard, so quietly that not even the water could catch it.

I didn't know how to respond. I know what I heard, though. He only said those five words, but there was more folded in with the words. *My dad hits me sometimes. I don't want anyone to know. I don't want you to tell your dad or anyone else. And I don't want to talk about it. But I want you to know that my dad hits me sometimes.* The meaning was there, whether or not he said it out loud.

107

I couldn't change the subject either, no matter how awkward the silence was. There was no way to make the change. And certainly no way to throw in a joke about "trouts." It was up to Pete to decide what would be said next.

Luckily, a trout did grab hold of Pete's line. Pete pulled him in and tossed him in our bucket. "Corn," he scoffed. We went back to fishing, and within a few minutes I was able to let what Pete said drift away as easily as if it were paper I'd placed on the surface of the water.

I was only about twelve, so there's no way I would have known what to say anyway. I might not know what to say or do today if Ronnie, Vivek, Emily, or Robin came and told me the same thing. I'd like to think that I'd come up with something or some way to help them, but I don't know that I could.

Pete and I fished for a couple hours before sneaking back to Ed's place and returning his boat.

The spring before last, we borrowed the Sunfish one last time before Ed came up from Florida, and when we put it back we left a note taped to the inside of the hull that read: IGNORANCE IS BLISS, ED.

At the time, it cracked us up.

Scratched, sweaty, and covered with mosquito bites, we pause for a moment at Whale's Jaw. Vivek slaps the back of the rock and shouts, "Olly olly oxen free!"

"Now that we're back, that was kinda cool," Ronnie mumbles, his eyes to the ground.

"Cool?" Robin asks.

"For us to see it, I mean. For us to all go out there. We finally got to see what was out behind the Hawthorns."

Robin shakes her head. "He thinks it's cool! Bugs and sweat and thorns ripping your skin! Evil old houses with things in the basement!"

She did see it! She must have! I spin around to look at her, but she's already stomping down the path toward the house.

"Well?" Ronnie asks, turning to the rest of us. "Am I wrong?"

"About this?" Vivek asks. "No, you're right about this. But you're wrong about so many other things, Ronnie, like how to comb your hair or start a fire or balance cinder blocks on your head. Those things . . . well, you just don't do them so well."

"Shut up," Ronnie says quietly. "Just shut up."

"Oh now, Ronnie," Vivek says. He throws his arm around Ronnie and leads him down the path toward home. "You're so serious. Your grandfather is about to see how dirty you are. Think of how awful your life will be then. These are your last few minutes to laugh. So laugh, bud! Laugh!"

"It was interesting," Emily says after they've gone. "We saw things. A rock with scratches on it. A collection of erratics. The remains of an old cottage. But I don't think we learned much. Nothing that proves anything. They could all just be bits and pieces of things Ronnie was told years ago, things that he then wrapped into a story."

"What are you saying?" I ask.

"Stucks, I don't know that I'm saying anything, really. I'm thinking." She turns and stares up at the Widow's Stone. "And I'm worrying. Worrying about you."

She gives me a moment to respond, but I don't say anything.

"You grabbed Ronnie and chucked him into that mud. That's not like you. It's more like . . ."

"Like who?"

She turns and looks me dead in the eye. "Like Pete," she says.

"You don't know what you're talking about."

"Maybe. I don't know a lot of things. But something here doesn't ring true, and I'd like to know what it is."

I grit my teeth, step quickly toward her. She doesn't back away. "I saved you back there," I say. "Back at the Hora House. You don't even know it. For all your thinking and your pondering and your analyzing, you don't know anything. You couldn't even see it! But I could. I saved you!"

She looks at me curiously but doesn't say a word. I turn away from her and head back toward the cottage.

I like the idea that I saved her. I like feeling it even if she doesn't know that it happened. I was scared out there at the

110

Hora House, but even so, I was the one who got her out of there. But there's no way for me to explain that to her.

"Stucks!" she calls after me, but I don't turn around.

Then again, louder this time, I hear, "Stucks!" But it's not Emily; it's Robin, running as hard as she can, Vivek and Ronnie following along behind her. Her face is flushed. "The Cricket isn't at the house! Your mom says he hasn't been there all afternoon. She thought he was with us!"

My mind goes quiet for a second, and then I realize what has happened. He wouldn't have stayed behind while "the big kids" were up to something in the woods. How could I have been so stupid to think that he would?

"Oh no," I whisper.

I start running back into the woods. I pass the Widow's Stone without pausing, rushing headlong into the thorns. I use my body to push them out of the way, hoping that I might clear a path for those behind me. I only worry about my eyes. I just need to protect my eyes.

"Cricket!" I shout. "Cricket! No playing! Come out now! No playing!"

From the back of my mind a little voice reminds me that this is how I have always imagined the Pricker Boy moving through the bushes, running at full speed regardless of the thorns. I reach the Hawthorns. I am about to run deeper into the woods when the others catch up with me.

"Stop!" Emily says. "Take a second! Think!"

"He's out there alone!" I shout.

"Stop for just one second!" Emily says. "You don't even know where he is. He could be anywhere."

"Yeah, what's the big deal?" Vivek asks. "He's a weird kid. Could be jumping at butterflies from the roof of your house for all you know."

I stop, breathe deep, then walk in small circles. I point at the rest of them. "You guys go back to the Widow's Stone! If he comes back this way, I want him to see you!"

"I'm not staying here," Robin says. "If you're going back there, I am too, and you can't stop me."

"Then keep up," I say. I reach up into the Hawthorns and pull down one of the dead branches, breaking off a thick stick about three feet long. I begin to break off the spikes so that it is easier to hold.

"Uh, Stucks," Ronnie whispers. "Stucks, do you remember . . ."

"What?" I ask him.

"What Emily said? About harming the trees?"

I have no idea what he's talking about. My mind is on one thing and one thing alone.

"It will bring sickness to the household of the offender," he whispers, almost as if he doesn't want the trees to hear.

"Let it bring sickness," I say. "I just want my brother back."

I swipe my stick through the air, knocking it against the thorn branches that block the path. The bulk of them break to the sides. I swipe again and step onto the path.

I feel the wind pick up, and the thorn branches begin to

sway. For a moment, they seem to intertwine, like a giant net, or like an angry trap whose jaws are just beginning to twitch. Evening is coming, and they are waking up.

I push forward down the path, shouting for the Cricket. I hack at the bushes, but the thorns take their toll on me. My arms and hands are covered with scratches, and I have at least one gash across my face. The salt from my sweat has gotten into the cut there, and I can feel it stinging.

"Cricket, no games! Come out now!" I call.

The muscles of my arm begin to burn. I look behind me. My cousin has been keeping up. And right behind her, keeping pace as well, is Ronnie. He's risking a lot by coming back out here—if not with whatever supernatural creature that might be lurking in the bushes then with his very real grandparents, who will surely kill him when he returns home. His good pants and shirt are snagged and torn, filthy with blood and sweat.

I hand the stick off to my cousin. She begins slapping at the thorns, her fresh arm hitting harder than my tired one could. After a while she passes off to Ronnie. I cringe. If his spindly muscles can't take the strain, I'll grab the stick from his hands and drive on ahead of him.

But to my surprise he does okay. Soon we pass the black puddle, stomping right on through the mud. We reach the spot where we strayed from the path, the part that leads off to the Hora House. I don't want to go back there. I don't want to imagine the Cricket back there alone.

But we have to, so we go.

Through the bushes, into the pines, past the sleeping stone giants, we call the Cricket's name the whole way, even as we pass around that last stone and head down the incline to the Hora House. Ronnie stumbles on the way down, loses his footing, and almost falls into the cellar hole. I grab him and he pulls at me like a panicked, drowning man. Clinging to my arm, then my shoulder, then pushing off, he climbs past me to get as far away from the hole as he can.

Robin and I check the area. She circles the house to check the basement. The Cricket is nowhere to be found.

The sun is just falling past the peaks of stone; in less than an hour the pond will blaze with the sunset. But now, here in the woods, as the sunlight disappears behind the boulders, dusk comes early to the Hora House.

"What now?" Robin asks. She shouts out for the Cricket, turning in circles as she does.

"Cricket!" I shout with her, but my voice only strikes weakly against the rocks.

"Guys?" Ronnie asks hesitantly.

"What?" Robin says tersely.

"I have to pee." He says it so pathetically, as if we're teachers and he's asking permission.

"Well, just go," Robin says. "I don't care."

Ronnie nods, turns his back to us, and unzips his pants. I look up at the tops of the stones, hoping to find the Cricket perched up there, just as Ronnie and I found him perched on Whale's Jaw two days ago. I see nothing. But I feel the darkness beginning to gather around us. A full minute passes before I notice that Ronnie isn't peeing.

"Ronnie?" I ask.

"I can't go," he says, his shame as thick as the heat. "I can't go if you guys are here."

"What are you talking about?" I bark. "You just . . . you just do it, Ronnie. You've been doing it all your life! So pee!"

"I'm not looking," Robin says impatiently.

Ronnie zips up his pants. "I can't. I can't go if people are around. Listen, I'll be okay. I'm just going to walk around this boulder. I won't go far. You guys wait for me."

"We shouldn't separate," I warn him.

"I don't want to. But I have to. Darn it, I feel silly."

Robin shrugs at me. "Do you have a better idea?" she asks.

I wave him off. "Go. But be quick about it."

Ronnie walks off through the boulders. I continue to search for any sign of the Cricket.

I hear a giggle.

A clear giggle. One that I am meant to hear. Where it comes from, I can't really tell. The sound bounces off the stones, seems to come from everywhere.

Robin spins around and points out a break between the stones.

I hadn't seen it before. I doubt that any of us had. But by stepping three feet to my right, I see a thin path through a split in one of the boulders. It's like a secret doorway.

I see something move in there.

115

I take off running. I hear Robin right at my heels. There's just enough room for us to squeeze through the break, and once through we find a hidden path twisting up and away between the rocks.

I'm not watching where my feet are landing, and a couple times I trip on the small stones that litter the path. The path starts to climb, and I catch sight of a little boy up ahead of me.

"Cricket!" I shout, scrambling over the rocks. "Cricket!"

I charge between two boulders, turn, and head uphill again. The path levels off. Small blueberry bushes cluster between rocks. Vaguely, I can tell that we've reached the peak of a hill, that off to my left there is a clear view over the woods. But up ahead I see a figure. . . .

A boy, but not the Cricket. Not the Cricket at all. He looks back at me with gray eyes in a gray face—looks back and giggles. He's young, but he's old at the same time. I see him but at the same time I can't. It seems as if a thin film of mucus has fallen over my eyes, blurring my vision and causing me to see the newly born and the ancient at the same time. He darts away and melts into the granite.

My feet freeze on the path; it feels like ice has gathered around my legs. All of a sudden I can feel the whole weight of the day—the walking, the heat, the frustration, the arguing. All of it settles in my thighs and calves, and I feel like I can't go any farther. If that gray thing shows itself again, I won't even be able to run away. It's as if a drug has hit my blood, cooling me all over with ice water, dragging me downward, begging me to lie down and rest at least until the cold night comes.

Another giggle wakes me from my trance. My eyes clear. I turn around. The Cricket is right behind me, his face one giant grin. I start back toward him, the older brother, the angry brother, ready to make it clear to him just what he has done to us.

Robin gets to him before I do. She grabs him by the shoulders, kisses the top of his head. "You're a pain in the butt," she says to him, gasping. He laughs, tosses a slow-motion punch against his jaw, and slaps his own behind. OUCH BUTT.

The Cricket reaches out and pokes my arm with his index finger, but I ignore him. I'm not going to laugh at this joke. In fact, this joke isn't over yet. We still have to get back. I turn my back on him and then . . . I see it all before me. Our path has ended at a rock cliff, and beyond the cliff, the woods stretch all the way back to the Hawthorns. In the distance Tanner Pond reflects the fading sun like a golden mirror.

Directly below me is the cellar hole of the Hora House and—and—and—

My whole body shakes. I couldn't see it from below, but up here it's so clear. The Hora House was built in a small depression in the ground. On all sides it's surrounded by the boulders. They fit together like puzzle pieces, forming rough walls.

It's a pit. A pit of stone. We did find the stone pit; we just couldn't see it from below because we were standing in it. If Vivek were here right now, I would yank him to the edge and make him look down into it. To hell with his "time-line problem." The stone pit wasn't the cellar of the Hora House. It wasn't built in the 1940s by Daniel Hora. It was built over ten thousand years ago by a massive receding glacier.

Hora didn't build his house over the stone pit. He built it down *in* it.

"Robin? Robin, look. Look down at the—"

"No, Stucks, look at this."

It's a magnet down there, pulling at my eyes. I force myself away from it, turn back to her. "What?"

"Well, look."

She is looking the Cricket up and down. He's dirty, but that's not unusual. He's smiling, but that's not unusual either. It takes me a second to realize it, but she's right: something is definitely wrong.

There isn't a scratch on him. Not a nick. Nothing. Not one sign of broken skin. Most of us hadn't made it a hundred paces past the Hawthorns without getting cut, and we were working together to get through the thorns. On this second trip, I got cut from head to toe. I look like an extra for a zombie movie. How has he followed us all the way out here without getting a single scratch on him? His legs aren't even that muddy, and there's no way he could have crossed the black puddle without thick mud staining his skin up to his knees.

I try to figure this out, but then I remember Ronnie.

Ronnie, who had followed us all the way back here again, who had without hesitation come back through the thorns to find the Cricket. Ronnie, still in his good pants, tired, knowing he is already in trouble at home, poor Ronnie who is too shy to pee with us watching . . . We left him alone in that stone pit.

"We forgot Ronnie!" I shout.

I take off down the hill, slipping on stones all the way. No one is at the Hora House when we get back there. "Ronnie!" I shout as loud as I can, but my voice doesn't seem loud enough. It's like the boulders can somehow capture and hold the sound. I try to shout louder. "Ronnie, where are you?"

No sound comes back to us other than the hollow echo of our own voices. I turn to Robin. "I don't know what to do," I confess.

Robin is holding the Cricket's hand. She's not going to let it go until after we pass Whale's Jaw again.

I wish that Emily were here to tell me what to do. She would be able to detach, to look at things rationally. "He wouldn't have gone too far alone. We can catch up to him on the path," I say.

"But I don't think he would have left us either," Robin says, shaking her head. "He wouldn't have abandoned us out here," she adds, and I ignore the slightly accusatory tone in her voice.

"You're right," I say. "Unless he thought that we had gone first. Think about it. Ronnie is always odd man out. If he came back and saw that we were gone, he'd think that it was just another trick, just another jab at him. He'd think we left him behind."

Robin shakes her head. "Out here? No, I'd never leave him out here."

"I know we wouldn't! But *Ronnie* doesn't know that."

Robin thinks for a moment, shaking her head back and forth.

"Look around!" I shout impatiently. "It's already dusk. In a half hour or so, we won't be able to see the thorns in front of our own faces. We have to head back."

"Okay," she says. "But keep calling out to him."

As we turn away, I see something terrible. A white worm of smoke snakes up over the edge of the cellar hole and then back down inside. Another two roll up the side. One gets up and out and begins to wriggle across the ground toward us.

I can barely speak, but I am able to get out one hoarse word. "Hurry."

"Oh God," Robin says. I can't tell if it's because she sees what I see, or if it's just the darkness pulling in toward us.

I lead the way, Robin follows me, and the Cricket clings to her hand. Going back is easier. The path that we hacked through the thorns is still fresh, though a few strong branches have found their way back into it. In my mind I can picture those slow-moving things at the Hora House, drifting around the boulders, trying to find the path that we disappeared down.

120

We are only halfway back when the real darkness comes. It comes quickly, and with it the woods change. Birds stop chirping, and the insects start calling. The wind seems louder in the trees, or maybe it is just our ears, which become more and more sensitive as our eyes become less and less useful. Either way, we find ourselves in another world.

I feel ahead for the thorns. With each step they seem to grow thicker, as if in the darkness they have gathered in the path again, despite my beating them back with a stick just an hour ago. We take it step by step, moving slowly now, and every few feet I call out to Ronnie. I shout as loud as I can. I shout to make my voice carry through the darkness, not caring if anything out there other than Ronnie can hear me. I shout so that if Ronnie *is* out there, he'll hear me and know that he is not alone. But no matter how loud I shout, it feels like something is knocking my voice down, like in a dream when you try to scream and nothing comes out.

It is pitch-black when I finally get an answer to my calls.

"Stucks!"

It isn't Ronnie's voice that calls back through the darkness. It's Emily's.

"Yeah!"

"Did you find the Cricket?"

"He's with us!"

I hear Vivek cheer through the darkness.

"Is Ronnie with you?" I yell.

There's a short pause, and then a slightly confused response. "No! Isn't he with you?" Emily calls.

We break out of the path to the small clearing around the Hawthorns. "Don't go near the Hawthorns," Robin warns the Cricket. "Those spikes are dangerous, and we can't see them in the dark."

In the distance I can see the Widow's Stone. One of them went back for a flashlight, and the beam shines to us through the darkness.

"We got separated from Ronnie!" I yell to him.

"He's not with us," Vivek shouts.

I watch the beam of light waver at us from the Widow's Stone. Going to it means abandoning Ronnie to the woods.

The thorns between us and the flashlight seem thicker than ever. They seem to have doubled since nightfall. Part of me wants to burst through, to just run for it, to try and make it to the back of Whale's Jaw.

I turn to Robin. My hands are shaking. "You take the Cricket home, and I'll go back for Ronnie," I say, not quite believing the words myself.

"Are you sure?" Robin asks. "We can take him home together. I'll come back with you to find Ronnie. But first we take care of the Cricket." It's the most sensible thing I have heard all day, and a more sensible idea than any I can think of at the moment.

We start moving toward the Widow's Stone together. I

tell myself that once the Cricket is safe, I'll have the courage to go back for Ronnie, that I'm not so frightened that I would abandon him out there altogether.

We're halfway to the Widow's Stone when I hear the noise.

"Do you hear that?" I ask Robin.

"Hear what?" she says.

"It's a . . . like a clicking. Can't you hear that?"

It's getting louder. Whatever is making the noise is getting closer to us, moving underneath the thorns off to our right.

"I don't hear anything," she says. "Please, Stucks, you're scaring the Cricket. Let's just keep going."

We take a few more steps, then I stop again. There's no way that she can't hear it. It's too loud now. Like a giant insect skittering along, its legs clicking together as it crawls.

"You can't hear that?" I shout at her.

"No," she says quietly. She starts again toward the Widow's Stone.

Now it's not one insect but hundreds of them that I hear, all of them swarming under the thorns toward us. I try to ignore the sound, but it just gets louder, it just gets closer.

I bow my head, close my eyes, and say out loud to myself, "I will not leave my friend behind, I will not leave my friend behind, I will not leave my friend behind. . . ." I raise my voice to drown out the clicking noises, but they just get louder and louder and louder. I start to shout, "I will not leave my friend behind! I will not leave my friend behind! I will not leave my friend behind!"

I feel something at my ankle. It cuts into my skin. I fall to the ground, and as I do, thorn branches wrap around me. Something nearby, something close to the ground, hisses at me through the darkness.

Robin is almost to the Widow's Stone. I try to follow after her, but something is wrapping around me, grabbing my clothes tight, digging into my skin through my pants, through my shirt. Thick thorns drag across my face. I shut my eyes. Sharp points press against my eyelids. I'm afraid to open my mouth to scream.

I hope that Robin has her arms around the Cricket, protecting him from whatever has gotten hold of me. I picture them rejoining Vivek and Emily. The Cricket is terrified, but he's safe behind my friends. They have each other, and the Pricker Boy only takes kids who are alone.

And I'm alone.

I hear a voice from far away.

"Stucks!" Ronnie shouts, his voice high and desperate. "Stucks, come back for me! *Stucks, I can't find my way without you!*"

9

The Poison Seeps

Mr. Milkes is pulling me from the thorns. I think that I might have blacked out for a moment or two. My leg is stuck, and Mr. Milkes has to do some twisting just to break it free. Robin has gotten my mother and my father. Whatever was pulling me under the thorns has left, but I am still tangled in the branches.

"Where's Ronnie?" Mr. Milkes asks me, his voice unsympathetic.

"I dunno," I blurt. I feel stupid. "We got separated in the woods. He's back there someplace, I think."

I feel my dad's hand under my shoulder, yanking me to my feet. "Then you go back there with Mr. Milkes and find him," my father says. He grabs the flashlight from Vivek and hands it to Mr. Milkes.

Mr. Milkes and I start walking. "Call out to him," he

commands. Ronnie immediately answers me, and I tell him to keep yelling and to stay calm.

I'm holding something tight in my palm. I loosen my grip. It's that ring that we found in the package yesterday. At some point I must have taken it out of my pocket, but I don't remember doing it. I start to put it back but then decide to tighten my fingers around it again.

"I don't know," Mr. Milkes says to me. "There's nothing simpler than, 'Be home in time for dinner,' is there? Huh, boy?" When I don't answer quickly enough, he says, "Huh, boy?" again.

"No sir, I don't think so. But it's not Ronnie's fault. We couldn't find my little brother—"

"Shouldn't have been out here in the first place. Poison ivy. Pine sap. Mrs. Milkes works hard washing his clothes, keeping them clean. Works hard to get dinner on the table on time. Are you listening to me?"

I keep nodding and agreeing, but I'm not really listening. We find Ronnie crouched down on the path, his arms wrapped around his legs. He's badly scratched from head to toe, and I don't think that Mrs. Milkes will be able to salvage his clothes. When the flashlight beam hits him, he turns away from it as if he's ashamed to be seen. I am pretty sure he's been crying, though his eyes have dried. Mr. Milkes turns his accusatory questions to Ronnie and leaves me alone.

Not that there aren't plenty of questions for me when we get back to the house. Robin sits at the dinner table, looking miserable and offers no protest to my parents' inquest. I explain to them exactly what happened. I say that we had gone on a "nature discovery walk" into the woods and had returned in time for dinner, but that we were afraid that the Cricket was lost in the woods, so we went back to look for him. After we found him, it got dark, and coming home I stumbled into the thornbushes and freaked out.

I leave out the part about the monster that lives back there. I don't think that they'd understand.

Through it all, the Cricket sits at the table and stares at his bare feet. The thrill of his joke has been replaced by guilt. He hates to see me get into trouble under any circumstances. When I finish my story, he taps his fist against his heart and makes the sucking sound with his mouth. I'M SORRY.

My mother glares at him. "If anyone is in trouble here, it's you," she says, her voice raised. "Why would you go off into the woods with your brother and then start playing your hide-and-seek game? You could get lost out there!"

The Cricket starts quietly crying, and I cross my arms and line my pinkies up. He sees me, smiles only slightly, but returns the sign.

My father calls around to the Milkeses, the Patels, and the Habers and explains to all the parents that we were late because we were in the woods looking for the Cricket. He apologizes to each family, and with the exception of Ronnie, we all get off without any punishment.

Or so we think. The itching begins on the afternoon of the next day. It starts on my arms, then spreads to my neck and onto my shoulders and the left side of my face. Within two days bubbles form, and my neck swells so much that I can't move my head. Robin gets it too, worse than I do. Her little trip to the bushes got her in the worst place imaginable, and within days she can't even sit down. Emily turns into something out of a horror movie. Her eyes swell shut, and her lips grow into a grotesque red bubbling mass. Her fingers swell into stiff claws, and only her first finger and thumb have any real movement. Vivek's legs are covered with oozing blisters. Ronnie has it the worst, though we don't know it at first because we don't see him. He is locked inside the Milkes Fortress, and his grandparents probably give him hell right up until the ambulance arrives.

I once tried to explain to a friend who had never been to the woods what it is like to have poison ivy. I said it's like taking thick molasses and spreading it over your skin and then dunking your arm down into a bucketful of fire ants. You let the fire ants swim in the molasses and then dig down into your skin, hundreds of them, digging down deeper and deeper. They sit there and wiggle, and when they wiggle it makes you want to itch so bad you think you're going to lose your mind. If you tried to scratch at them, you'd only succeed in popping them like little blisters, and their skins would quickly grow back and swell all the more. After a couple days, they'd all start to ooze yellow gunk, and a crust would form over the whole mess.

My friend looked at me. "It ain't like that," he said.

Well, it is. At least for me. For nine days it feels like fire ants have infested my neck, face, and shoulders, and for nine days Robin has fire ants on her upper thighs and Emily has them on her lips and the flesh around her eyes and Vivek has them crawling all over his legs.

The Cricket gets nothing. No scratches, no poison ivy. He goes right on playing. Meanwhile, the first real summer heat wave comes, settling in on us like a heavy wool blanket and driving those fire ants insane. We don't sleep; we don't play; we just try to keep from sweating at all costs, because the salt and sweat only make it worse. When it gets really bad, the others crawl into the pond, where the cool water quiets the maddening itch for a while.

I don't go in the water. I won't go in the water.

The ambulance comes on the fourth day. I figure that's when Ronnie's blisters start to ooze. I'm sure that's what sends Mrs. Milkes over the brink. I stand in the backyard with Nana, watching them walk Ronnie to the back of the ambulance.

"If that boy can walk, he doesn't need an ambulance! All he needs is a little jewelweed and peppermint!" Nana shouts to Mr. Milkes, who ignores her.

Ronnie sees me as he steps into the back of the ambulance, but he doesn't say anything. He doesn't wave, and his eyes quickly dart away. The driver closes the ambulance doors behind him.

"I only rode in an ambulance once," Nana says after the vehicle leaves. "And I didn't need it any more than that boy."

"What's that, Mrs. Cumberland?" Mr. Milkes says, stepping to the edge of his yard.

"I said *I only rode in an ambulance once, and I didn't need it any more than that boy!*"

"Serves him right for being out there," Mr. Milkes responds, then turns to head back into his cottage.

"Thirty years!" Nana shouts at him, and he turns back around. Nana holds up her left hand so that Mr. Milkes can see the stump where her index finger was. "Thirty years I've been without that finger. Lost it at work in a grommet press." Mr. Milkes nods and pretends to be interested. "You put your left hand in, you take your left hand out," Nana sings. "Then whack! Your finger ain't yours anymore. It belongs to the grommet press!"

"And is that when you got to ride in the ambulance?" Mr. Milkes asks, glancing once at the doorway to his cottage.

Nana scowls. "They forced me. I could walk! I could drive! I wasn't ready to go to the hospital. You know what they say about having on clean underwear when you go to the hospital?"

Mr. Milkes nods politely and then checks his watch. "Is that right? No clean underwear?"

"It was clean, all right! Only it wasn't mine. I hadn't done laundry in a few days, and when I was getting ready for work and opened the dresser drawer—whoops! No underwear. So I looked in Mr. Cumberland's drawer. He had clean underwear."

Mr. Milkes forgets about his watch and the door of his

cottage and stares at Nana. "You wore your husband's underwear?"

"If I had it to do again, I'd do it differently, but yes."

"I can tell you truthfully, Mrs. Cumberland, that my wife has never worn my underwear."

"Don't be so sure! A man never really knows what his wife is up to while he's out of the house."

Mr. Milkes's eyes flicker with anger. "What are you saying about my wife?"

"I'm not talking about sex," Nana says, shaking her head. She turns to me. "Is that all men think about?"

Mr. Milkes starts toward the door of his cottage, but he only makes it a few steps.

"Anyway, there they were, walking me out to the ambulance, and I was just desperate to get to my car so I could go home and put on my dirty underwear, which at least was for females." Nana chuckles. "I'm so glad I married that old fool. God bless Mr. Cumberland!" She kisses the stub of her missing finger. "Nice talking to you, Mr. Milkes! I'll brew up something for Ronnie and send it over with one of the boys." I help her inside the house.

One summer we raided the wild grapevines that grow all over the woods. When the grapes grow ripe each year, they become mushy and sour, and they leave purple stains on the bottoms of your feet after they drop to the ground. Early in the summer they're green, and they're hard little pellets, hard enough to sting if thrown with enough force.

Vivek got a handful, and he chucked some at Pete. Then Pete got a handful, and he chucked them back at Vivek. Emily wanted to stay out of the fight, so she climbed to the top of Whale's Jaw with a book. I only had to fire a single barrage at her before she climbed down and chased me down the paths. And that was it: the Great Green Grape War had begun.

Ronnie and I teamed up for a while, and he disappeared into the woods to "gather more grapes." I could have killed him for leaving me alone to defend myself, but when he returned he had a whole grocery bag full of them, and together we were able to overtake Whale's Jaw and drive Vivek and Pete back onto the paths. But then Ronnie kept talking about how we were "partners," so I turned on him and joined Emily. Pete turned on Vivek, so Vivek went to Ronnie, and on and on.

I'll never forget the look of horror on Vivek's face when he spun around and whipped a handful of the hard green pellets at what he thought was a Pete Morgan sneak attack. He had released his fist before realizing who he was throwing at, and with the sting of the grapes the Cricket started screaming bloody murder. I stood up from my hiding place and went to him, picking him up off the ground and rubbing the spots where little red welts had begun to form. I walked him back out of the woods. I walked quickly. I wanted to get the Cricket to safety, but I wanted to be back in the fray as soon as possible.

I wasn't back from the house for five minutes before

the Cricket was back to watch the big kids again. I got angry with him, and I tried to ignore him. In a few minutes he was gone again. I ran a full-out assault on Ronnie, using the same grapes that he had gathered for us earlier in the day. I grabbed another handful of grapes and let loose on Vivek. It became a free-for-all, but Pete was long gone by then. He was at the pond, sitting with the Cricket by the water's edge and building drip castles in the mud. I remember being ashamed when I found out how nice he'd been to my little brother.

The poison ivy scabs are healing. I'm sitting on top of Whale's Jaw. The woods have changed over the past few weeks. The summer heat has moved in. With it has come a dry spell, and the rich, humid air that we breathed under the trees just a week or so ago is now lighter and dustier. The smell of earth has been replaced by the smell of dry leaves and pine needles, and under our feet the ground no longer feels cool and damp, but dusty and loose.

I reach into my pocket and pull out the ring that we found in the Hawthorns. No one's claimed it, so I've kept it. It's mine as much as anybody's, I guess.

Small green pellets rain onto me. I figure it's one of the others sneaking up on me, but I thought I was alone out here. I spin around to see Pete smiling at me. He launches another handful of green grapes my way.

"Oh, it's you," I say, tucking my head in as the green hail falls around me.

"*Oh, it's you,*" he mocks me. "Some friend. You haven't seen me in a week and all you can say is, 'Oh, it's you.' "

"I thought you were someone else," I say, settling back down on the rock. He eyes the ring I keep fiddling with but doesn't ask me about it.

Pete climbs up and sits next to me. "Who'd you think I was? Ronnie? Or Emily? You know, the other day I was up on the hill behind her cottage, and you know how they have that outside shower? Well, she came out to take a shower, and I could see everything . . . everything."

I try to ignore him, but it's difficult when he's sitting right next to me. He takes the green grapes one by one and drops them down the back of Whale's Jaw, watching them bounce down to the dirt below.

"Last year she was just a kid, but look at her now. I almost walked right out of the woods and gave that townie a real country welcome, you know."

"Pete, stop."

"I'll stop when I feel like stopping."

"Why do you have to talk like that? She was your friend."

"Yeah, well . . ." is the only answer he has to give.

I shake my head. "Sometimes I don't understand you."

"You got something on your mind?" he asks me. "If you've got something to say, just say it."

I don't respond right away because I don't want to confront Pete on anything. He reaches over quickly and snaps the ring out of my fingers. I try to grab it back, but he holds

134

it out of my reach. He laughs. "What? I can't see it? I just want to look at it, Stucks."

"Give it back."

"Give it back! Give it back!" he squeals. He holds out the ring to me, but when I reach for it, he yanks it away.

"Friends for life, and I can't even look at a stupid ring." He takes a quick look at it, then obviously loses interest, but he doesn't give it back to me.

"Do you know who it belongs to?" I ask.

"Don't know, don't care," he says. He stands up and chucks the ring off into the woods.

"Don't!" I spring to my feet. "Pete! Why did you—"

Pete laughs and holds out his hand. He had only mimed the throw. The ring is still in his hand.

"Give it back."

He doesn't respond.

"Give it back now."

He stares at me. He offers it twice, each time pulling away at the last second. On the third offer, he drops it down into the brush on the steep side of Whale's Jaw. He sits back down.

"What's the matter with you?" I ask him.

"Same thing that's always been the matter with me." He laughs as if he understands things that I'm incapable of seeing. "My doctor told me that I was, uh, how did he say it? He gave me some disorder or something. Hyperactive defiant something or other. 'With potential for violence.' That was my favorite part. 'With potential for violence.' "

I'm scared to sit back down next to him.

"Your family's as batty as all hell, but I'll bet none of you has 'a potential for violence'—am I right?" He stares at me for a minute. "Anyway, so there's this pill and that pill and 'keeping a journal of your thoughts' and 'reconnecting with your family' and the bottom line is that it's all crap."

I climb down the back of Whale's Jaw. Pete watches me as I push through the brush to the steep side and begin searching the ground for the ring. "Is it magic? You lost your magic ring, little boy?"

I ignore him. I move the low branches of a young maple tree out of the way so that I can see better. I spot a glint of gold and grab the ring. I stand and brush it off.

Suddenly Pete jumps from the top of Whale's Jaw and lands right near me, knocking me backward. I look up and wonder how he did that without breaking his ankle.

"So what do you think?" he asks.

I stick the ring back into my pocket before he has a chance to steal it away again. "About what?"

"Do you think that I have a potential for violence?"

I turn around and push through the brush back to the other side of Whale's Jaw.

"Sure, I guess. I don't know. Maybe everybody does."

He grabs my shoulder, spins me around. "But everybody doesn't have it written down on paper, where your teachers and parents can see it, do they?"

I don't answer. He'd grabbed my shoulder pretty hard, harder than was necessary. I take a step backward. He smiles and steps forward. He locks his eyes on my eyes. He reaches out and slams his open palm into the center of my chest, kicking the air out of my lungs and knocking me off my feet.

I try to scramble away from him, but he follows after me. He drags his feet in the dirt and kicks the dust up at me. I feel my back bump hard against Whale's Jaw. I place my arms over my face to protect myself. "Leave me alone!" I shout at him.

He starts laughing. "I'm just messing with you!" He reaches down and helps me up. "But you should have seen the look on your face."

I brush myself off but I keep my eyes on him just in case he jumps at me again.

"You sure were ready to run away. Like a little bunny rabbit. Your family's got a rabbit and a cricket. A rabbit, a cricket, and a crazy old grandma."

Again he goes silent. He's studying me. Studying me the way you'd study an anthill before kicking it. Studying me the way you'd study the ants afterward to see how they'd react.

"I can't tell you how glad I am that my father didn't raise me to be like you," he says.

Now I don't care how much potential for violence he might have. He can say what he wants about me, but he should leave my family out of it. "My family has always been good to you. They've always kept a seat at the table for you. My father . . . well, he's been like a second father to you."

"Maybe," he says. He reaches into his pocket and pulls

out a pack of cigarettes. He lights one and pulls a few drags off it as he watches me.

"Enough of this," he says. "I'm going to ask you one last time. Are you going to hang with those little brats all summer? Come out with me tonight. We're not doing anything except driving around, maybe heading up to Tucker's Corner. There's a lake out there that people go out and party at. Or maybe we'll all just drive . . . wherever. It doesn't matter."

"No. No thanks."

He walks up to me very slowly, watching to see if I'll back away. He doesn't stop until his face is inches from my face. "You smell, you know. You smell like, I don't know. Like flowers?" He takes a long breath in through his nose. "Not perfume. Like some woman's lilac water or something. Something someone's grandmother would wear. You smell like an old woman trying to cover up her stink." He takes a long drag off his cigarette, blows the smoke over me, then looks me up and down like I'm the most disgusting thing he's ever seen. "I don't like you anymore. And that's something that you should remember the next time you see me."

But this time it's me staring. This time it's me studying him. "That's not true," I say firmly. "And just so you know, our table is still open to you."

He backs off, shaking his head. He turns and walks up the hill toward the Widow's Stone. "I'm not that hungry anymore," he calls back over his shoulder.

10

Lanterns

I reach into my pocket and pull out the ring. I press it hard into my palm and pull it away. There's an imprint of a circle left behind. It's way too big for a kid to have worn, but that doesn't mean that one of us didn't treasure it for some reason. Found it in the leaves or in the shallow water of the pond. Picked it up and gloated about our lucky find. But if it was so important that it was sacrificed for a widow's walk, then someone should remember it.

"So I guess it's just a normal summer from now on," I say to the others.

Light from the Japanese lanterns flickers off the ring. Earlier in the evening, my father pulled me aside and told me that we couldn't have a fire out at Whale's Jaw. I was going to say, "What are you talking about, Dad? We don't have fires out at Whale's Jaw." Instead I said, "We keep buckets of water out there. Just like you used to when we were little. We're careful."

"It's been dry," my father said. "So use the lanterns."

The lanterns are a pain in the ass, and I told my father so.

"I wouldn't even let you use the lanterns if there was a breeze. Look, I don't care what you guys do out there. Roast marshmallows, tell ghost stories, curse and call your parents assholes . . . whatever. But if I take a walk into the woods and see a fire tonight, then I'm coming out there, and the party's over."

"I'll make a deal with you, Dad. Ronnie's planning on telling a pretty scary one tonight. Lots of blood and gore in this one. Could you keep the Cricket home tonight?"

A little white lie never hurts, and if it keeps the Cricket from hearing anything about what's really going on, then it's worth it.

"That won't be easy," he said.

"Just one night. And I won't be out late, so it's not like you'll have to hold him for long."

Dad agreed. I carried the lanterns out to Whale's Jaw, Boris wheezing and panting by my side. I hung them by Christmas-tree hooks on the branches around the fire pit and lit them with votive candles.

Now we're sitting by the fire pit and watching dusk fall. The lanterns are becoming red and green and yellow orbs glowing in the trees. They're pretty creepy. I'd really rather have a fire.

I close my fist tightly around the ring and look up at Vivek, Ronnie, Emily, and Robin. "How about it? Normal summer? Catchin' fireflies and swimmin' in the pond and playin' tag?"

Emily reaches over and pinches one of the accordion-like rice-paper folds on a green lantern. "There was nothing that happened out in the woods that can't be chalked up to overactive imaginations," she says. She releases the fold and then gently taps the side of the lantern.

I have a tough time holding back my anger. "Overactive imaginations! The package, the words carved in the stone, even the Hawthorn Trees! What was it you said? *Those fairies get very upset if the tree is harmed in any way.* Something about sickness to the house of the offender? And what's the first thing you do? Pluck the berries! Well, look around! We've been scratching at scabs for a week now."

"Don't you point that one at me," she shoots back. "You know poison ivy better than any of us. You must have seen it. So let's not blame the Hawthorns."

"I told you it was poison ivy, you jerk," Robin chimes in. *"You wouldn't know poison ivy if your own name was written on the leaves."* She folds her arms, leans back in her seat, and looks off into the trees. She continues talking, but it sounds more like she's talking to the lanterns than to us. "I learned my lesson. I'm not going back there again. Poison ivy in my crotch! If they want to go back, they can, but I'm no dope."

"I can't go back," Ronnie says. "My grandpa says—"

141

I sneer at him. "Your grandpa says what? Did he offer you a cookie if you promised not to go back into the woods again?"

I shake my head. I slide the ring over my thumb and pick up my fire poker. I jab at the ground, and the soil crumbles to powder. There hasn't been a drop of rain in three weeks, and there isn't any expected for some time. You can almost hear the ground beneath us crying with thirst.

"I don't believe in fairies or woodland demons, Stucks," Emily states. "I'll admit that when I was a kid it scared me a little, but I never believed in the Pricker Boy any more than I believed in Santa Claus or the Easter Bunny. And I gave up Santa and the Easter Bunny a long time ago."

"I'm Hindu," Vivek says. "I never had to give up Santa or the Easter Bunny. Just women with lots of arms. Whole lots."

I glare at him. "You know, I'm getting pretty sick and tired of your dumbass jokes."

"I don't know any other kinds of jokes. Sorry!"

We look at each other over the fire for a moment, and then Emily interrupts our staring contest. "Santa Claus and the Easter Bunny aside, I'm still . . . interested," she says. Boris wanders over to Emily and sticks his nose into her palm. She scratches his head. "And if one of you is orchestrating this whole thing—the package, the carving on the stone, the things you claim that you've seen—then now's the time to stop. Because if it turns out that one or both of you set this up as some kind of prank, then I'm going to lose interest pretty quickly. Both in this story and in you."

"She's talking about us!" Ronnie says, looking over at me.

Emily ignores him at first. She reaches into the pouch of her sweatshirt and pulls out a dog biscuit. She sniffs it once before handing it over to Boris. He flops to the ground and begins crunching. Finally Emily says, "Yes, I'm talking about you."

"Hey, I know this is my story, so I guess that makes me the prime suspect for putting that package out there, but I wouldn't do that. I wouldn't leave any of you out there on your own either."

Robin releases a sad sigh, then reaches over and squeezes Ronnie's arm. "We told you, Ronnie. We thought that you'd headed back. We never would have left you out there on purpose. I swear, Ronnie. I feel so bad about what happened."

"If you knew how to pee properly, then it never *would* have happened," I say.

Vivek raises an eyebrow and turns toward Ronnie. "You don't know how to pee?"

"You're all just trying to embarrass me again!" Ronnie blurts. "You left me out there! You left me!"

At first, I think Vivek's going to make another dumb joke. But then something in his face changes.

"It's not their fault, Ronnie," he says. "It's mine."

Ronnie looks confused. "But you weren't even there."

"Exactly. I was the one who said that we would all stay together. I should have been back there with you guys, but I wasn't. And I'm sorry about that, bud. It never should have happened. Never."

The way Vivek says "never" stretches his apology back further than our one-day trek out into the woods. Ronnie looks like he wants to say something, but no words come out.

So I speak first.

"I guess I'm the only one here who still believes in the Easter Bunny, because that thing out there scares the hell out of me," I say. "Emily, do you really think that I've set this up? How could I have gotten hold of the old baseball cards, the locket, the book? I believe that there is something in those woods, something I can't explain, and maybe I'm supposed to be too old to believe in it, but I do anyway. I told you, I saw that stone pit. You could see it from the ridge above! Are you saying that I rolled those boulders over so that they surrounded the Hora House? Or maybe I went back in time and actually *built* the Hora House?"

Emily turns to Robin. "Did you see this stone pit?"

"No," she admits. I am just about to chuck a few choice words at her when she adds, "but I wasn't looking down. I was too worried about the Cricket. I can't say that it was down there . . . but I won't say that it wasn't."

"Fair enough," I say, nodding. I have to admit, I'm surprised by what she just said. But because no one else seems willing to give me the benefit of the doubt, I add, "There's one thing that no one here is considering. If there is any truth to the story—"

"That's a good question," Emily says, picking at the flaky remnants of poison-ivy rash on her jaw. She turns to Ronnie. "The time for 'stories' is over. You've been telling us for years that this is a true story, one that you did not make up. I want the truth."

Ronnie slumps down in his chair. "Parts of it are true. Parts are made up. Those kids really died. My grandpa told me so when I was little so I wouldn't go too far into the woods. And I know people have claimed to have seen him. A lot of the details were made up, filled in."

"Why the hell didn't you tell us that before we went out into the woods?" Robin asks.

"Because it's my story," Ronnie says, sulking. "I made it. It's mine. But it's beginning to feel true. I didn't tell you guys, but I thought I saw something out there too. That's why I wasn't at the Hora House when you got back. I saw a little boy and thought it was the Cricket and pushed through the bushes after him. But then it laughed and vanished, and for a few minutes I couldn't find my way back. When I did, you guys were gone."

"But you couldn't have gone far," Robin says. "Didn't you hear us shouting for you?"

"I didn't hear anything at all." He shivers, then whispers, "I'm scared."

A curious expression comes over Vivek's face. He leans over and looks at the ground. "Did one of you guys start smoking?" he asks, plucking a cigarette butt off the ground and tossing it into the fire pit. He finds two more and picks them up—

Boris leaps to his feet, the hair on his back rising. He looks up toward the Widow's Stone and barks. Just like before, just like on the first day of summer.

I reach down and try to calm him, but he spins in the dirt, takes a few steps toward the path, and looks back over his shoulder.

Then a sound rises from the woods, a gruesome sound, frightened and sobbing. We all jump to our feet. Ronnie's chair falls over. Robin knocks into one of the lanterns, and it falls to the ground. The votive topples out, snuffing itself out in the dirt.

"What the hell?" Vivek says. Emily actually steps forward, turning her ear in the direction of the sound.

We hear it again. It is a single voice, wailing from the woods. At first I think that it might be Pete out there, hiding out in the darkness and trying to mess with us all, but there is something unreal about the sounds, and I know that Pete could never produce them.

Vivek stumbles backward down the path. I hear Boris's growl rumbling.

The voice yelps—excited and happy. It isn't forming words, just releasing sounds into the night. It's human, or at least it sounds human. My skin prickles cold in spite of the heat. This is clearly a child's voice. A child's voice mixed with blindness, blackness, and blood.

"My God," Ronnie says. "I've never heard anything like that before in my life."

The voice calls again, almost forming words before dissolving into nonsense. Now it's a voice of madness, of gibberish. It says nothing rational, but it delights in every squeal it produces, as if it has been bound and gagged for a hundred years and some dark angel has finally reached down and ripped the muzzle from its mouth.

And it's getting closer.

"Come on, let's go!" Vivek shouts at us.

Robin joins him on the path. "Guys, let's get out of here!"

"No," Emily responds softly, as if she is in a trance. "Let's wait a moment."

Another voice joins, just as sickly as the first, and the two of them echo through the woods together. Any lingering suspicion that Pete is the cause of the noises evaporates, and I find myself crossing my fingers and praying that if Pete is in the woods tonight, he is far away from whatever is making these noises. Another voice joins, and another. Four in all, whooping with delight, happy together in the darkness out near the Hawthorns.

"It's children," Emily says, stepping toward them again. "They sound like children."

They rush at us from over the hill. Emily doesn't move. I push Ronnie down the path and grab Emily by the arm. I pull her along behind me. Boris follows at my heels.

We sprint halfway down the path, but just past the twin

climbing trees, Emily yanks her arm out of my hand. "Let go of me!" she says. Again she turns toward the noises. "I want to know what they are." She starts to jog back toward them.

I know what they are. They're those things that rose up around Emily in the cellar of the Hora House. Those things that were sleeping in the leaves. We woke them up, and now they've come back to the woods. And if I need to save her from them again, I'll do it. I'll throw her over my shoulder if I have to. I run after her, but just before I get to her, she reaches up and grabs hold of one of the branches of the climbing trees. She pulls herself up and disappears into the darkness above. From behind me I hear, "I've got to see too." Ronnie pushes past me and climbs up behind Emily.

"Are they nuts?" Vivek says. "I'm getting out of here!"

I look at Robin. She looks back at me. "Let's go," I say.

"Okay, Cousin."

Vivek is a few steps away before he realizes that we've taken to the trees with the others. He curses, looks toward the safety of home, stamps his foot, shakes his head at our stupidity. Then he follows us up.

I look down at Boris. He's growling, whining, pawing at the dirt. "Boris," I call down. "I'm fine. It's fine. Go home!" He looks up at me. I can see genuine concern in his eyes. "Go home!" I shout at him. He obeys and runs off down the path.

I take the right tree with Emily. Robin follows Ronnie up the left one. Vivek pushes himself into the crook between the two. The voices haven't followed us. They've stopped somewhere up around Whale's Jaw. But they're still screaming.

They do sound like children playing in the woods, but there is something else to them, some other quality that is impossible to put my finger on. Their voices are hollow. They sound like children whose minds have been torn apart and then sewn back to rag dolls. Unable to form words anymore, they simply scream out for each other, scream out and sing and laugh in the darkness.

"They sound like demons," I say. "They sound like devils. Playing in our woods."

Then I see something. In the dim light of those lanterns I see a large figure moving around the fire pit. The figure screams, and all the other voices go silent. He goes into a rage, furiously smashing at the lanterns and throwing our chairs off into the bushes. One of the lanterns catches fire, and in the flames' yellow glow I can see the thing more clearly. He looks as if his shoulders are covered with short, sharp antlers. His hips look more like haunches.

The Widow's Stone doesn't mark a boundary anymore. We went into his lair, so now he's come into ours.

He lifts his head. His chin is one long spike. He releases a sustained howl and then strides off up the hill. The voices answer, yelping as they follow behind.

The woods go quiet. After a few minutes Emily climbs down, brushes her hands together, and starts back toward Whale's Jaw.

"Where are you going?" I whisper, jumping down behind her.

"Where do you think I'm going?" she replies. The others climb down behind us.

"Are you crazy?" I ask her.

"No," she says, still walking away from me. "My shoes. I took them off when we started talking. So I'm going back for them. Oh, and they left one lantern burning, and I'd rather not see the woods burn down tonight. I'd also rather not go alone. I'd like your company. All of you. So come along."

I make myself go, and the others follow silently behind me. Once we're back, Emily picks up her shoes. I stomp out the smoking lantern, then check all the others to make sure they haven't caught fire. I'm not sure what I'm going to say to my father about this. There's only one that survived the destruction, swinging on a long branch and casting a shifting green light over everything.

"Now then," Emily says. "Who do you think did this?"

"Who?" I say. "What do you mean, 'who'?"

Vivek shakes his head. "You really are nuts, aren't you?"

Emily continues. "We all saw someone. The question is who? If we can figure out who they were, then I think everything else will fall into place."

"Who *they* were?" I ask. "You mean you didn't see him?"

"I told you, I don't know who they were. I couldn't see clearly enough. But I saw three, so we know that much."

I march up to her and grab her by the shoulders. She doesn't try to wiggle away. "Do you mean to tell me that you didn't see a creature covered with giant thorns?"

"Come on, Stucks, don't start that again," Vivek says. "In fact, let's all of us just get out of here before those things come back."

Emily takes my hands from her shoulders and then gently holds my forearms. "Things?" she asks Vivek. "What did you see?"

"I saw coyotes," Vivek said. "Five, maybe six of them. Running in circles around the pit. Look down! The tracks are all over the place."

Emily lets go of one of my arms but holds the other. "Of course there are animal tracks, Vivek. Boris has been here since Stucks came up to light the lanterns."

"I saw coyotes! Plural! With an *s*! Running in circles and yapping at each other's heels and making that god-awful noise!"

"Emily? What did you see?" I ask.

"I saw three women. They plucked the lanterns from the trees, blew out the candles."

"And this?" I say, pointing out the destruction around us.

"Well . . ." She hesitates. "Ronnie knocked his chair over. Robin hit a lantern. Perhaps in our panic—"

I spin around. For no reason, or some reason, I don't let go of Emily's arm. "Ronnie?"

Ronnie is cowering at the edge of the path, shifting from one foot to the other. He looks like he's about to be sick. "Can we go, please? I don't want to be here anymore."

Emily lets go of me and walks over to Ronnie. "What did you see, Ronnie?" she asks him, so quietly that I can barely hear her.

"Don't make me say," he whispers back.

"It's okay. Tell us."

"I saw babies."

Gooseflesh crawls down my arms, and I feel a muscle twitch in my stomach.

Vivek starts to shout. "Okay! Okay! This is so messed up! I'm getting out of here."

"Shut up and listen to him," I say.

"I didn't see what wrecked the lanterns and the chairs," Ronnie continues. "All I saw were babies. A fire started in the fire pit, a tall fire that lit up the whole area. And then something crawled over the rocks around the edge. It looked like a baby, only its legs weren't fully formed. It fell into the dust and wiggled like . . . like those eels we used to catch in the pond. Like those eels looked when they started dying in the sand. Then more started coming, a dozen or so, crawling up over the rocks and making those horrible noises and dragging themselves into the bushes."

I don't want to hear any more of what Ronnie has to say. I just want to get back home and get back inside the house. "I agree with Vivek," I tell them. "Let's go."

We all start to leave, but then Ronnie notices Robin sitting on the edge of Whale's Jaw. Her back is to us. She's crying as quietly as she can, hoping that we won't hear her. Emily goes over and sits next to her.

"What did you see?" Emily asks.

"No, no, no," Robin sobs.

"Tell me," Emily says, just as quietly as she did to Ronnie.

"I don't want it to be true. I don't want him to be so angry. Why does he have to hate us so much? Why would he want to scare us like this?"

"Who did you see?" I ask.

She turns around, wipes her eyes, looks directly at me. "You don't care. You're the only one who feels anything, remember? I don't have the right to feel anything because I don't know anything about trees or vines, and this place isn't mine and these people aren't my friends—isn't that right? Isn't that what you told me?" She starts crying again and turns away.

"Tell me what it was," Emily says to her. She places a hand on Robin's shoulder.

Robin leans into Emily and composes herself as best she can. "I saw Pete," she says. Emily holds her for a minute, then helps her up. They move down toward the path. I reach over and grab the last remaining lantern. I lead, using the lantern to show each of them the rocks and roots that might trip them.

But as far as I'm concerned, Robin shouldn't be crying.

I think she's just pretending. Just trying to get attention. And it works. Emily keeps an arm around her all the way back to the cottages. Vivek and Ronnie offer comfort with their silence.

And me? I'm left lighting the way.

11

Nana's Crow

I try to sleep that night, but I don't like what I see when I close my eyes, so instead I lie awake watching the ceiling. I can see the slight sliver of the moon through the branches of the pine trees outside my window. I lie back on my bed and pull the covers up over my lips.

"That's how they get you, Stucks. They get in through your mouth when you're asleep."

I know that the voice isn't in the room with me, but I hear it next to my head anyway. When we were kids, Pete and I used to sleep out in a tent in his backyard. He wasn't afraid of being in the woods at night. But I was. And Pete knew it.

"They're like elves, or little trolls," he told me on one of the first nights we were out there. "They come out of the woods at night. If they find you, they'll try to get in

155

through your mouth. But if you keep your mouth covered, they can't get at you. If they do get inside you, Stucks, they'll crawl up and eat your brains a little bit at a time, and you'll slowly go crazy. This one kid I know lost his mind and killed his whole family. He's in a crazy house now."

I remember wanting to run back inside the house, but I was too scared to even step outside the tent into the darkness.

"Of course, when you fall asleep, that cover may slip off your lips, so it's not the best way to protect yourself. There's only one thing that can really protect you from them."

"What is it?"

"You won't like it. It's terrible."

"What?"

"Well, if you gotta know . . . it's dog turds. You put them under your pillow at night, and you never have to worry about trolls."

I giggled a little, so Pete went on.

"Oh, those little guys just love dog turds. Can't get enough. They crawl up the bed to get you, and they smell those dog turds, and they forget all about little-kid brains. They grab those turds and take off. They're so happy, they go home screaming to all the other little trolls, and then there's a big dog-turd troll party. . . ."

By then I was laughing out loud, and then Pete was laughing too, both of us not able to stop, and I didn't even notice that I wasn't scared of being in the woods anymore. And if I did begin to get even a little scared, all I had to say was "dog-turd troll party," and we'd start laughing all over again.

Still, before I went to sleep that night I made sure that my chin was tucked into the neck of my sleeping bag. And I even did it some nights when I was in the house. Sometimes I couldn't get to sleep until that sheet was pulled up over my lips.

I still do it sometimes when I wake up from a nightmare, or sometimes at night when I get that feeling . . . that feeling that I'm not alone, that something unhealthy is nearby. I know I probably look stupid with the sheet up over my lips. Maybe there is a Pricker Boy, but there are certainly no demonic gnomes running around the woods, trying to get into my head and eat my brains. I know that, but I keep my mouth covered by the sheets anyway.

Sometimes you couldn't tell if Pete was trying to scare you or just trying to be funny. Whether he was trying to scare you or stop you from being scared. You had to be careful. He could be nice one minute, and the next he'd slash at you and slice deep enough to scar.

It had started small. Last summer Pete was fine on some days, not so great on others. He liked Ronnie's stories, and he enjoyed swinging from the rope swing that hung over the pond in front of Ronnie's grandparents' cottage. Some days, Pete accepted Ronnie as one of the gang.

But other days, Pete wasn't fine. A tiny match can set paper, which sets kindling, which sets logs aflame. Pete's moods were like that. On those days, it was always better for Ronnie to just go home and read a book or work on a new story and forget hanging around with us. Everybody got mad at Ronnie at one point or another. Ronnie's that kind of kid. He gets under your skin. He's a little too clean, a little too smart. It's like he thinks he's just a little bit better than the rest of us. Not a lot, but a little. And that was enough for Pete to really hate him on some days. Pete, who wasn't book-smart at all, and who didn't own a shirt that ever needed ironing.

Last summer during one of the worst heat waves we were all over at the rope swing. Pete was doing his usual crazy flips and dives. Sometimes it looked like he would come down in shallow water and snap his neck. Ronnie got hold of the rope and was about to swing out when Pete said, "Hey, Ronnie, do a flip. Just go up and flip backward into a dive."

Ronnie shook his head. "I don't do that stuff."

And that was it. I'm sure it was those five words that set Pete off. Something about Ronnie's tone that Pete didn't like. Something that registered in Pete's brain as, "I'll leave that stuff to dumb assholes like you."

"I don't do that stuff." Not "I can't do that stuff."

"I don't do that stuff."

A second passed, and in that second I could feel Pete change, feel his personality shift. Ronnie turned to jump, and Pete said, "That's 'cause you're queer." Ronnie stopped and blinked at him, then laughed a little and swung out over the water. I remember his skinny arms straining just from holding his own body weight up. He reminded me of a scrawny old man as he let go and flopped into the water. Ronnie always looks like that whenever we're swimming or climbing trees or running around. He's never been all that coordinated, and he always looks awkward when we get to sports and other physical stuff. His body favors a clean shirt and a good book. His movements hold no grace.

Of course, Vivek is no better. He swung out after Ronnie. Whenever Vivek lets go of the rope, he likes to stick out all his arms and legs and scream like a demented Tarzan. This time his flapping appendages and garbled yodeling ended with a crack as his body slapped the surface of the water. When he surfaced, he moaned, "Ohhhh. That one hurt." I knew that it wouldn't stop him from doing the same thing the next time.

I swung out next. When I got to the surface of the water, I could see Ronnie and Pete talking. Pete had this sick smile on his face. Then Pete swung out and did a flip in the air, the same one that he had suggested that Ronnie do. I climbed out of the water, and Ronnie shook his head. "Sometimes I hate that guy," Ronnie muttered, but I ignored him. I was hoping it would all go away so we could just go on swimming. I only wanted to swing and swim and try to stay cool in the sickening humidity.

Pete broke the surface of the water and shouted with joy, more to rub Ronnie's face in it than anything. He climbed out of the water, and Robin swung out. Pete started in on Ronnie again, and Ronnie finally said, "I wish you'd just leave me alone."

And Pete said, "That's 'cause you're queer."

It went on like that for a while. No matter what Ronnie said, Pete responded, "That's 'cause you're queer."

At one point Emily followed behind me, holding her nose and turning back to face the shore before doing a pin drop into the water. She surfaced, and before I could swim back, she caught me by the elbow.

"What's going on with them?"

"I dunno." I guess it was lie, and I guess I lied because I wanted to convince myself that I didn't know enough to do anything about it.

When we climbed out of the water, I heard Ronnie say to Pete, "That's a dirty word. I don't like that word." I winced when he said that. He sounded like a prissy librarian.

Pete responded, "That's 'cause you're queer."

A few minutes later Robin asked what time it was, and Ronnie said, "I think it's about three."

And Pete said, "That's 'cause you're queer." Every time Pete said it, he laughed at Ronnie. It was like those nights in the tent. I couldn't tell if Pete was trying to scare Ronnie, or if he thought it would make us all laugh. No one was laughing.

Finally Ronnie had had enough. He tried to kick Pete out of his grandparents' yard. He didn't want to look like a little kid saying, "You can't be in my yard anymore," but that's exactly the way it came out. "Why don't you just go home? I don't want you here anymore," Ronnie said. But Pete just laughed.

"What are you going to do about it, queer?" Pete asked.

Vivek jumped in. "Pete, when you say queer, do you mean that Ronnie's weird? Because let's be honest, we're all pretty weird, and I'm the weirdest. Or do you mean that he's happy? Because in that case we're all gay, and I'm . . . the absolute gayest!" Vivek leapt into the air like Peter Pan. As he landed he twirled, grabbing the rope swing and swooping out over the water, shouting with joy until he slapped the water in a full belly flop.

"What I mean," Pete said, smirking at the rest of us, "is that he's a fag." He sat down on the ground and started pulling up tufts of grass from Mr. Milkes's perfect lawn. "So why don't you kick me out of here? Run me out of town, Sheriff!"

"Pete, what's the matter with you?" Robin asked.

"Pete, what's the matter with you? Pete, what's the matter with you?" he mimicked right back at her.

"Pete, stop. Come back over to our house with me," Robin told him.

"No," he said stubbornly, sticking out his lower lip like a four-year-old.

"Pete, please," she pleaded.

Vivek climbed back up out of the water, and I could tell by the look on his face that he was annoyed that his antics hadn't put a stop to what was going on. All he had to show for his silliness was a red, bruised stomach.

Emily stared curiously at Pete. "Do you know where the word 'fag' comes from?"

"Don't care."

"I'll tell you anyway. 'Faggots' are bundles of sticks used to start fires. More specifically, the fires used during the Middle Ages to burn people at the stake for supposed crimes like witchcraft or homosexuality. Of course, in the Middle Ages people also burned polydactyl cats because they thought they were evil spirits."

"Poly-what?" Pete asked.

"*Polydactyl.* Hemingway cats. Boston thumb cats. Double-pawed cats. Let me make it simpler: cats that have extra toes. Would you call a cat a 'fag,' Pete?"

"Emily," Vivek said, "you're acting kinda queer."

"I suppose so," she said.

Pete just shook his head at her. He stood up. "So you think I'm gonna light Ronnie on fire because he's queer? Is that what you're saying?"

"I'm saying that I don't like words that suggest that people—or cats for that matter—should be burned alive."

"I don't care what words you don't like." He laughed. Then he looked at me. I think he expected me to be laughing with him. But the cold look on my face must have been the final straw. He started to walk off.

Ronnie should have left it at that, should have kept his mouth shut. Maybe seeing us take his side had bolstered his courage. "Not that it's any of your business," he said, "but I'm not gay."

Pete swung around. "Wanna prove it?" he asked eagerly, and he walked right up to Ronnie. I saw Ronnie take a step back, but Pete just grinned wider.

"Don't worry—I'm not gonna light you on fire." Pete smiled and a little of his trademark charm came back into his voice. That charm always worked on all of us, kept us all loving Pete even when he got into one of his moods. "Just hold your hand out, like this." Pete dangled his hand out, letting it go limp at the wrist.

"Cut it out, Pete," I said, but Pete ignored me.

Ronnie held out his hand, keeping his wrist rigid. Pete's arm flashed out, and he grabbed Ronnie by the hand from underneath. He didn't twist the arm, but he held the wrist tight so Ronnie couldn't pull away.

"Okay," Pete said. "First one to give in is queer? All right?"

Ronnie's brow creased. "Give in to what?"

Pete extended his index finger. It hung right over Ronnie's wrist, right over the spot where all the veins run near the surface. His finger darted out and scratched at Ronnie's skin with his nail. "See, you scratch at me. I scratch at you. We keep going until one gives in. Whoever gives in first is queer. It's called a fag burn. Didn't you ever do this as a kid?"

Ronnie's face looked like a sheet of ice had gathered across it. "No," he said.

"That's 'cause you're queer." Pete smiled.

"Come on, Ronnie," Emily said. She grabbed Ronnie by the elbows and tugged him away from Pete.

"No!" Ronnie pulled away from her, walked back to Pete, and grabbed him by the wrist.

I'm not proud of it, and I doubt that Vivek is either, but he and I both took a single step away from Pete and Ronnie, signaling to them that we weren't going to do anything to interfere.

Robin started crying. "Pete, don't do this! This is stupid! Ronnie, you don't have to do this."

"Yes, he does," Pete answered drily.

Robin shook her head and walked away.

"I'm not interested in watching this," Emily said, and followed after her.

"Well?" Pete asked. "First one to stop has to say, 'I'm queer.' "

Ronnie looked down at his hand. He looked back up at Pete. His finger shot forward and dug into Pete's wrist.

The two of them attacked each other. Pete dug into Ronnie's arm, and Ronnie just tried to keep up, digging as fast with his nail as he possibly could. Ronnie kept looking down at their arms locked together, focusing all his energy on doing as much damage to Pete as quickly as he could. In less than a minute, their skin got raw and shiny.

"Look at me, queer!" Pete shouted at him, and Ronnie pulled his eyes up to meet Pete's. It became a staring contest as well. Ronnie's eyes started to tear as the layers of skin fell away. Pete just kept smiling, that darkness growing on his face with every strike of his finger. I could tell that

Ronnie was scared, but he wouldn't give Pete the satisfaction of giving in so easily.

Their arms were shaking, their grips so tight I thought one or both of their wrists would snap from the pressure. It wasn't long before the blood started. First it was tiny droplets, but it instantly smeared underneath their fingernails, making it hard to scrape at the skin. Ronnie started to sweat, the tendons of his upper body standing out under the pale skin. Pete gritted his teeth and continued to stare at Ronnie, all the while trying to dig in harder. "I did better than you when I was in the second grade," he taunted.

Ronnie wasn't ever going to win, and he knew it. By the time he finally pulled away, their wrists were pretty raw. Ronnie gasped for breath, clutching at his wounded wrist. He looked right into Pete's eyes and said, "Fine. I'm queer. Is that what you wanted to hear?"

Pete turned and walked away through the woods. He got into the trees, turned around, and called back, "You're a faggot, Milkes!" Then he strutted off. I turned to say something to Ronnie, but Ronnie was already walking away. He was going to have to come up with some story to tell his grandmother, who would surely fuss and fret over him like a mother cat fretting over a muddy kitten.

Ronnie is still wearing that scar today. Since the start of the summer, he's tried to tuck it away whenever someone notices it. I guess to him it's a reminder of having to say those words. But not to me. It reminds me of the day that

Ronnie finally stood up to Pete, stood stronger against him than I ever have. I should tell Ronnie that, but I probably won't.

I don't know why I'm lying in bed and thinking about this again, but tonight it's probably better than sleep.

I drop my feet over the side of the bed, grab my book from the dresser, and lift the latch on the door to my room, being especially gentle so as not to wake anyone else. I'll read until dawn. I like a good sunrise.

I head down the hall and cross through the family room and am startled by the black figure seated in the front room.

The figure is looking out the picture window. For a moment I think I'm asleep, and that this is a dream and that whatever it is can stand up and do anything it wants to me. For a moment, my heart doesn't beat and I don't breathe. The figure turns toward me. "Stucks?" it calls.

"Nana? Nana, you scared the life out of me!"

She points a listless finger up at the ceiling. "There's spiders up there, Stucks," she says. "Get a broom and get them down for me, will you?"

I retrieve the broom. In her four-fingered hand, she's clutching her glasses, holding them tight to her lap. "Where are they, Nana?" I ask her.

"Up there." She points to the crossbeams that span the ceiling. "They're dirty. I don't mind spiders, but they leave webs and traces, and the dirt gets in them. Like charcoal. They spin charcoal."

I follow her finger and pass the broom over the spots she points to. "Is that better?" I ask.

"No. I guess . . ." Her voice trails off. "I know they're there, Stucks. But you tried. Thank you."

There are no spiders on the ceiling. There never are. The natural wood of the beams has knots and rings in it, and Nana sees figures in the patterns of the wood. Most often it's spiders, but sometimes it's other creatures. As a kid I saw them too, the way you would see shapes in clouds. I could see birds sometimes, and bats with huge wings. In one corner I had always seen a man screaming furiously at an invisible tormentor. I saw other faces too, and bees, and hooves. They were simply there, and even as a kid I never let them disturb my imagination too much.

I place the broom by her chair and sit on the floor next to her. "What are you doing up, Nana?"

"I couldn't sleep because of the crow. He wants my glasses."

"A crow?"

"He was in the ceiling before, but now he's out in the trees. He wants my glasses. I can't see without my glasses."

The things Nana sometimes sees make my father nervous. Once she saw an old woman in the backyard and went outside to invite her in for dinner, but there was no one there. Other times, she sees children playing. Dad points out that there's nothing there, that nothing could be there. With the best of intentions he tries to organize a mind that is slowly losing all sense of order, but it only reminds her of just how old and frail she's become, and she curls up inside when he does it. In younger days, she traveled the world alone by ship, car, plane, and foot, and she raised my father and my uncle on her own while working full time when Grandpa was in Korea. She will never come to terms with her withering faculties. So when she sees things, I let her see them. I never argue.

I reach up and take her hand. "Do you see the crow, Stucks?" she asks me.

"He's in the tree?" I ask.

She nods, pointing to the branches of the pines shifting with the night wind. For a second I do see something, a raven with harsh angry eyes and wide wings, looking straight down at the both of us. Then it vanishes, and there are only pine branches before me.

"I can't see him from here," I say. "But he won't get at your glasses. I'll make sure of that."

"Oh, he's a bad one." She shakes her head and clicks her tongue against the roof of her mouth. "He's looking at me with bad eyes. He wants my glasses. But he's scared of you, Stucks. He won't fly down as long as you're here. He's afraid. Oh, see him! See him! He just hopped over . . . over . . ." Her arthritic hand waves in the air, loses its focus, then falls to the arm of the chair. "I can't see without my glasses," she whispers.

"Nana, don't you want to go back to bed? I don't think he can get inside."

She considers it, then shakes her head. "I need my glasses. It's too much of a risk with him up there."

"What if I hold your glasses? I'll put them in my pocket, and then he won't be able to get them. He'll never come near me."

Nana's eyes brighten up. "You'd do that? Oh, Stucks, you're such a good boy. Thank you." She quickly presses her glasses in my hand, and I place them in my pajama pocket.

"I'll give them back to you in the morning."

"Oh thank you. I can't see without my glasses," she repeats.

I take her hand and help her get to her feet. We shuffle through the darkness to her room, and I help her get back into bed. I tell her where I'll be if she needs me, and then I return to the chair by the window. Her glasses safe in my pocket, I pick up my book and start to read, all the while waiting for the dawn.

12

The Numbers and the Glass

A couple of years ago Pete and I found an old Atari 2600 in his parents' basement. At first we had no idea what the thing was. Then Pete spotted the cartridges and the joysticks, and we realized that it was an old video-game system.

Luckily, his parents had an old TV in the basement as well, or we wouldn't have been able to figure out how to hook up the connectors. Even then we couldn't get an image. Frustrated, Pete grabbed the Space Invaders game cartridge, yanked it out, and then slammed it back in again. The screen flashed, and suddenly these chunky things that looked slightly like bugs started jerking their way across the screen. I pressed the button on the joystick and zapped one of them. I couldn't believe that anyone used to play those games. It was like playing with blocks, except that it was on television. One of the games was exactly that. You threw a ball against blocks. That was it. That was the entire game. Throwing balls against blocks.

Finding that game system was like discovering the sticks and hammers left behind by cavemen. We actually enjoyed ourselves, even though the TV was black-and-white and we had to whack it if the picture went out. Our favorite game was called Berserk. You were dropped into a maze and had to kill a bunch of robots. The robots shuffled like the monsters in old science-fiction movies where the actors were afraid they'd trip over their rubber suits. It was easy. The real fun of that game was laughing at ourselves when one of us accidentally got shot.

Pete's parents weren't home. I know because he started giving the video characters profane names and shouting at them when they got zapped. He never would have done that within earshot of his mom, but between us it just made it all the more funny. And my family couldn't have been around either. I know because of what happened next.

We were playing our bazillionth game of Berserk when Pete turned down the volume on the TV. He paused and listened, holding up his hand to quiet me when I asked him what was wrong. Then I heard it too. The whine of an engine fighting against its driver. Wheels spinning. The rise and fall of the RPMs as the gas pedal was rocked up and down.

Pete and I grabbed our coats and left through the basement door. It was one of those dry winter nights when the air slaps your cheeks as soon as you walk out. We hadn't even bothered to put on our caps or gloves, but we weren't about to run back inside to grab them. Somewhere down the edge of the pond someone was trying to drive a car out onto the ice.

Pete and I ran across the frozen ground toward the car. As we got close, the car's wheels must have caught hold of something, because the headlights bobbed and started moving across the ice. The car fishtailed out over the deeper water.

Dad had told me earlier that day that the ice was probably safe. He emphasized the word "probably" by saying it very slowly and then repeating it again in that annoying way that parents have of explaining why they're about to tell you not to do something. It's as if they think we're from a foreign country and that we're struggling with this troubling new thing called the English language. "So I think it would be better to wait for a few more days of cold weather before you go out there," he'd said.

That afternoon Pete and I had tested my father's theory by going down to the cove, out of sight of the house, and hacking through the ice with a hatchet. We stayed over the shallow water. We're not *that* stupid. But we also decided that the ice was a good six inches thick, which was plenty safe, so we did some runnin'-and-slidin' for a few hours. That's what Pete and I always called it. Runnin'-and-slidin', a name that avoided any unnecessary confusion.

Just in case, we'd stayed over the water that was five or so feet deep. Okay, maybe seven feet. Okay, maybe ten.

The car started heading out toward the center. Luckily for

the driver, the wheels lost traction again, and even though he gave it all the gas that he could, the car didn't budge.

Runnin'-and-slidin' over the shallows is one thing, but that car was maybe a hundred yards out in the darkness, and it wasn't smart to head out that far until the ice fishermen had been out there for at least two or three days. The ice fishermen are good indicators of how thick the ice is. If they're out drinking beer in the center of the pond while boring through the ice with a giant drill and they don't fall in, then it's probably safe. Even then I'd give the ice a good stomp every now and again to make sure that it didn't crack even slightly under the blow.

"Is this safe?" I asked Pete. My ears were beginning to sting, really sting, and I knew already that when I got back to the house and finally started to warm up, I'd get an earache like you wouldn't believe.

"Probably not," Pete said. "Not for us, and not for him."

I've never understood why ice breaking in movies sounds so lame compared to the real thing. In movies, cracking ice sounds like the crackling of dry leaves, just magnified. You hear a *crack crack crack,* and then one big *crack,* and then the water swallows a person or a car or whatever is stupid enough to be out on ice that even drunken fishermen would be afraid to walk on.

In real life, ice rumbles. It squeals in wobbling spasms that start at one end of the pond and ripple all the way across. Usually the spasms are harmless, just the ice shifting and expanding like miniature tectonic plates. But when the ice made those sounds that night, underneath the body of a car that was spinning its wheels, that was another situation altogether.

I stopped about thirty feet from the car. "I don't know, Pete," I said. "I think that thing may drop at any second. It could take us down from right here when it goes."

"Stay here," Pete said. "I'll go." He started inching his way forward, all the time calling out, "Hey!"

It was Hank Paulding's Impala. I could smell thick exhaust coming from the motor. It was a monster of a car, long and wide and a guzzler of gas. Hank always told us that he was going to fix the rust spots and paint it cream yellow and take it out to car shows.

"Hey!" Pete called out to him.

Hank stopped gunning the engine and rolled down the window. "Oh hey," he said. "Hey, hey."

"It's me, Hank. Pete?"

"Oh yeah. Pete. Hey, Pete." His voice sounded thick and sleepy. It was clear that he had found his way to the bottom of a bottle of something. "Hey, Pete, give me a hand. I gotta get out of here. She's back. I gotta . . ."

"I think you're stuck, Hank," I heard Pete say. "How about we leave the car here and worry about it in the morning? Come on, I'll walk with you back home." Pete spoke to Hank as if Hank were a kitten he was trying to coax down from a tree.

Hank started wailing. "No, no, ain't gonna go back, no way!" He started hitting the gas again. I heard ice spasms radiating out from underneath the car. One of them passed right between my legs.

Pete looked back at me and shrugged his shoulders. I thought he was going to walk back and tell me that we should just go to his place and call the police. If Hank fell in before they got out there, at least he wouldn't take us down too. But instead Pete walked right up to the open window.

"How about I give you a push, Hank?" Pete asked.

"Yeah!" Hank said. "We'll get it moving. You and me, Stucks. I mean . . . Pete? Is that you, Pete?"

"Yeah, it's Pete. Tell you what. You give it a little gas, and I'll go to the back and give you a push. But gentle on the gas, Hank. Just a little bit."

"Okay, just a little."

I thought Pete was crazy. Even if he did get the car moving, it would only send Hank out farther, and then Hank might hit a thin patch over one of the springs that fed the pond. Pete sometimes had a sick sense of humor, but this wasn't funny. It might even be murder or something. I ran up to Pete as he walked to the back of the Impala.

"Pete, what are you—"

"Stucks, stand here next to me. Hey, Hank? Stucks is here with me! We're going to push you together!"

"Okay. Good, good," Hank called back.

"Give it a little gas, Hank! Just a little!"

Hank pressed the gas pedal, but Pete didn't touch the car at all. He waited a few seconds while the wheels fought

175

the ice, then told Hank to ease it off. I heard more squealing and popping from the ice.

"I don't know, Hank," Pete said as he walked back to the open window. "Stucks and I pushed as hard as we could, but the wheels didn't budge. I have an idea, though."

"Yeah?" Hank said. His eyes were glassy from the booze. Tears had streaked his face.

"Yeah," Pete said. "How about this?" Pete's voice was still calm, as if it were a spring afternoon and Hank was just stuck in the mud. "I think your wheels have gotten too hot. I think they've been spinning so much that the heat's built up in the rubber. So now they're hot and they're just melting the ice and you can't get going over wet ice, right?"

"Yeah," Hank said. "Wet ice can grab tires on ice when it's hot. . . ."

I heard a sharp *ping* in the ice followed by several crunching rumbles. Pete shifted his feet from side to side. I saw his hands shaking. It was only then that I realized just how scared he was.

"So maybe we get out and take a little walk, and we let those wheels cool down. In twenty minutes or so the wheels will be cool"—the ice wheezed and then wailed like a giant banshee—"and we'll come back here and give it another shot. That sound good?"

"Uh, sure, Pete. That's a good plan."

Pete pulled open the Impala's rusted door. He quickly reached into the car, shut off the engine, and stuck the keys in his pocket. Hank stuck one foot out, but he kept slipping so bad that he couldn't even get the other foot out of the car.

"Stucks, I need your help here," Pete said desperately. I rushed over and we grabbed Hank under the arms. We pulled him from the car, and he immediately fell on his face, smacking his cheek against the ice.

"Oh, oh," Hank moaned. "Please help. I can't walk too good." He was bleeding out his mouth. The guy stank. It was worse than his usual stink. Now he had hard-alcohol breath on top of it. We reached down and hoisted him back to his feet.

"Cars are a bitch, huh, Hank?" Pete said as we stepped away from the car. He was trying to sound calm so that Hank would come along with us easily, but he was straining against Hank's weight. In my head I was pleading with the ice to hold out for another minute or two.

"Yeah, cars are no good," Hank slurred.

We were about ten feet away when the ice under the car started shrieking. I could feel the vibrations up to my knees. It wasn't just a single explosion this time, though. They continued in smaller, individual aftershocks as the fault lines expanded.

We started moving faster, but we had no traction, and Hank was dragging us down. I think . . . I think that for a second I considered dropping Hank and making a run for it. If it had been anyone else but Pete with me, I probably would have.

Thirty feet away and we heard what I can only describe

as a dragon groaning, and then the most terrifying sound yet. Water splashing.

The cracks were still traveling along under our feet. We let Hank fall to the ground and started dragging him by the shoulders of his coat, but we had waited too long. The ice under our feet split, and all three of us dropped down into the water.

It took a second for the cold of the water to hit me. When it did hit, it knocked the breath out of me as surely as a punch to the stomach would have. For a brief instant I remembered Ed Giles, our local loudmouth, telling me that "when you fall through the ice on a really cold winter day, you're actually better off, because that water is always going to be warmer than the air." Well, I can tell Ed Giles for a fact that when you hit the pond water in the middle of winter, the cold takes a quick breath and then starts ripping your life away. No exaggeration, Ed. I don't know what your winters are like down there in the Florida Keys. Up here, the cold air plays fair, but the water takes the cold right to your soul.

My legs were kicking against the water and the broken ice. It had to be less than ten seconds before I stopped feeling my legs altogether. I was flailing.

"Stucks!" I heard Pete shout. "Stucks, put your feet down!"

I barely heard him through my panic, but I did as he told me to do. My foot didn't reach the sandy bottom of the pond. But it did reach the submerged edge of Hank's rock pile.

Pete and I clawed over the rocks to the shore, pulling Hank along with us as we went. I looked back and saw the Impala slide sideways under the ice.

We dropped Hank and collapsed onto the ground. Our breath flew out in clouds. Behind us the pond gurgled and belched as it swallowed the Impala down.

"Hey, Hank!" Pete wheezed. "Don't forget where you parked!"

Once Pete and I got our breath, we helped Hank up and got him walking. We caught him whenever he stumbled. Our clothes stiffened as the water in them froze.

Hank's house is built on the side of a steep hill, and long stilts level out the front. The house loomed overhead, but the windows let out a lot of light from within. At night Hank's place always makes me think of a really bright streetlight. You don't want to look at the light, though, because Hank often walks around naked up there.

Hank looked up at his house and fell backward to the ground. "No, no, no!" he wailed. "I can't go up there! Don't make me go up there!"

Pete's voice was still soothing, gently coaxing. "But Hank, it's your house. And we can't go out driving any-more, because we don't know where the Impala is. You gotta go home."

"No, she's up there! She won't leave me alone!"

I felt my skin prickle, and it wasn't from the cold. Every once in a while Hank would tell us that his house was haunted by a pale, long-haired young woman. Sometimes he would wake up at night and she'd be standing at the foot of the bed, staring at him. Sometimes she would stand in the corner and wave her finger at him. Perhaps strangest of all, she would sit down and watch television with him. He spoke about her so matter-of-factly that we never considered that he was pulling our leg. We knew that he believed it, and that meant either that he hallucinated, which seemed beyond even Hank Paulding, or that his house really was haunted.

"I can't go back there!" Hank shouted. "I gotta get out! Where's my car? Stucks, can you see my car?"

"No, Hank, I can't," I said, and it couldn't have been any further from a lie.

"Come on, Hank," Pete said. "You gotta go home."

Hank started to crawl across the ground away from his house. "No, no! She's up there!"

Pete smiled at me. "Well, maybe it's not so bad. When was the last time you had a date, Hank?"

I laughed, but Hank was too far gone to catch the joke. "She's been following me all night. Right at my elbow! Her face is rotting but she keeps staring!"

"Damn, I'm cold," Pete said to me. "My coat's frozen stiff. Really. We need to get inside." He pulled at the edge of his coat, and it didn't bend. "Hey, Hank! What if I stay here with you, and Stucks goes up to your house to make sure she's gone?"

If Pete thought I was going up there alone to possibly

come face to face with a ghostly corpse with a rotting face, he had another think coming. "No way," I whispered.

"There's nothing up there, Stucks. The guy's drunk as hell."

"He's seen her when he's sober, Pete!"

Hank kept whining. "She keeps telling me I'm no good. Over and over, 'You're no good, Hank.' Where's my car? I gotta get out of here! Where's my car?"

It was no use. We couldn't get him to go back up to that house.

Hank passed out on the couch in Pete's basement. I grabbed my sleeping bag from my house and left a note for my parents, and Pete and I stayed up playing Berserk until we fell asleep on the floor in front of Hank. In the morning he was gone.

We decided that we wouldn't tell Hank what happened to the Impala. We were pretty sure that he wouldn't remember, and if he did he'd be too embarrassed to say anything to us about it. Chances were he'd think it was stolen or that he'd lost it in a poker game.

That was how a '72 Chevy Impala got to the bottom of Tanner Pond. And more importantly, that was the lonely, bitter night that I watched Pete risk his life to save a sad man who would have otherwise found his way down under the ice.

It wasn't me. I was just following along, and I was ready to run with the first snap of the ice.

*   *   *

I've been reading by the pond for only a few minutes when the Cricket sneaks up behind me with a bicycle horn and honks it right in my ear. I scowl at him. He sits down beside me and mimics my scowl face. Eyebrows dragging low, bottom lip jutting out, he sits on the ground beside me and pretends to angrily turn the pages of an invisible book. I laugh. I close the book and lay it by my side.

I wiggle my thumb and little finger in the air, then run my index finger across my outer ear, then finish by rubbing my thumb across the fingertips of my right hand. CRICKET, LISTEN TO STUCKS.

The Cricket lifts his fist and nods it.

I make the Cricket sign again, then shake my fist back and forth. I wiggle two fingers at the ground, then put my palms together and open and close them like a whale's mouth. CRICKET NO GO TO WHALE'S JAW.

"No more this summer," I add out loud, and he covers my mouth. He lifts his fist and shakes it back and forth.

I make the signs again. CRICKET NO GO TO WHALE'S JAW.

He again shakes his hand back and forth. He is in what my mother calls "toad mode," meaning that he is being a pain for the sake of being a pain.

I run my thumb across my fingertips again. Using both hands I pretend to pull my chest open. STUCKS AFRAID. I follow it with the original instructions. CRICKET NO GO TO WHALE'S JAW.

Again he shakes his fist no. He wiggles his pinkie and thumb in the air, shakes his fist, and pretends to split his own chest open. CRICKET NOT AFRAID.

I want to say something, but I have no signal for it. It's something that I have never asked him before. Unable to think up a sign and too annoyed to create a new pantomime for it, I speak out loud.

"Why?" I ask. I make the sign for his name, then shake my fist, then trace my index finger over my outer ear again. CRICKET NOT LISTENING. "Why?" I repeat out loud.

He doesn't cover my mouth. He just looks up at me and repeats his signs. CRICKET NOT AFRAID.

I make the sign for my name, then pretend to pull my chest apart. STUCKS AFRAID. I make a tight fist in front of my chest, then pull it apart again. VERY AFRAID.

We had all walked Vivek and Emily home on the night of the sounds. We were terrified, but we figured that it was easier to be terrified in a group of five than to force any one of us to walk alone. After they were safely in their cottages, Ronnie, Robin, and I made our way back down the hill.

In the days following, Robin tells me four times that she is not going into the woods again under any circumstances, not even to Whale's Jaw. For almost a week, no one goes into the woods, even in the daytime. Then Ronnie comes to me. I ask him what he wants, but he stutters, whispering so low I can't hear him.

"What do you want, Ronnie?"

"Will you do a widow's walk with me?" he asks.

"Are you serious?" I ask him.

"Yeah. Listen, I know you don't want to. But it has to be you. Emily will try to talk me out of it. Vivek will just make a joke. I can't trust him not to run away. Robin is too upset to go back there. But you'll understand. You know about bad dreams. And I know that if you promise me you'll do it, you won't run away on me."

"Ronnie, what happened?"

We are down at the water's edge. I'm sitting on the shore while Nana takes her daily swim. Ronnie sits down and lowers his voice.

"I've been having this dream, Stucks. A bad one."

Ronnie looks out at Nana in the water, and when he is convinced that she isn't listening, he whispers, "I've never had a dream like it before. It was one of those dreams that when you wake up you're not sure exactly where you are because it was so real."

"I know the feeling," I say quietly. "Tell me."

"It was just you and me in the dream. We were in your house. I don't know where everyone else was, but it was nighttime. But it felt like it had been night for a while, for days and days, and that everyone else . . . well, that they were all *gone*. And that they weren't ever coming back. It was like—"

"The end of the world," I say, nodding quickly. "Judgment Day. And everyone else had faced judgment except you."

"Yes! But . . . you didn't seem scared. You pulled out a piece of paper and wrote numbers on the page, but not in any order. 9, 3, 8, 2, 7, 5 . . . Then you took a clear glass and turned it over on the paper. We were sitting across from each other, and we each reached out and placed a finger on the edge of the glass. It started to move."

Ronnie looks around to make sure that there is no one in the bushes eavesdropping. I want to point out that the only person who does things like that is . . . well, Ronnie himself, but I figure it's best not to interrupt him.

"The glass chose five numbers before it stopped moving. Then you looked at me and said, 'Go ahead.' There was a phone on the table. I picked it up and dialed the numbers. But there was nothing on the other end. No sound at all. I remember laughing, and I said, 'Nobody home.'

"So we did it again, and this time it picked three numbers. You dialed this time, and you listened, and your eyes lit up. You passed the phone to me. I could hear static, and behind the static I could hear voices. Little kids talking back and forth to each other. Then we did it again, and it chose six numbers. I dialed. This time a voice answered."

Ronnie stops and grits his teeth. His voice quakes. "It was a kid's voice, but it was from far away, like he was on the other end of the yard and he was shouting over a storm. He said, 'Can I come visit you?' "

I look away from Ronnie and check on Nana. She is floating blissfully in the cool pond water. Overhead in the trees, cicadas buzz in the heat.

Ronnie continues. "I said, 'Who is this?' And the boy's voice said, 'You know who this is.' It sounded like a voice from Hell, Stucks. Worse than those noises the other night. It was like it was laughing at me. Then it said, 'I'm coming over for a visit right now.' I said, 'You don't know me.' And it said . . ." Ronnie fights against his shaking voice.

"It's okay," I say, "just tell me about it." I've felt the fear of a nightmare so strong it doesn't fade as the day goes on. I wouldn't wish it on anyone.

"It said, 'You bled out here. I can smell you. I know what cottage you're in.' He said it again: 'I can smell you.' Then the line went dead." Ronnie wipes his eyes and laughs nervously. "It's the same dream every night, every night since . . . well . . . you know. Last night I woke up, and I didn't go back to sleep. Unless we do something, I'm not going back to sleep at all. I'll stay up all night for days if I have to."

"Ronnie, if a widow's walk cured bad dreams, I'd have asked you to do one with me years ago."

"I know it's just a dream, but I want to do it anyway. Be my watcher while I do a widow's walk this afternoon. Please, Stucks."

I turn away from him, check on Nana.

"You said you'd do it, remember? When I bled out there?"

I nod. "Okay," I say.

"Just between you and me, okay? No one else needs to know."

"Don't worry."

Nana flaps and splashes in the pond water. "No one else needs to know," she sings. "No one else, no one else, no one else needs to know. . . ."

A half dozen thorn branches droop over the top of the stone wall around the Widow's Stone. I gently run my hand over them. They have the feel of plastic, and the plant they sprout from is shiny, as if it has been polished. I let the branches glide through my palm. I can feel their desire to cut me. I pull Pete's knife from my pocket, pinch one of the branches firmly with my first finger and thumb, and cut off about two feet of it. Then I realize that damaging the thorns might not be the best idea right now.

"I hope this works," Ronnie says.

"Ronnie—"

"It's just got to make me feel better," he says. "That's all, just make me feel better, let me sleep."

Ronnie pulls out a stack of postcards held together with a rubber band.

"Postcards? You're supposed to pick something that has meaning, Ronnie. Something of importance. If you want this to work, you have to—"

"I like them," Ronnie explains, avoiding eye contact with me. "They're from all over."

Now I feel stupid. When you've known someone since you were really little, you sometimes forget. You just take their families for granted. You never question. So-and-so has no father, so-and-so has two mothers, so-and-so has a brother and a sister, but they're not related because one's mother married the others' father. It's just the way it is. So I never ask Ronnie about his parents. I know that his father travels a lot for work, that sometimes his mother travels with him. Vivek said once that Ronnie almost never sees them. That's why he spends so much time with his grandparents. Those postcards do have meaning. Maybe a little pain too. I shouldn't have doubted them, and I feel pretty lousy about it.

Ronnie steps away from the Widow's Stone and then pauses. "Promise me one more time that you won't run away?"

"I won't. I promise."

"Okay," he says, more to reassure himself than anything else. I place my hand on the top of the Widow's Stone. Ronnie turns and starts walking.

I look at the field of thorns, all their branches intertwining in a heaving, swirling sea of pain. I imagine what it would be like to be dropped into the center of them. I wouldn't be able to get back to the Widow's Stone without substantial slices to my skin and clothes. I'd have to protect my eyes if I could. But I'm not sure that I could. Lifting my arm to my eyes would leave the side of my body open. . . .

Why am I even thinking about this?

I reach into my pocket with my free hand and pull out the ring. I rub the outside of it, feeling the gentle weave of the etching. Lately I've been fiddling with it more, rubbing the edge, hoping to wear the tarnish off.

A gentle breeze shifts the bushes, and one of the thorn branches rubs along my arm. I pull away. It doesn't cut me, but it leaves tiny red lines along the skin. Being careful to keep my hand on the Widow's Stone, I try to shrink from its reach.

Ronnie's made it about halfway to the Hawthorns. He walks quickly and cautiously, picking his way past the thorn branches one by one. The sun's out, and I'm watching for him, but he's still terrified. I know because I did the walk several times myself when we were little, and it spooked me each and every time. That dream freaked him out so much, I doubt it's any easier for him now than when we were kids.

There is something about the way Ronnie freezes on the path that stops my breathing. He has been moving too smoothly, and the way he is frozen there, his body locked awkwardly and his head turned to the side, tells me that something has gone wrong. I slide the ring back into my pocket.

I can barely hear him push my name up from his throat. He bends over. The postcards drop by his side. He turns back toward me. He is gagging. He retches on the side of the path. He tries to move forward, but the retching hasn't stopped. He vomits again. He inches forward, too scared to realize that he is shuffling through his own puke.

I want to move forward, but my legs don't respond.

"Stucks!" he calls out when the choking has stopped. "Stucks!"

I remove my hand from the Widow's Stone and force myself out onto the path.

"I'm coming, Ronnie!" I shout to him. He starts to run, using his forearms to push the thorns out of his way. I feel the thorns scraping along my own arms, and I regret having used those clippers on that branch earlier. I hear their voices in the back of my head. They hiss in unison. *You took one of our fingers. . . . How many can you spare?*

I get to Ronnie, grab his hand, and shout at him. "What's the matter? What's happened?"

He is sweating and wheezing. He looks back down the path. "Oh, Stucks, don't go! It's filthy! What it did, that thing is filthy!"

"Go back to the Widow's Stone, Ronnie," I tell him. "But don't you go past. Promise me you'll stay at the Widow's Stone. I need you to watch for me."

Ronnie seems to get his breath, and he stands up tall. He wipes his mouth. "Okay," he says, gathering himself. "Okay."

We separate. He takes my place as the watcher. My steps slow to a tentative crawl. I'm worried about the thorns, but I'm more worried about what I'll find farther on up the path. Whatever is up there, I want to glimpse it first and turn my eyes quickly away, then look back when I am ready. I don't want to be shocked like Ronnie was.

I turn to check on Ronnie. He has one hand on the top of the stone, and he has turned back to watch me. Still cautious, I take another step forward, holding my breath and carefully picking my way around the spot where Ronnie got sick. Keeping my eyes on the path and the thorns, I reach down and pick up the postcards. I tuck them into my waistband. I take one more step forward.

I can see it out of the corner of my eye, and I slowly turn my head to look, then quickly look away.

The death of a pet is horrible enough, but what I see doubles that horror. Triples it. It is an image that I will never forget, an image that I am sure Ronnie will never forget. Morangie, the Milkes family pet, the hunter, the cat who had beaten up poor Boris on more than one occasion, is lying in the thorns just off to the side of the path. Large portions of her are missing. She has been torn apart not by something hungry, but by something fierce and angry. I steady myself, then look back at her. I can see her back legs, but her middle has been chewed away. I'm not sure if her spine is still connected. Insects have gotten at her, and her open stomach cavity crawls with worms, flies, and maggots. Half of her head is also gone, and her remaining eye, as quiet as the moon, as still as a noontime shadow, stares at nothing.

"Morangie," I whisper. I look back at Ronnie, who is still watching at the Widow's Stone. I crouch down next to Morangie. I take off my T-shirt, then carefully reach through the branches and lay it over her. I close my fist over her head and gently lift her carcass. My hand expects some warmth. It expects the body to move at the joints. But Morangie is as cold as the ground, and with the exception of the nearly severed hind section, she is stiff. She doesn't feel like flesh, but not like plastic either. Wood is the closest thing I can think of, but still this is like something I have never felt before.

Pulling her from the bushes, I scrape my hand against the base of one bush, and my hand bleeds. The thorns are still quite alive. Morangie is stone-cold, but the thorns are still alive and ready to fight.

"What are you doing?" Ronnie shouts. "Just leave her!"

"I can't," I call back, wrapping her carefully in my shirt. I start back toward the Widow's Stone. "If we leave her, she'll just rot there. She'll become fertilizer for the thorns. She deserves better than that."

Ronnie nods. He keeps his hand on top of the Widow's Stone, but his eyes follow the wrapped thing I carry along with me. I know that his mind cannot connect this object to the warm, living creature that was his grandmother's pet.

"Go get a shovel," I say to him when I get past the Widow's Stone. "I'll stay with her. We'll bury her together."

Ronnie can barely take his eyes off her. I hand him his postcards. "Go," I say.

He nods and disappears down the path. I lay Morangie down on the far side of Whale's Jaw and sit next to her on the parched ground. Overhead the cicadas scream.

I look down at Morangie. "What the hell happened to you?" I ask her.

· Ronnie comes back with two shovels. "Let me pick the spot, okay?" he asks. We walk down one of the paths. He finds a small clearing, a place that is usually pretty sunny. "Here," he says, and sticks his shovel into the ground.

We work side by side without talking for nearly an hour. Stones and roots make the digging difficult, but obstacles do not stay in our path long. Ronnie kneels down next to stones and digs in his fingers around them, and when he gets a handhold, he tugs with all the strength in him, releasing small crying sounds as he strains. He hacks at roots with his shovel until they are severed, then he reaches down and tears them from the ground. At times I stand aside and let him do the job alone, holding his shovel and stepping away as he kneels and wrestles the earth with his fingers. Dirt gets ground into his clothes, dug under his nails, smeared up his arms. It even gets into the scar on his wrist, making it all the more noticeable, but he doesn't seem to care.

We create a hole deep enough to prevent any animals from digging Morangie up. I lay her in the hole myself, wanting to save Ronnie the horrible wooden feel of her body. I let him throw the first shovelful of dirt over her.

Ronnie forgets about the widow's walk. It wouldn't have helped him anyway. I think our situation is a bit more serious than that. I think so because the same thing has been happening to me every night. The same dream. Night after night. And if he thought his was bad, then I'm never going to tell him mine.

But I'll tell you.

In my dream I'm hiding in an unfinished room about

fifteen feet by fifteen feet. There's no plasterboard—in fact, the windows haven't been put in yet, and where they should be there are just square holes leading to the outside. There is no door. I'm alone, and this one boxed room is the last safe place. Everything else has been overrun. The locks on the gates of someplace worse than Hell have broken, and everything inside has gushed out and infected the Earth. Everyone and everything is gone.

For whatever reason, I am safe so long as I stay in that room. But outside the room there are things that want me to come out, or they want me to invite them in. I can see them moving around through the windows. They've brought my friends to the windows to try and lure me.

Vivek is dead, and they're dragging him around the outside walls, dragging him in circles over and over again.

They're just talking to Robin, but talking is enough because the things they're whispering to her are making her cry, loud at first, and then slowly weaker and weaker until her cries sound like strangled mewls.

Emily is still alive, but she can't be, but she is, but she can't be because those things have ripped her body apart, pulled her insides out, and they're crawling all over her. She's trying to scream, but they're crawling inside her mouth.

They have the Cricket, but they've turned him into something else.

They're forcing Ronnie to . . .

I don't want to talk about this anymore.

13
Flames on Water and Stone

Not one cloud has disturbed the sun all day. Another day's worth of moisture is being leeched away from the parched ground. A little more green is being sapped from the leaves and grass. The cicadas are screaming to each other in the trees.

We're all down near the water together, but no one is saying much of anything. Vivek is lying back in a lawn chair. Every few minutes he leans forward and scratches at his legs where the poison ivy used to be. Ronnie is pretending to read, but he hasn't flipped a page in his book for fifteen minutes. Despite the heat, Robin is wearing jeans and a sweatshirt, and she's just staring at the pond. I don't think she's aware that any of us are here.

The Cricket is the only one who seems normal, but he's certainly not going to break the silence. He's wading in the water, turning rocks, scooping up algae, grabbing at critters.

I'm sitting in a patch of sun next to Emily. My blood feels thick in my veins. My neck and shoulders ache. I have a slight headache, and it's making me nauseous. I haven't let myself sleep for two nights now. The buzzing of the cicadas feels like it's crawling over the surface of my mind.

Emily is wearing a one-piece bathing suit. She came down to swim but decided against it, so she placed a towel in the sun, lay down on it, and started shucking her way through a few handfuls of peanuts. Halfway through her snack she fell asleep, her head lolling to the side, one arm flopped up next to her ear.

The belly of her bathing suit is covered with peanut shells. I reach over and begin flicking off the larger shells one by one into the grass. The smaller ones I gently pluck and toss away. When those are gone, I decide that it would be best to just leave the dust of the peanut skins alone.

Emily's body jerks. She gasps. Her head lifts off the towel. She reaches up with one hand and grabs my wrist. Her other hand closes around my fingers. Her sudden grip pulls me toward her. It's as if she's grasping my arm and pleading for me to pull her up out of some deep pit. She shouts something I can't quite make out. She opens up her eyes and looks at me. "Stucks," is all she says. She rubs my hand, pulls it closer to her. She hugs my hand against her cheek. I feel a tear there. I've never known Emily to cry, even when we were little.

"Are you okay?" Ronnie asks.

Emily lies back down on her towel and shakes her head. "I try to stay awake, but I can't do it."

"What do you see when you close your eyes?" I ask, letting her cling to my hand.

She shakes her head again. "I don't want to say."

I squeeze her hand. "No one wants to."

"This has never happened to me before. I rarely even remember my dreams, and I've never had a nightmare." She sits up, brushing off the last of the peanut remnants from her bathing suit.

"I, uh, sort of, brushed you off," I say awkwardly, trying to explain myself. I point at her stomach and then the peanut shells lying in the grass.

"Yes, thank you," she says, then adds, "These nightmares are driving me insane. I don't know how you deal with it, Stucks."

"I'm used to them. Tell me about the dream. You'll feel better."

"Do you know the outside shower in the back of our cottage?"

I am suddenly as scared of listening to her nightmare as I am of having my own.

"I dream that I wake up. I'm in my own bed. It's morning, just like any other morning. I grab my bathrobe and go outside. I turn on the water, take off my bathrobe, and step under the shower. It doesn't even feel like I'm dreaming. It's so real, and it's so normal, at least up to that moment."

I don't need to know any more. I have a pretty good idea where this is going.

"Then the door to the shower is kicked open, and someone comes in, hits me in the back, and grabs me by the hair." Her voice trails off. I don't know how she can keep herself steady telling us about this. Knowing how vivid my own dream has been, and knowing how disturbed Ronnie was by his, I can't imagine how she can live through this each night.

"I guess that's it," Emily says. "You get the picture."

"Can you see who it is?" I ask.

"No," she says, but I'm pretty sure that she's lying.

I look around. We all look sick, all desperately tired. Except the Cricket of course. He looks fine. He comes up from the water to show me a handful of freshwater mussels that he pulled from the sand. He gives me a few.

"Is it all of us?" I ask. "I know about me, and I know about Ronnie." Ronnie sits up, staring at me as if he didn't want me to tell, but under the circumstances I think it's the right thing to do. "And now it's Emily."

Vivek's eyes are bloodshot. They jitter from side to side. "Every night I dream that insects are chewing at my legs. They're made of fire, and they burn and gnaw through my skin, into the muscle, and then they chew through to the marrow. I feel every bit of it. Even when my shinbones snap in two." He reaches down and scratches his legs again. I thought it was just the last of the poison ivy that was bothering him, but I guess I was wrong.

Ronnie relates the story of his own dream. As he does, Emily lies back down, placing her arm over her closed eyes.

"Robin?" I ask.

She doesn't look at us, doesn't stop staring out at the pond, but she nods. "But I'm not going to talk about mine, so please don't ask."

"What about you, Stucks?" Emily asks.

"I see us all standing in a circle, putting this all to rest," I say. I impress myself with how convincing I sound.

"*That's* your nightmare?" Vivek asks. "You wanna trade?"

"Stucks and I tried to get rid of mine," Ronnie admits. "I asked him to do a widow's walk, but all we found was the body of my grandmother's cat. Something had ripped her apart."

"Good God," Vivek says.

I look over at Robin, expecting her to jump in, to talk about how upset she is, to claim that she's more scared than anyone, but she doesn't move.

"I have an idea," I say. I start chucking the mussels back into the water.

I'm tentative. I have to sell this, and I'll only get one shot. "I think that my dream, as frightening as it is, is trying to tell me something."

"What's that?" Emily asks. I can tell that she's ready to analyze. She's "interested."

"First, we all need to admit that whatever this is, it's gone beyond anything that we can explain. There's no way to explain what happened to us in the woods—"

Emily breaks in. "It was dark. There was no light to see by. We were all frightened. We heard animals making noises."

"And you saw three women come out of the woods and kick our lanterns and run away. Now we're all having nightmares, the same nightmares each time we go to sleep." Emily doesn't have any response to that, so I continue. "If we can agree that we're beyond what can be explained, then maybe our response needs to include the unexplainable. The symbolic. The spiritual."

"The paranormal?" Emily asks skeptically.

"No, the supernatural. And when I say that, I mean it literally. Super, as in great. Nature on a deeper, more powerful level."

"You're getting this from your nana," Ronnie says.

Beside me, the Cricket nods.

"Nana once told me a story," I say. "She and my grandfather had a daughter after my dad was born. The child was stillborn. They were devastated. They had already named her. They tried to get over it, to be grateful for the two healthy sons that they had. But a year later, they still hadn't recovered, and their pain was beginning to wedge them apart. So on what would have been their daughter's first birthday, they rowed out to the middle of the pond. They brought a stack of paper with them. My grandmother took a piece of paper and wrote her daughter's name at the top, and then she wrote that her daughter would have been walking by now. She folded the paper into a cup, set it in the water, lit it on fire, and watched it float away. Then my grandfather did the same, writing down what her first words might have been. He placed his folded cup into the water and lit it on fire. They took turns writing out everything that they hoped their daughter would become as she grew older: her desires, her loves, her fears, her dreams. And one by one they set them adrift and watched the flames take them away."

The Cricket has stopped throwing mussels and is listening intently to me.

"It took them hours to let go of a future that would never be, but it worked. Grandpa and Nana were able to let go of her after that and get back to their family."

"That story always breaks my heart," Robin says.

Ronnie heard this story once when we were younger, back when we used to help Nana in her garden. He probably doesn't remember all of it.

"So you want us to row out into the pond and—" Vivek starts.

"Not the pond. They chose the pond because to them the pond had always been a place of magic. We need to go to our own place of magic. I say we go up to the Hawthorns at dusk tonight, we write our nightmares out on slips of paper, and one by one we burn them in the hope that they will be exorcised from our minds."

"But it was more than just that," Robin chimes in. "Don't you remember, Stucks? Nana and Grandpa threw sprigs of pennyroyal over the water to protect the baby from evil. They floated morning glories so that she would know peace."

"We don't have to worry about all that," I say. "Not to take care of the dreams. We just need a ritual."

I'm expecting them to scoff. Maybe not Ronnie, who has already tried the widow's walk. But Vivek might toss a joke out there. And this idea of placing ashes on the wind is not Emily's style at all.

But Vivek doesn't say anything, and Emily just nods her head. "I'll try anything," she says.

I don't feel well. It will pass.

I wait by Whale's Jaw for the others to arrive. I listen to the cicadas. It was better when I didn't notice them. They used to be just background noise, the sound track of summer, but lately I haven't been able to ignore them. Maybe it's the heat. Maybe it's the lack of sleep. But I keep hearing them, and when I try to focus on something else, they only seem to get louder. And it's not just the cicadas. The other day a hornet flew past my ear, and the sound seemed to slice my face. At night I try to ignore the crickets, but their chirping sounds like crying—relentless, monotonous weeping.

I can't not hear them.

The others show up just before dusk. Ronnie has brought a stack of paper and a handful of pens. We march up to the Hawthorns together.

Emily was curious the last time we visited the Hawthorns. She would say that she was "interested." This time she seems reverent. It's as if she recognizes the trees from somewhere, somewhere other than this spot where they have always grown.

"How do we do this?" Vivek asks. "Is there a script? We don't have to get naked, do we? Cover ourselves with pine sap and feathers?"

"If you're going to mock this," Robin says, "then we'd rather you just leave."

"Sorry," Vivek says.

Ronnie hands out sheets of paper and pens to everyone. I give them all instructions. "Everyone write down your dream with as much detail as possible. Write everything that you can remember. Don't leave anything out, because if you leave something out, if there's something so troubling that you don't want to put it on paper, then that one thing will stay with you. You won't be able to get rid of it."

I find myself in a dilemma. Do I write down the nightmare that I actually had, or do I write down the dream that I told them I had? I look around. Ronnie is scribbling furiously. Emily appears to be making a list. Vivek is done. It'll serve him right if he only gets rid of part of his nightmare.

Robin is writing and crying. It seems that she can't do anything without crying anymore.

I decide to write down the dream that I lied about. I can't purge the other one just yet. I'll need it later on tonight.

"Roll your dream into a scroll," I tell everyone after we're done. We stand in a circle around the offering stone. "There's a way to do this, and a way not to. We shouldn't make up our own rules. It's important that we do this right, otherwise it may not work."

"This is getting cree-ee-eepy," Vivek says. Robin glares at him and he quiets down.

"What we're going to do is—"

"Stucks?" Robin says. "Can I go first? They'll get the picture. There's no need to turn this into a big production." She turns to the rest of the group. "Watch what I do, do as I do, listen to what I say, repeat what I say, and go in order around the circle. Clear?"

Robin steps forward. I hand her a rag and some matches that I'd stuffed into my pocket. She places the rag on the offering stone and lights it. She holds her scroll up to the flame, and once it catches fire, she drops it onto the stone. "I release my pain into the fire. I trust the fire to turn my pain to ashes. I trust the ashes to rise onto the wind. I trust the wind to scatter my pain away."

She remembers the whole thing. I'm impressed.

She waits until her scroll has completely burned and then steps back to her place in the circle.

Vivek is next. "Whoa," he says. "What is this? I mean, uh, I read up on the Salem witch trials, and those people were crushed under stones, so—"

"Stop!" Robin says.

"Haven't you figured this out yet?" Emily asks Vivek.

"What?" he answers. "This is weird. This whole business has been freaking me out for days, and I don't see how this is going to help. Who made this up anyway? 'I trust the ashes to rise onto the wind'?"

Ronnie tries to explain. "Their nana . . . well . . ."

Robin turns to Vivek. "Let's just say that it's a family thing and leave it at that."

"Oh," Vivek says. He looks at Robin and me as if we're animals in a zoo. I'm not sure which one of us, me or Robin, is going to lose our patience first.

"Look, Vivek," I say, "either do this or don't. But make up your mind now."

"Okay," Vivek says. "But you might have to talk me through this. I didn't get everything on that first run." He steps forward, lights his scroll on the burning rag, then drops it onto the stone. "I release this pain to the wind."

"Fire," Robin says.

"Fire. I trust the fire to—to turn my—to turn my . . ." Vivek stumbles over the words. Now that he's in front of us, it's not so easy to make fun of what we're doing. This kind of thing has a way of flowing into you. You begin to feel it pulling your burden away. Pulling at you, like that thing that is pulling at me, making me feel sicker. It's something in my head, something loud. Something making my stomach tighten.

"To turn my pain to ashes," Robin says.

"To turn my pain to ashes. I trust the ashes to rise onto the wind. . . ."

"I trust the wind to scatter my pain away."

"I trust the wind to scatter my pain away."

Vivek watches his scroll disappear and then sheepishly walks back to his place in the circle.

Ronnie goes next, at least I think he does. I feel like I might fall over, so I can't be sure. Maybe not, maybe I missed him, because now I see Emily up there, see a flame in her hand, hear her saying something like, "Fire to speak to wind to speak to ashes to speak . . ."

She's getting it all wrong, or maybe I am, because she's too smart to get it so wrong. Too smart, too beautiful.

I can't hear her anymore. The screaming of the cicadas has grown too loud. The others don't notice. Why can't they hear it? I turn and look up at the trees.

The next thing I know Robin is staring at me. "Stucks?" she says, but I can barely hear her. I don't know what she wants, why she is calling my name.

"What?" I say. But my voice is drowning.

I feel someone grab me under the arm. I think that it's Robin. Someone else is on my other side; I can't tell who it is. They carry me. Robin takes my wrist and pulls it forward. I feel a burning near my fingers and instinctively let go of whatever is in my hand.

There are voices next to me. "He releases his pain . . . turn his pain . . . trust the wind . . . scatter . . . away."

The buzzing seems to crawl inside my head; it feels like a thousand hornets inside my skull. I open my mouth to speak. I think I'm shouting; I have to, so that they can hear me over the buzzing.

Hornets rush from my brain and fly out my mouth and nose and sting them all over their bodies and drive them to their knees drive them rolling to the ground burning stinging flames smoking blackened dying writhing everything ashes gone away—

I see black, I see lies, I see black, and I see . . .

"Stucks? Stucks, can you hear me?"

It's Robin. I can hear her. I can hear her fine. I just can't open my mouth yet to tell her.

The next voice I hear is Vivek's. "What happened? Is he possessed or something?"

"You're a fool," Robin answers.

"I'm serious. I'm worried about him."

I open my eyes. "Fine," I say. "I'm fine."

"No, you're not fine," Robin says. "You know it and I know. Nana warned us about things like this. We should have asked her to help."

"Just water," I say. "It was hot. I didn't drink enough water today. And sleep. I need sleep. We can all sleep now."

I force myself to sit up. Nausea almost knocks me back down, but I shake it off. I push myself to my feet, stumble a bit. Vivek catches me, steadies me.

There are leaves in my hair, dirt on my elbows. Grit is stuck to the backs of my legs. I notice for the first time in a long time just how dirty my feet are.

"Nope, nope, fine," I say. "Just need sleep. Water and sleep."

"Help me get him home," Robin says.

They're all concerned. I can see it in their faces.

By the time we step out of the woods, my head has cleared. I can walk on my own, so I pull myself from their hold. "I just got overwhelmed. It all swam into my head at once. I'll go home now."

"Thanks, guys," Robin tells them. "I'll take care of him. And with any luck, we'll all sleep better tonight."

"Your Nana wouldn't call it luck, would she, Stucks?" Ronnie says. There's something in his voice. Suspicion.

"You're right, she wouldn't," I say.

Robin and I walk away. At one point she reaches out for me, but I pull away from her. She holds her hand out behind my shoulder anyway, just in case I lose my balance again.

I look back at the others. Only Ronnie is still standing there. He's watching me. He knows something.

Back in the house, I head toward the bathroom. Robin asks me where I'm going. "The shower," I tell her. My mother asks me why I don't just swim in the pond instead of taking a shower.

"I'm kinda dirty, Ma. I'd like to use soap and hot water."

She's reading a book in the living room, and she doesn't even look up as she talks to me. "But it's been so dry, and we're beginning to worry about the well. I'd rather you went in the pond."

"You can't get clean in the pond."

"But, Stucks, you always used to—"

"I'm not going in the pond, Ma. I'll stay dirty before I go in the pond."

She puts her book down and looks up at me. "Okay, Stucks," she says.

"Ma, I am not going in that goddamned pond!"

"Oh, Stucks," Robin says. I think she's going to cry again, and at this point I don't really care if she turns on the tears or not. She's like a damned water park this summer.

My father stops what he's doing in the kitchen and steps into the living room. He is about to say something when my mother rises from her chair and comes over to me. She puts one hand on my shoulder and another on the side of my head. "Okay, okay," she says. "Take a shower. It's fine." She's petting my filthy, matted hair. Only a mother could love a kid when he's this dirty. "It's just that you used to love the water, and I'd hate to think that you're never going to go swimming again, that's all. I wasn't thinking."

I know I should apologize to her, but I can't. I turn away and go into the bathroom. I lock the door and turn on the water. I begin to peel away the rind of sweat and dirt and clothes that has attached itself to me over the course of the day. I step in and duck my head under the shower, spread my arms out, and turn my face up to the water. My ears fill with cottony silence. I let the water have my body because it doesn't feel like my body belongs to me anymore.

There are bees at the window. I can hear them buzzing, clawing at the screen.

14

The Pond in Black and White

Two years ago on the last day of summer, the others were up at their cottages packing up and getting ready to go home, and Pete and I were down by the water in front of his place. He had gone to his father's shed and grabbed an old grass sickle. It worked like a normal sickle, but you swung it like a golf club, and the blade flew horizontally through the surface of the grass and cut it to whatever length you wanted. Pete's dad never used the thing anymore, probably never had. He had a small lawn mower that gagged a bit as it cut, but it got the job done. As far as I could tell, the grass sickle served no real purpose. It was just one of those useless things that lean against the wall inside a shed.

Pete was swinging the sickle back and forth across a tuft of long grass at the edge of the pond. The grass started out at eight inches, then Pete whacked it down to six. Then three. Then a half-inch. When the grass was gone, he started whacking at the ground, spraying dirt out into the water.

I had planned on wandering from house to house to say goodbye to people, but Pete didn't want to do that. I asked him if he wanted to go dig around in the woods, but he said no. I asked him what he wanted to do, but he said that he didn't know. We wandered down to the edge of the pond, and Pete starting his aggressive pruning.

He kept smacking the edge of the sickle into the dirt, and when it bent he stood up and with both hands chucked it as far as he could out into the water. I watched it go, and its fall drew my eyes directly across the pond to Noah's Beach.

Noah's Beach had always seemed like some sort of foreign country where quirky people went about their business in strange and mysterious ways. On our side, we had our yards and our rope swing and our paths to the water. On their side, a half-mile away, they had grass and sand. We had the waterfronts of multiple cottages, and where we jumped into the water on any day depended on our mood. They had one single beach, with a raft that a couple dozen families from a couple dozen houses in some sort of association used. I never understood how someone could even consider swimming there. I mean . . . it wasn't home.

"You think we could make it all the way straight across to Noah's Beach?" I asked Pete.

"Hell yeah," Pete said. It was stupid of me to ask because the full answer was obviously, "Yes, but who would want to?"

"I think we could too," I said. I also thought that the swim might help to distract Pete from whatever had gotten under his skin. I stripped off my T-shirt, threw it on the ground, and then emptied my pockets onto it. I shouted to my mother up at the cottage.

"Yeah?" she yelled down.

"Pete and I are gonna swim down the cove!"

"Okay!"

She didn't need to know the truth of where we were going. It would only make her nervous. Little lies are good for a mother's mental health.

I jumped into the water, and Pete jumped after me. As we swam, we shifted to keep our muscles from getting too tired. We started with an overhand swim, then turned to the backstroke. Most of the time, we just did a cross between the crawl and the doggy paddle. It was the slowest, but it was also the easiest on the muscles.

I've never understood anyone who says they don't know how to swim. You just swim. You get in the water and you swim. To me, saying that you don't know how to swim is like saying that you don't know how to breathe or swallow food. Sometimes I think that when me and Pete were babies, our mothers threw us into the water in June and didn't come to fish us out until September. We could swim all day, and the idea that anyone would ever get tired and start to drown was the craziest idea in the world. In order to drown, either you had to get drunk and pass out in the water, or you had to get dragged under by a Volkswagen-sized snapping turtle. What other excuse could there be?

Swimming to Noah's Beach took a lot longer than we expected it to. The water can make things seem closer than they are, and when you only move a yard with each kick of your legs, the process can get pretty monotonous. It took us forty-five minutes to get over there, and while my legs and lungs could have gone on for longer, I was happy to finally be there.

We climbed up onto their raft to rest and wait for someone to kick us off their private beach. We got a look or two. Of course we would. We were illegal immigrants in cutoff jeans.

"What are you thinking about?" I asked Pete.

"Richie," he answered.

"Richie Nunes?"

Pete kicked up water with his feet. "Do you remember when he didn't come back?"

"Yeah," I said. The Nuneses had a cottage down past the Patels. One spring they sold their cottage so they could buy one on a lake a little closer to where they lived. A new family bought it, but the kids were really little, so we never got to know them all that well.

"I hated the start of that summer," Pete continued. "I remember asking my mom what happened to Richie, and she said that he wasn't coming back. Just like that. Like it was no big deal."

"My parents too," I said. " *'Oh, by the way . . .'* "

"I guess because our parents didn't know his parents, to them things didn't change much. Richie was just one of the kids, and there were plenty of other kids, so what did it matter? But to me, well, I hated the beginning of that summer."

"It felt like something was missing. Like a car—"

"With only three wheels, right?"

"Yeah."

"But . . . ," Pete said, and then he kicked at the water a little more before going on. "By the middle of the summer it was like he'd never been there. Like he'd been erased. And the next summer, when his parents let him come and stay with the Patels for a week? It was weird having him back. It didn't feel right. I felt better after he left."

I knew exactly what he meant. Richie wasn't part of the summer that the rest of us were building that year, and trying to wedge him into it just didn't feel natural.

"It was like he was erased, and what scared me about it was that it was so easy. It just happened. At the beginning I wanted to keep him. Like water cupped in my hands. I wanted to hold it there, but . . . And then it didn't matter anymore."

"If it doesn't matter, then why does it bother you?" I asked. It seemed like a logical question. I was hoping that the answer was short, because the Noah's Beach natives were starting to get restless. I heard one of them say, "I don't know who they are." I think they were trying to elect a border-control officer to swim out and send us back to where we came from.

"I can't believe that you haven't thought about this," Pete said.

I shrugged.

"If it can happen like that with Richie, then it could happen with any of them," he said.

Something cold crawled across the inside of my rib cage. I wished that I could get it out, but it was one of those thoughts that once inside would never go away.

"Think about it. Ronnie, gone. Emily, gone. Vivek, gone. Someone new might move into one of their cottages, and in no time they would have taken their spot. Or maybe some old folks would move in, and we'd just have more old folks and fewer kids. And you and me, we'd just rewrite things like our friends were never here."

I wanted to tell him that he was wrong, but I knew that he wasn't. Richie had been there, and Richie was gone. He probably has new friends at his new lake. By now his new lake isn't the new lake anymore. To Richie, Tanner Pond has become the old pond.

"This isn't going to last," Pete said. "And you'll never know when it's coming. Ronnie's grandparents might sell in a month—who knows—and then we'd never see him again. So maybe we should swim back, because who knows if today isn't really the last day for them."

Pete hopped off into the water, and it was a good thing, because some guy had started swimming out, probably to find out what we were doing swimming in their personal water at their personal beach. I jumped in, and we started back. I didn't know if we should swim faster or slower on the return trip. I wanted to go and see my friends, but part of me couldn't bear to look at them, just in case.

When no one is looking, I steal a canister of salt from the kitchen. I take a box of matches, a large candle, and a mason jar. I stuff these in my knapsack, then toss in a thick, misshapen ceramic bowl that I made in pottery class in middle school. I throw the knapsack out my bedroom window. I tell my parents that I'm going for a walk, grab my flashlight, and leave the house. I retrieve the knapsack. I go to the shed, siphon a pint of gasoline from the lawn mower into a water bottle, and close it off as tightly as possible. I wipe it down with a towel and wrap it in a plastic bag to keep the fumes away from the other things that I'm collecting. I walk around the house to Nana's garden.

The pond is black, but the moonlight on its surface is holy white, a flickering path across the water. I raise my hand for a minute, waving my fingers as if I can play the light like a flute. So long as the sky remains clear, that white will never leave the water alone, even if the wind were to pick up and try to peel it away.

Robin is down by the pond. I thought she'd be in bed by now. They should all be in bed now, all of them fast asleep, getting the first good night's rest they've had in a week. She's wrapped herself in a blanket. It's too warm for a blanket, but Robin has wrapped one around herself anyway, almost as if the sharp blacks and the whites on the water's surface are too stark for her to bear.

Her feet aren't in the water. In fact, I don't know that she's been in the water all summer long. I thought that she had, back when the poison ivy was burning into us all, or perhaps with Nana on one of her early-morning swims, but now I don't think so. I don't remember her ever going in at all.

Not that it matters to me. She has her reasons, and I have mine.

I find that I can do my work without the aid of the flashlight. I can see every bush around me. The mugwort that Nana says brings dreams of future events. The sage, which Nana asked Ronnie to plant because it's bad luck for a gardener to plant sage in her own garden. The mints, which have too many uses for me to remember. The yew bush in the back, whose every green needle is poisonous. Only the birds know how to eat the yew berries without killing themselves. When used correctly, they say yew can raise the dead.

I pull Pete's pocketknife from my pocket and cut handfuls of horehound. I clip the longest sprigs of rosemary that I can find. I place them carefully into my knapsack.

"I couldn't figure out why you lied to us."

I drop the pack, whirl around.

It's Ronnie. He's standing about four feet above me on the slight hill that runs up from our yard to the Milkeses'. The moon is behind him, so I can't see his face, just a black silhouette speaking from above.

"Why aren't you asleep?" I ask. It's more an accusation than a question.

"Because I was thinking about your nightmare. Vivek was right. Your nightmare was pretty mild compared to ours. All of us standing around in a circle, putting this to rest? That's a pretty convenient dream."

"Go home. Go to sleep." I grab the knapsack.

"Your nightmare should have been the scariest of all. Every one of your nightmares is."

"I said go home."

He's persistent. "You lied, didn't you?"

"I guarantee that you'll sleep well tonight." I shoulder the pack and head up out of the yard. He jumps down into the garden and follows along behind me.

"What are you up to, Stucks?"

"You're tired, Ronnie. Aren't you tired?"

"You didn't even mention the pennyroyal or the morning glories in the story you told us about your grandparents. Robin had to do that. It was almost as if you didn't want us thinking too much. You wanted it simple. Dusk, a quick burning, everyone goes home and goes to sleep. You even made up a dream that would tell us what we needed to do."

"How would *you* know what I dreamt?"

"Because when I first told you about *my* dream, you said it was like being alone on Judgment Day. And there was something about the way you said it. Like you'd been seeing something just like it, and you were relieved that someone else was seeing it too. What have you really been dreaming about?"

"I have all kinds of dreams, Ronnie."

"Come on, Stucks. What was your dream? What does the end of the world look like in your head?"

I spin around. "Go home!" I shout, and then immediately curse myself for raising my voice so close to the houses.

His voice is quiet, but I've never heard it more resolute. "No."

I march across the road. He stays on my tail the whole time, telling me over and over again that he's not going to leave me alone. I pick up my pace, hoping that I can lose him. He probably knows where I'm going, but if I can move fast enough, leave him behind, he'll get scared and go home.

Except that he won't get scared, and he won't go home. I learned last year that Ronnie is a hell of a lot fiercer than I give him credit for.

I'm nearing Whale's Jaw. When I get there, I really will turn on him, really will start screaming, because out here no one will be able to hear me anyway. I'll tell him what people really think of him. I'll be as cruel as I can possibly be, even if I have to make things up. I'll tell him that we never really liked him, remind him of times when we sent him home because we didn't want him around anymore. I'll point out that most people don't want him around, even his own parents, and probably his grandparents for that matter. I'll say whatever I have to say to turn him around and send him back home, send him crying if I have to. It doesn't matter if I believe what I'm saying or not, so long as he leaves the woods tonight.

But as I reach Whale's Jaw, I see two other figures waiting for us there. I try to run past them, but Vivek grabs me by the arm.

"Where you goin', bud?" he asks.

"Nowhere!" I shout, trying to shake him off. But he's stronger than I am. While I struggle with him, Emily pulls the pack from my shoulder.

"Give it back!"

Emily hands the pack off to Ronnie. She walks up and pulls Vivek's hand from my arm.

"Go home! Please just go away and leave me alone!"

Emily takes both my hands with hers, looks directly at me. In the moonlight, I can't see the color of her eyes, so I fill in the blue from memory. "We're not going anywhere, Stucks. And neither are you. That's just the way it's going to be."

"You're in charge now?" I ask her.

"If I have to be."

"Oh yeah?" It's stupid, but I can't think of anything else to say. She's taken the fire out of me.

"Yeah," she says. And for her there is nothing else that needs to be said.

I sit down on the edge of Whale's Jaw. "You can't be here. You just can't."

"Well, we are." Emily sits down next to me.

They shouldn't be a part of this. It's too dangerous. If I can't protect myself completely, then I can't protect them either. They should be home. They should be in bed. They should be away from this place. That simple purge of their nightmares should have sent them off into the deepest sleep.

"You have to let me go."

"Nope," Vivek says.

Ronnie starts sniffing my backpack. "He's got herbs in here."

"And I'm guessing that he's not going up there to make soup," Vivek says. "I don't know what the hell you've got planned. If someone explained it to me, I'm sure I wouldn't understand it anyway. But I do know that I'm not going anywhere until I'm sure that you're not going to . . . go up and make soup, or anything else."

"You all have to go home sometime."

"Nope," Ronnie says.

"Are you kidding me, Ronnie? You're lucky that your grandparents even let you out after dark! You know that they'll completely freak if you stay out—"

"I don't care," he says. It's dark, but I can see his eyes, and it's the same look that he gave Pete last summer.

Damn.

"What about those . . . noises? The women? The coyotes? The things wriggling out of the fire? If those things come back?"

"We don't care," Emily says, and she means it.

Three hours later, and we're all still here. Just my luck to have friends this stubborn. The moon has moved across the sky, but other than that nothing much has changed. I'm sitting in the dirt at the base of Whale's Jaw. Emily is right next to me. She has a handful of cheese crackers that she's pecking at, and to my surprise she offers me one. I accept.

Ronnie is staring up into the sky, watching the stars.

Vivek is balancing himself on one of the damaged lawn chairs. He's trying to hum a song, a Beatles song I think, but he doesn't know the tune. He tries to sing the words to help him figure out the tune, but he doesn't know the words either. It's a bit annoying.

"Stop it," I say.

"What tune would you prefer?" he asks.

"A very quiet one."

I don't need some song stuck in my head. My head is full enough already with the noise of the night woods.

I suppose I should be thankful. Their intentions are good. They're putting us all in more danger, but they came here because they think that they're saving me from something, so I guess that means that they're good friends. All of them except Robin, of course. She's back at the pond.

"Let's see," I say. "Who showed up to 'save' me tonight? Ronnie!" I point at Ronnie. "Vivek!" I point at Vivek. "Emily!" She's close enough so that when I point at her, my finger is an inch from her hand. "Who isn't here? Let me see. Hmm . . ."

I can see Vivek across from me in his lawn chair. He's shaking his head. "Bud, you just don't get it."

"What? It's no mystery. I can't stand her, and she hates me. I'm sure you guys have figured this out by now."

"Sure," Ronnie says condescendingly.

"You guys don't like her much either. You can admit it. You know where she was when I left the house? Where she probably is right now? Down by the pond, staring out over the water. As if her life is just too dramatic for words. She's all wrapped up in her own little world. She's blind to anything that doesn't have to do with her."

Vivek pretends to be alarmed. "She's blind? Like Amelia Earhart?"

"You mean Helen Keller, you idiot. And no, I don't mean literally blind. She just doesn't care about anybody but herself. If you were to break your arm, when you got back with your cast on she'd tell you all about the hangnail she had while you were gone."

Emily gives me another cracker, then asks, "You don't know anything about women, do you?"

I kick my feet in the dirt. If it were daylight out, they'd all see my face getting red. "Sure I do."

Ronnie laughs.

"Well, I know more than you do!" I shout.

Ronnie laughs again.

"You really think you know something about women?" she asks.

"Yeah," I say.

"Then why aren't you holding my hand right now?"

Ronnie goes back to watching the stars. Vivek joins him. Everyone is dead quiet for a full thirty seconds.

"Why?" I finally ask. "Are you scared or something?"

"Oh my God," Vivek says. "Look, Stucks, I'm not too bright, so if I have to be the one to point this out to you, then you're in deep trouble. You see, when a boy really likes a girl, and the girl really likes him, sometimes they start out by holding hands. And you should have started out a while ago."

Is he saying what I think he's saying? Do I like Emily? As in *like*? And what does this have to do with Robin?

I think another thirty seconds have passed, but I can't be sure. Vivek is trying to hum the Beatles again, and this time I recognize the tune.

"Hold my hand, Stucks."

I hold her hand. It feels nice. Vivek is right. I should have done this a long time ago. I've wanted to. I'm confused.

Vivek leans back in his lawn chair as he looks up at the sky. "Holding hands is fine," he lectures us, "but don't be getting all hanky spanky over there."

His hobbled lawn chair collapses under him. Serves him right.

Emily's hand is warm. No, not warm. Something different. Light. Touching her makes my fingers feel light. Weightless.

She gently squeezes my fingers. "You hold on to information that works for you, Stucks. And the rest you just ignore. Polish the blemish away like it doesn't matter. You erase it like it doesn't exist."

"What are you talking about?"

"Tell him," Ronnie says.

"Tell me what?"

Emily places her other hand over the two that we're already holding together. "Robin was in love with Pete. They were dating all last summer. They tried to hide it from you, but I don't know how you never saw it. We all saw it."

I pull my hand away from her. I look at Ronnie, then at Vivek. Surely one of them is going to chime in. One of them is going to say, "That can't be possible." One of them is going to say, "No way, Emily." But neither of them says anything.

"It was hiding in plain sight, bud," Vivek says.

Of course. I'm so stupid. I saw it, but I didn't want to believe it.

"She was so deeply in love with him," Emily says. "And she saw how that part of him that was always so angry was taking him over, how it was getting easier and easier for him to be cruel to people, and how he hated himself more and more inside each time that it happened."

Why didn't he tell me? I'm not sure whether I just said that in my head or whether I said it out loud to them.

"Come on, Stucks," Emily says. "Do you think that you're the only one who misses him? Do you think that you're the only one who is hurting because he's gone? He may have been your best friend, but that doesn't mean that there weren't other people who were crushed when he died."

And Emily is right about my ability to hold on to information that works for me and to erase the rest away, because just like that I erase away those last few sentences.

Around us the night insects get louder.

And louder.

And louder.

And I wish I could just stick my head underwater and let the water fill my ears so that I can't hear them anymore.

15

Purification

A slobbering tongue is lapping at my cheek. I open my eyes. Boris looks down at me. He whines.

I don't know how long I've been asleep. I don't know what time it is. I'm face to face with Emily. I turn to the other side to see Vivek's hairy toes. Ronnie's head is next to Emily's feet; Vivek's head is next to Ronnie's feet. They've got me penned in on three sides, but we—all of us—could only stay awake for so long.

And then along comes Boris, my faithful friend, to rouse me.

I scratch Boris behind the ears, tell him to follow me as I head back to the house. I make one more trip to Nana's garden, gathering up a few sprigs of lavender. Its smell seems to sink through the skin of my hands and settle on my bones; it's like smoke that leaves soft talcum on your arms, your chest, your face, inside your nose and mouth. According to Pete, lavender makes you smell like an old woman. To me, it smells like earth with all the grit rinsed away. It smells like the best that soil has to offer.

Robin is still down by the water. I don't think that she's fallen asleep. I should say something to her, but it will have to wait until tomorrow.

On my way back to Whale's Jaw I pause by the twin climbing trees and pull up some of the bloodroot that grows around the base. Boris sticks his nose in the leaves but can't figure out what I find there that's so interesting.

Once at Whale's Jaw, I quietly open my knapsack and take out my heavy ceramic bowl. I pull some leaves from the lavender and place them in the bowl. I take a match and light the leaves, letting the smoke drift over my friends. Around all of them I place pieces of the bloodroot. Even in the moonlight I can see the stains the bloodroot leaves on my fingers, stains that will show up red by the light of day.

Lavender smoke to deepen their sleep even further. Bloodroot to protect them.

Boris is thumping his tail in the dirt. "You're going to stay," I tell him. "Stay with them."

I turn toward the hill, but I hear him follow after me. "No. You stay here tonight. Bark if you see trouble. Wake them."

Listen to me. It's not like he's Lassie. He's faithful, all

right. But he's not smart. Still, he lies down at the base of Whale's Jaw, places his head on his paws, and watches me as I walk beyond the Widow's Stone.

The spikes of the Hawthorns are pretty horrifying by moonlight, and if they really are the three old ladies of the woods, then I hope that they too are fast asleep.

I place the bottle of gasoline in the bushes. I open my pack and take out the salt. I lay down a line of salt from tree to tree, forming a large triangle with the Hawthorns at its points. I scatter the horehound leaves along the salt lines.

I pull leaves from the rosemary, place them on the offering stone, and light them. The smoke wafts over the bark of each of the three trees.

Salt to form the walls. Rosemary to cleanse the site before evil is brought forth. Horehound to help banish.

I kneel on the ground outside the lines of salt. From my pack I pull out the candle and mason jar. I light the candle, put it inside the jar, and place the jar on the offering stone next to the smoldering herbs.

The wind picks up for an instant. The branches of the Hawthorns waver back and forth. The flame in the jar flickers slightly, but it does not blow out. It should remain lit for a good long time.

"The stars will pierce the darkest night, the moon above will give me sight. Mother bless this simple ground that evil led here may be bound."

I stand at the opening to the path that leads back into the woods. I close my eyes and concentrate as hard as I can. In my head I picture them all: the Cricket, my parents, my nana, Emily, Vivek, Ronnie, even Robin. I picture them all in my head as clearly as possible. I let my feelings for them fill me from my forehead to my feet and out to my fingertips. I imagine that they are a white light around me, protecting me from what is waiting out there. Though I go out there alone, I imagine that their light goes with me.

It's hard to concentrate with all this noise, this summer's never-ending cacophony. It's hard to picture all of them together, to feel each of them, to generate a white protective shell. It's there for a moment, but then it wafts away like vapors, and I have to draw it back together. I guess it will have to do.

I place the remaining lavender in my pocket. It brings sleep when burned, but when carried with you allows you to see spirits.

It's time.

I'm about to turn on the path when a piercing scream stops me dead. Somewhere far off in the woods, something cries out. I can't tell if it's a scream of joy or pain. The voice rises to a high pitch, then falls back down again, snickering and sobbing as it descends. The wind picks up, and with it the branches of the trees and the brush begin to sway. I wonder if I can really do this.

The first step is the hardest. I take another step, then another. I pause.

The woods go silent except for the swishing of the trees in the wind. I step forward again.

I use the clippers to cut the thorns away, clearing my escape path. When the thing that made that noise finds me, I will be able to move over fairly open ground.

Somewhere out there in the woods is a screaming thing, a thing with a voice like a child, but also like a wild animal. He could be around any corner. He could be hiding in any bush. For all I know he could be circling around to close in behind me. I try not to think about it, but the more I try the more difficult it becomes. I begin to feel like someone else is running the movie projector in my brain, and I'm locked down in the theater with no way to stop the images that are rolling on the screen. I can see in front of me by the light of the moon, but my brain takes what I see and adds to it, twists it, makes it appear to be more than it is. It lashes out and grabs at the most horrible thing that it can, and try as I might, I can't get it out of my head.

I reach out to grasp one of the thorn branches to cut it away, and I feel the cool, smooth skin of it. It feels like the leg of a giant spindly insect. In my brain, I see that I am not standing in the middle of a thorn patch in the woods. Instead, I'm in a nest of giant insects. Thousands of them, all moving slowly in the darkness around me, reaching out with long, spiked legs. They're waiting until I am far enough away from my friends that I can't call for help. The projector in my head runs the images in obscenely sharp focus. I hear the projector noise, but then it's not projector noise; it's buzzing. The buzzing of the insects. And in my head I can listen so closely, I can hear words in their humming machine.

Every branch I reach for has segments like a hornet's leg. It feels like they're shifting, trying to bend and pull away from me. I grab them tightly and cut them anyway. Every time I cut one, I see it oozing black blood onto the forest floor. Behind me a hundred stumps dangle, each one dripping and wiggling. I can see them, not with my eyes—the moon only shows so much—but in the projector in my head. In my head I see them clearly.

But I don't see the rocks or the hole between them.

My left foot comes down on a large stone on the path in front of me. It slips into the hole, jams in there. I fall forward, and then to the side. I feel something tighten and then snap.

I try to crawl but—

my ankle lodged in there—tug—doesn't move—

like a—trap has closed—like teeth—

like metal—I yank—

twice—three times and—it pulls—

Rock slides along the bone knub on my inner ankle, ripping off the skin, but I'm free.

But pain . . . sick . . . grit my teeth . . . sick . . . pounding my fist . . . dirt, but the pain . . . sick . . . draining . . . sick . . . not going away, it isn't going away, it isn't going away, it isn't going away, it isn't going away—

I get to my knees, but I can't see. I trip, fall again. Sick.

I feel so sick. All the white, light, life draining. I can't concentrate on the light.

I can't do this.

It hurts too much.

All I can do right now is roll around on the ground.

I can feel the darkness gathering on all sides.

It's as if the moon went out, as if it means to leave me alone out here in the dark.

Somewhere in my head a small voice, like a little boy's voice, reminds me that the moon can't make decisions. It's not on anybody's side. That small voice suggests to me that I've swum too far below the surface and I'm not seeing things correctly.

And with that, the moonlight comes back. It was the trees blowing in the wind and leaning out so far that for a moment they took the moon away. The moon hasn't left me, but she's fighting with the trees. I can see her. Even with the pain trying to push my eyes closed, I can see her.

Then I hear a sound that shouldn't be heard in the woods at night. It's a sound that might make a person smile in other circumstances. But this time I'm not smiling.

It's the sound of a playground, of children running and playing. But these children are doing the impossible. They're running on either side of me, straight through the thickest part of the thorn patch. They run as if they were in an open field. As they pass they giggle, call out to each other, but I can't make out any of their words, just their high squeals and tumbling laughter.

I reach into my pocket and pull out the ring . . . no, I pull out *my* ring. I don't know who it belonged to before, but it's mine now. I place it on my left thumb. It may be too big for my finger, but on my thumb it's snug. It could have been anybody's. It could be a person living or dead, good or downright evil. I shudder and immediately pull it off.

But it feels better—I feel safer and stronger—with it on my hand, so I slide it back over my thumb. I fidget at it with my middle finger, rubbing at the etching on the outside. I force myself to stand and find that I can keep my balance. But God this hurts. It hurts so much.

I limp forward toward the Hora House. Along the way I have to stop several times and wait for the pain to subside.

I reach the spot where the black puddle should have been, but it has long since disappeared during our dry spell, and all that is left is cracked mud.

As I make my way toward the old ruin, I realize that I'm not really limping anymore. It's more like I'm dragging my injured foot behind me, hopping with all my weight on the right leg.

I pass the ancient stone boulders. They remind me of beasts, not rock, not "glacial erratics" left ten thousand years ago. Something older. Dinosaurs. Dragons. Things that slept through the great Ice Age and still sleep. I can see the monsters softly breathing. I imagine that if I step on even the smallest twig, they'll wake and rise to their feet to see what has finally disturbed them after all these years.

I pass around the last boulder and into the hollow

where the remains of the Hora House lie. Everything here is quiet. No children. No creature crying out. I find a large rock near the open cellar and sit, grateful to take the weight off my foot. I sit and wait.

I pick a few pebbles off the ground and begin chucking them one at a time into the square wound that the foundation cuts into the earth. At first the silence and the wind calm me, but then I realize it isn't the wind. I can hear them swirling in the air above, can feel the air sweep across my cheek as they skim by. Together they cry with one voice, and then all at once they dive down into the foundation. The next thing I know, a hand is reaching up from inside the wreckage of the Hora House.

"Bastard," I whisper, and chuck the rest of the pebbles in his direction. I stand and move back up the path.

An arm appears and flexes, and with one push the Pricker Boy leaps up from the hole in the ground. He crouches down near the edge of the hole. He wheezes, he cries, and he chuckles. He sniffs the air for me.

He is about twenty paces away, and I can make out his outline in the dark, can see the tangle of sharp thorns growing across his back, can see the long spike of his chin pointing down at the earth. He appears to be crouched over and walking on all fours, more like a spider than a boy. His breath is broken and desperate. He finds my scent. He freezes and locks his eyes on me. He lets out a light, rambling whine, a tone that rises and falls and cuts through the darkness toward me.

I back away and stand among the boulders. I see him rise to his feet. He twists his neck, spreads his fingers wide. He stretches his back and his skin crackles. He wavers back and forth as if trying to get his balance after a long, dry, restless sleep. He treads sideways and falls down on all fours again. His legs buckle and morph and become more like an insect's than a human's. He moves on his knuckles, sniffing the air and clicking softly at me.

I turn to run back down the path, but my foot can't support my weight, and I end up facedown on the ground. I force myself to stand and try to steady myself, but I only fall on my face again. I can't walk. I turn around. The thing, the Pricker Boy, is getting closer. He is not bolting toward me; he is not running. With my leg gone, he could catch me in a second. But from the projector in my mind I can see, and I know. He's been waiting quite some time for me. He's been waiting since he killed Pete and dumped his body in the pond last winter. And he knows that I'm wounded, and that there is time, plenty of time, left for killing.

I begin to crawl, using my hand to steady myself as I lurch forward. I must look like an animal crawling along, broken and helpless. Behind me the Pricker Boy is laughing. He knows that my foot was torn apart by a trap in the woods. He knows about traps and what they can do to a leg. He knows from so many years ago, back when he felt the snap and crunch of his father's trap closing around his own ankle. But he had been saved by the thorns. I will not get the same treatment from them. Even the dead thorns can get at me. The branches that I clipped earlier cut into my palms as I struggle back over the path. The branches are still oozing, and my hands start to bleed. Our blood mixes together. Pain registers somewhere, but I don't slow down.

Twice I accidentally throw myself off the path and into the thorns, then scramble back out, my face and arms sliced by the bushes. At one point the creature is less than two yards away. I can hear his stuttered breathing, but he chooses not to pounce. He actually stops and stands. He watches me struggle to drag myself across the ground, cocking his head to one side as if wondering why I'm even bothering to try and get away. He is planning, I can tell, to pull me into the woods, to make me just one more voice in his collection of children's souls living in the broken-down basement of the Hora House.

I break into the clearing of the Hawthorns, and I scramble forward to the space in the center of my triangle. He enters the clearing, pauses, sniffs deeply at the air. Overhead the sky rumbles, and the wind rises until I hear the tree branches begin to crack together.

But he doesn't step forward. He just stares down at me, his anger rolling over me in waves. The spikes across his body glow orange by the light of the candle. Every inch of him is covered with spikes, even his eyelids, even the palms of his hands.

"Come get me," I taunt. "Haven't you waited for this? Haven't you always wanted one of us? I'm offering myself to you, offering myself in place of my friends. You can take me back there, lock me into that basement of yours like all the others you've taken."

He doesn't move. He walks around the outside of the Hawthorns, staring at the ground, smelling the air.

I find a fist-sized rock on the ground. I hurl it at the creature, and I must strike him dead-on because I hear a small cry and he jumps back a few steps.

"You're weak, aren't you?" I ask him. "You want me to believe that you're stronger, but you're just a frightened little boy, a little boy so easily fooled—"

He leaps so suddenly that I can't get out of the way. I'd let down my guard, and he knew it. I try to turn, but he grabs at my wounded ankle. Thorns rip into the already torn flesh. I scream. I kick at him with my other foot.

"I'm not afraid of you!" I scream. "I'm not afraid of you! I'm not afraid of you!"

He lets go for just a moment, leans back and prepares to leap, and that is all the time that I need to push myself off and up—

Even with my crushed ankle—with the blood, with the cracked bones—up and over without breaking the line of salt and horehound and out of the triangle.

I roll on the ground, and the pain is there, but adrenaline is driving it away. The Pricker Boy leaps forward, but just as I expected, just as I planned, he hits an invisible wall in the air and is knocked backward. He leaps again, but again is driven back. He howls against his cage, spikes snapping against the invisible wall as he struggles against it.

I crawl to the bushes and retrieve the gasoline. I get to my feet and face the creature.

He's desperate, scrambling in circles, hissing, kicking, throwing himself at me, but he's locked behind the wall of salt and horehound. He moves faster and faster, struggling so hard that I hear pieces of him cracking, as if he'd gladly break off one of his own limbs to get out of this trap.

I have to hold my voice clear, hold it steady. I want to shout, but I have to restrain myself or my anger could release him. "The fire of the sun has fed me. The light of the moon has guided me. The strength of wind has driven me. The might of thunder, of storm, I bring to crush thee. The stars in the sky I call down to swarm upon thee."

I pour a line of gasoline just outside the boundary of his trap. "The power of Heaven and Earth I hold over thee."

He begins to struggle so fiercely that I can no longer see him clearly. His limbs blur, his eyes become white coals smeared into smoking trails of hate. He throws his entire body at me, but all I see are blazing golden trails against the candlelight.

I can't help it anymore. I have to scream. "The power of fire I carry with me, and I use it to drive thee away forever!" I light a match and drop it into the gasoline.

I hear a loud noise like a giant sucking of air. A blinding flash of pure white light knocks me to the ground. The trap fills with flame. For a second I see the creature silhouetted against the fire. His head spins as the flames roar up. He looks pitiful and sad and beaten, a hopeless thing startled by the flash of light.

He stands erect. He is just as vulnerable as Ronnie, just as clever as Vivek, just as wise as Emily, just as kindred as Robin, just as torn as Pete. He looks just like me.

The flames widen, obscuring him from my view. I hear a horrible thrashing, an agonized creature crying with a child's voice. There is one last loud, tripping squeal, and then all is silent.

Flames crawl up the Hawthorns, devouring their thorns. Tiny sparks rise into the air, and where the sparks land, fires spring to life in the parched leaves.

Overhead, the sky rumbles. The wind stirs the flames. I call out to the fire, order it to recede, but it doesn't listen. I planned everything perfectly . . . everything but the power of the fire.

I try to stand, but I fall to the ground. The pain in my foot is too great. I cannot move.

The flames rise in front of me. With deliberate fingers the fire crawls past the boundary I drew on the ground. In the projector inside my head, I see that it is not the fire reaching out of the burning Hawthorns, but the Pricker Boy himself, born again in angry flame. He rises out of the hole and spills fire toward the vast sea of thorns around us.

The pain in my foot is unbearable.

I feel all the light going away . . .
blackness pours—
numbing—
projector flicker slows—
and then—

The Life I Didn't Save

I remember Pete sitting at the fire last summer and laughing at Ronnie over the flames.

"You claim that crap is true?"

"Okay, Pete," I shouted back. *"If it's all crap, why don't you go back there right now? Go back there in the dark and leave your pocketknife in the Hawthorns. If there's nothing to be afraid of, then you should have no problem walking alone past the Widow's Stone, back through the prickers all the way to the Hawthorns."*

I don't know what made me take Ronnie's side over Pete's that night at the fire, but I do know it took Pete by surprise. He started to pull away from us after that night, little by little. But by then we didn't mind.

He answered my challenge, though. He walked out in the dark and left the knife there on the stone in the

Hawthorns. And as far as I know, he never went back to retrieve it.

I saw him in the woods the next day. I think the only reason he came to the woods was to find me.

"I went out there. I did it," Pete told me, stepping close to me.

"I believe you," I said. I moved away from him.

He stepped closer. "Go out there and see. I want you to see it."

"No," I said. "I believe you."

"What are you going to do now? In a couple of weeks they all go home. Who's going to sit with you and tell little stories around the fire then?"

I didn't answer because I didn't know what to say. He was right. The others would go away and then it would be just me and Pete, and that thought was beginning to frighten me. Part of me wished it were Pete going away and the others who would stay through the winter.

He pushed me and I stumbled, flopping backward onto the ground and hitting my tailbone. It knocked the wind out of me. Pete waited for me to do something, but I just sat there in the dirt trying to get my breath. He walked away, shaking his head. As he passed out of sight, he leapt into the air, grabbing the hanging branch of a small tree and pulling the trunk toward the ground. He released it, jumping into the air as the tree whipped back upright. I heard him whoop and shout like he had just scored a winning touchdown, and then he was gone.

He showed up a few days later with some older kids from town. I knew them from school. They were the kind of kids who liked walking in numbers, walking in numbers and hoping to find smaller groups of kids. We were all swimming over near Ronnie's, and they showed up to use the rope swing. It became clear pretty quickly that they weren't there to swim. They had names for all of us. They made fun of Vivek's ethnicity, and they said things to Emily that I won't repeat. We left them alone there, all of us heading back over to my house and hiding inside. We watched them out the window and asked each other what had happened to Pete. It wasn't long after we left them that their fun ended, and they headed off into the woods toward Whale's Jaw.

After Emily and Ronnie and Vivek and Robin went back to their winter homes at the end of the summer, Pete seemed better. We hung around together, and sometimes it was almost like old times. Almost. Pete was never quite all himself. In school he hung around with older kids, and I knew that he started getting into drugs. He never tried to get me into them, though. One day his friend Dean tried to pick a fight with me, but Pete called him off.

Pete went missing in January. It was so cold then, and the weatherman said that it was only going to get colder. The daytime temperature was hanging around five, and the wind ran reckless across the flat, smooth ice of Tanner Pond. It cut into your blood no matter how many layers you put on. Ice punishes in many ways. I've slipped and fallen on the ice before, and given the choice, I'd rather fall on concrete or pavement any day. They'll both hurt you, but ice will shock your bones too. Ice waits a long time to come into being, and when it finally gets there, it doesn't care about you. It doesn't care about anything.

I was confused that January afternoon when I saw Pete head out onto the ice just as the sun was going down, but I didn't spend too much time thinking about it. I didn't care where he was going or what he was doing. I had already decided that I never, ever wanted to see him again, and that if he ever got close to the Cricket again, I'd kill him with whatever I could get my hands on.

I am conscious enough to know that the fire has reached me. One leg of my pants has caught fire, and I know that I should try and get out of the way, but my legs don't seem to work. A hand reaches out and grabs my elbow, yanking me backward. My arm twists. In the socket a sudden shock of pain—

Rolling my body in the dirt—put the flames out—foot flopping back and forth—too much—

He has me over his shoulder. He is running with me down the path away from the fire. I can taste the smoke in my mouth, and I feel pain in my chest when I try to breathe. The fire is following us, riding the wind and sprinting through the dry brush. We can keep ahead of the flames, but the smoke is another matter altogether. I can barely breathe, and I don't know how the person carrying me can run with no air and my body weight over his shoulder.

He has carried me away from the Widow's Stone, far beyond the Hawthorns. I can't tell just how far back we've gone. The fire has turned the night woods a haunting orange. It's not the peaceful glow of campfire light. It's the smooth, steady light of a fire too enormous to flicker or to play or to ever be controlled. I lift my head up. The fire has spread out across the thorn patch. The Hawthorns are triplet towers of flames reaching thirty feet into the sky. The woods squeal and cackle as they burn. The wind blasts through it all, urging the flames on toward us. Everything is dying in this monstrous fire. I hope that my friends got away safe, because I can't stand the thought of losing another one.

"Hold on," the person carrying me shouts over the flames. "It's almost here. It's coming." I recognize the voice as Pete's.

There is a sudden, violent burst of light, and a split second afterward a sound like a giant sheet of ice being cracked in two. A few seconds later, I feel the first huge drops of rain strike me. The thunderclouds split open, and we are drenched in a wall of water. The flames hiss, but the lightning and thunder drown their anger. The smoke grows thicker as the fire dies.

Pete runs with me through the mammoth boulders to

the Hora House, but he does not stop. He somehow squeezes us through the fissure in the stone wall and carries me over the jagged rocks to the far side of the hill before he puts me down. The wind continues to drive thick smoke at us, but the hill offers shelter from it. Pete and I huddle together against the rocks as the rain pours down. Soon muddy water is running down the sides of the hill over the loose stones. I am soaked through. I can't feel my foot anymore. I try to breathe in clean air, but my breath is broken by blackened coughs. As odd as it sounds, the dull throb in my shoulder feels good. At least it's not my foot anymore.

"Did I do it, Pete?" I scream over the rain. "Did I kill it?"

"Yeah, you killed it!" he shouts back. He leaves me then, walking up to the top of the hill to watch the storm.

I struggle along behind him, but I can barely move. It's a slow crawl over the rocks. Twice I ask him to come back and help me, but he doesn't respond.

A half hour later, it's all over. The rain has slowed to a steady drive, and the fire seems to have died out entirely. The night is dark again. I made it to the top of the hill, and Pete and I are overlooking the scorched thorn patch. Smoke continues to blow past where we are sitting, but the earth is too drenched for the fire to ignite again.

"Thank you," I say. "No one is going to believe this. No one is going to believe that you came out of the woods and saved me. But maybe if I tell them about this, they'll forgive you for all that other stuff, and you can come back again. It wouldn't be like before, I know. But maybe it could be something new, and—"

"Stucks, I told you. I'm never going back there."

"But you could. It's safer now. The Pricker Boy is gone now. You could come back."

"Stucks, I'm never going back there. I can't."

I don't want to ask him the question that's in my head, but I can't stop the words from coming out. "Pete, what were you doing that night out on the ice? I saw you go, and I saw what you were carrying. You have to tell me what happened."

"That's why you've been bugging me all summer? Messing with your nana's stinking plants? Stucks, you already know what happened," he says. "You have all the pieces, but you don't have the guts to put them together. You're too scared. You'd rather hide behind some bullshit ghost story."

"You have to tell me it was an accident, because I'm more afraid of what you did with that ax out on the ice than of any monster that might be here in these woods."

"You still think there was a monster?" he asks. When I don't answer, he slaps me hard across the face. "I asked you a question!" he shouts.

"Yes!" I scream back. "I saw him! And yes, I'm afraid of him! Why aren't you?"

"You want to know when I stopped being afraid of the Pricker Boy? It was one night last fall. I was just taking the garbage out. You know how your mind plays tricks on you and you begin to think about what might be there when you turn around in the dark? Well, I had just had a fight with my parents, and I was so pissed off, but it wasn't at them really. I was . . . I dunno . . . pissed and thinking about everything. And then I realized that it wasn't really anything that was making me mad—it was something in my brain. Something that just made me angry. Like I'd always been angry. It was the thing that made me want to hurt people that I cared about. Like the way my dad would do to me. Anyway, I got this quick flash thought: 'What if I turn around and the Pricker Boy is right there?' And then I thought that if he was there and he dragged me off into the woods, he'd be doing me a favor, 'cause there's plenty of real things to be afraid of that are a lot scarier than he ever was. I wish there *was* a Pricker Boy, because it was so much easier being scared of him."

Pete takes his index finger and stabs it into my temple. "Your Pricker Boy is only real here," he says. "Here. Only here. So kill him here."

I cover my head to protect myself from his jabbing finger. "But he has to be real! We all heard him!" I protest. "We heard him that night in the woods, playing with the souls of the children he killed. We heard him!" I can feel my anger beginning to rise, but I try to hold it back because I know that he won't like it.

"You know the sounds of the woods at night. Those other kids don't know because they live in the city ten months out of the year. Owls, bullfrogs, bugs that scream when the darkness comes. Coyotes sound like Hell itself when they start whooping, and you saw what happens when they get hold of a cat. Remember that night we camped in the yard, and two raccoons got in a fight and we thought it was witches screaming at each other? And what scared Boris that morning? A fox? Maybe a bobcat was in the area this summer. Hell, it could have just been another dog. It could have been anything."

"Anything? Then it could have been ghosts too," I say, almost begging.

"Believe what you want to believe. I don't care. I'm sick of arguing with you."

I begin desperately throwing out ideas. "It could have been a ghost, or maybe it was some kind of soul trapped out there. A wood nymph, or a demon. Maybe, just maybe, because we believed in him, that's what brought him to life, and—"

"Shut up!" he screams. "What do I have to do, Stucks? Tell me what I have to do to get you to leave me alone. Do you want me to tell you that it wasn't your fault? Fine, it wasn't your fault! But let me go. After all these months just let me go!"

"I should have . . . I should have done something. I should have done more. That's why everyone needed to be safe this summer. I should have done something."

"That night I disappeared? Even if you had said some-thing that night, you couldn't have saved me. It wasn't your fault. Let me go, because if you don't, I'll kick you away. I'll knock you down. I'll break your bones. I'll spit on you, I'll put out my cigarettes in your eyes, I'll do whatever it takes to get you to go back to your life and leave me alone."

I try to crawl away, using my elbows to drag myself through the mud. "I can't have imagined it all. I can't be imagining you right now."

"Maybe you are and maybe you aren't." It feels like he's really here, even though I know that he can't possibly be. "It doesn't really matter."

I want to ask him so many more things, but I can feel him fading away. I would give up anything if it would just keep him here for another five minutes, because I know that when he goes this time, he won't be coming back.

But I have to keep telling myself over and over again that he's dead. He's dead and gone. He's dead and gone. He's dead and gone.

"That's better," he says. "Hey, you keep my knife, okay? But don't stick it in a drawer somewhere. Use it for stuff. Whittle things with it. Carve your initials into the trees. You and Emily. In a heart or something."

His voice is getting farther and farther away; it's unraveling in the smoky air. "I'm sorry," he says. "Tell them all that I'm sorry." I can barely hear him. His voice is disappearing into the trees, disappearing into the brooks, disappearing into the old stone walls. He's calling to me from his backyard, calling to me from the top of Whale's Jaw, calling to me from the deep waters he was never afraid to swim out to.

"You're a better friend than I ever deserved," he says, and though he doesn't say goodbye, I know that I am alone.

Except for the sound of a dog barking in the distance, and the sounds of voices, calling my name, getting closer and closer.

17

Family Gathering

When Pete went missing last winter, the police and the firefighters searched the woods and the frozen pond, but they didn't find any sign of him. It was so cold those first few days. I remember wondering where he was, and knowing that if he was outside somewhere, he couldn't survive in all that cold.

Pete was missing for forty-four days. In March, when the ceiling of ice cracked on the pond and the wind drove the huge pieces over toward the dam, two boys were chucking rocks out onto the ice. They saw a bit of someone's jacket poking through the shifting chunks of cold glass. They told their parents, and within two hours the police had pulled Pete's body from the frigid water.

They never found the ax. I assume that Pete dropped it down the hole in the ice after he chopped his way through.

By morning the hole he had chopped had frozen over, and over the next few days the snow and the deep freeze removed all traces of what he had done.

I want to believe that it was an accident, that he went out there in a rage, and that he planned to take out his rage by swinging an ax against that implacable floor of ice. I want to believe that he just walked across a thin patch that wheezed and cracked and gave out beneath his feet. I don't like imagining him grasping and clawing at the edges of the ice. But the alternative, that he went through purposefully, willfully, is even more horrible to consider.

And until now I've never been ready to tell anyone what happened on the afternoon before he disappeared.

It's been three days since the fire, and in that time I've been questioned by police and firefighters and doctors. I told them what I saw in the woods. I told them how it shifted and giggled and wheezed and lurched at me in the darkness. Then they asked how I was able to escape the fire, and I told them about Pete carrying me to safety. After that they didn't believe anything I said.

I don't care what they believe. They weren't there. I was. I was there when the Pricker Boy crawled from the basement of the Hora House. I was there when I trapped him in the Hawthorns. I lit the fire, and I saw it get out of control. I heard the storm destroy the fire. And I was there when my friends found me, led by a fat, faithful dog who is right now asleep at my feet.

Everyone's over at my house. Ronnie, Vivek, Emily,

Robin. We're in the family room with my parents. Nana is the only one who isn't here. She's pretty ticked off at me. She lectured me all afternoon about messing around with things that I don't understand, about making things up as I go along, about taking things from her garden without asking her. Then she went outside and dug up some horseradish. She ground it and made me smell the stuff until I choked. Then she scattered it in bowls around the house. After an hour my father couldn't stand the smell anymore, so he declared the house clean of evil spirits and carried the bowls outside.

I've got my foot propped up on the footstool in front of me. The Cricket is decorating my cast using his Magic Markers. I've just finished telling them yet again what happened the night of the fire. This feels like an inquisition. I'm present for the discussion, but I'm also the subject of the discussion. I'm not happy being stuck out here on display in front of all of them.

No one speaks for a long time.

Ronnie clears his throat. "You keep telling us that he was there."

"He was."

Emily looks me right in the eyes. "That's not possible."

"Okay, Emily," I say. "Then explain to me everything that's happened to us this summer. Starting with the package in the woods."

"I can't," she admits. But she doesn't break eye contact with me. She doesn't back off.

"Look, I understand what all of you are saying. But if Pete wasn't out there in the woods with me, then who carried me away from the fire? Even the doctors said that I could barely crawl, let alone walk."

No one says anything. No one has an answer. I know in their minds they imagine that I somehow crawled away, or that in the face of the fire my instincts took over and I ran on my broken foot through the woods. But that isn't what happened. I know that's not what happened.

"I'm sorry that I put you through all this," I say.

Vivek cuts me off. "You kept things interesting." My mother glares at him, but the rest of us laugh.

Robin reaches out a finger, places it on my cast, gently taps it twice. "I'd do it again," she says. "So long as you promise not to light the woods on fire. I don't always like you, but when we all thought you were dead . . . well, it was the scariest thing that I've felt all summer."

I didn't expect her to be nice to me. I don't deserve it. I feel the urge to cry, but I bite it back. It flickers inside me for a moment before settling down.

"But there's one more thing," I say. "Cricket, come here." He ignores me, so I make the appropriate signs in the air. He puts down his markers and climbs into the chair next to me. "I'm going to tell them what happened," I say to him.

The Cricket stuffs his fingers in my mouth and buries his face in my shirt.

"No, I have to tell them," I say.

The Cricket lets out a sound that resembles a muffled "no." I put my arms around him and begin to tell the story.

"The day before Pete went missing, he was over here at the house. You guys weren't here," I said, motioning to my parents. "It was just me and Pete and the Cricket. We were playing some cards and listening to music. Pete had just heard this new song and he wanted to listen to the radio so that he could hear it again. He said it was awesome. He said that I would love it. The Cricket was humming and scribbling on newspapers with some crayons.

"I think that Pete'd been up all night with some of his friends. He smelled like cigarettes. I think they'd been drinking. When he first came over, he seemed really tired, but other than that he was . . . well, the regular Pete. But then something changed. Like that day he gave Ronnie that scar. Something just changed. The Cricket was humming, and Pete was trying to listen to the radio, and he was losing the card game, and he said to me, 'Shut that kid up.' "

The Cricket whines and hides his face more. I put my hand on his head and rub his hair.

"I tried to laugh it off. But I was scared because I could see him change. Could see it so clearly. I said, 'You know the Cricket. I can't make him do anything.' And Pete said, 'I could shut him up.'

"I just wanted to forget about it and get back to the card game and the radio. I said something about the song coming on soon, and Pete said that the Cricket had better be quiet by then. I said something again about not being able to shut him up, but Pete said he could do it. I didn't know what to say. So I laughed, and oh God I wish I'd never said it but I did. 'I'd like to see you try.' I just hoped that he'd start laughing too and say, 'You're right, Stucks, he never listens to anybody.' But he didn't."

I kiss the top of the Cricket's head. He isn't whining anymore. He's just lying still and quiet in my arms and listening.

"He turned to the Cricket and told him to be quiet. The Cricket didn't listen. It was almost like he wasn't even paying attention. And then . . . it was so quick . . . Pete reached out and slapped him on the side of his head. It was hard, and there was a sharp snap when he connected. I didn't know what to do. I remember standing up. The Cricket was too shocked to even cry. Pete screamed, 'You listening to me, kid?' and he whacked him again, closed-fisted, this time in the ribs. It knocked the Cricket right out of his chair and onto the floor. I don't know why it took me so long to react."

I can't look at my parents anymore. I can't even look at my friends.

"It was like I couldn't move. I wanted it all to stop. Then I saw Pete heading toward the Cricket again, and I jumped between them. At first I thought that Pete was going to come after me. But he just laughed. I wanted so bad to say something, but I couldn't think of a single word, and when I tried to open my mouth, all that came out was a shaky whisper. The Cricket was on the floor, screaming bloody murder. Pete went toward the door. He turned around again and said that if my parents did that to the Cricket every once in a while, the Cricket would do as he was told and we wouldn't have so many problems with him. Those were his exact words. 'Wouldn't have so many problems with him.' "

"I didn't know that we had many problems with the Cricket," my father says. I look up at him. His face is deep crimson and his eyes look ready to burst.

"Pete left, and I locked the door. I took care of the Cricket as best I could, and after a while I got him calmed down. He had a huge bruise on his side. I told him I was sorry and that Pete would never, ever come into the house again.

"About twenty minutes later Pete came back. He stood at the door and begged to come in. He apologized and shouted and pleaded with me to unlock the door. When I wouldn't do it, he started pounding on the door frame. He screamed at us to let him in. I remember I went to my room and got my baseball bat just in case he broke down the door. I was standing next to the door with one hand on the Cricket's shoulder and the bat in the other, waiting to see what Pete would do. Finally he went away.

"That night I saw Pete head out onto the ice with an ax. But I was so angry with him that I didn't care where he was going. I didn't even think . . . it never occurred to me . . . I swear it never occurred to me what he might do. But now it seems so obvious. And then he was gone. I supervised bath time and bedtime for the Cricket for the next week or so. That's why you guys never saw the bruises. And when the Cricket stopped talking, I told you it was because of a game we'd been playing."

Ronnie stops me. "Stucks, there's no way you could have known what was going on in his head. You can't read minds. I probably would have done the same thing."

"You can't say that. You don't know. You've never even seen the winter out here, Ronnie. Pete and I used to use a hatchet to chop our way through when we wanted to check the thickness of the ice. What else would he have gone out there to do?"

When no one answers, Emily steps in to speak for them. "You still couldn't have known."

They're right. But knowing that they're right and feeling it are two different things. "That's easier to say than to believe," I say. I have to force myself to believe it, though, because I'm not the only one who's locked this up so tightly, and if I can't accept it, then I can't help him accept it either. I pull the Cricket away from me so that I can look him in the face. "What happened to Pete. It had nothing to do with you. Do you hear me?"

The Cricket doesn't respond. He also doesn't stick his fingers in my mouth to stop me from speaking. I try again because I need to know that he hears me. "It had nothing to do with you. You didn't do anything wrong."

Ronnie comes over and kneels by the chair. He holds

out his wrist toward the Cricket. "You see this?" he says, pointing at his scar. "Pete hurt me too. He did it long before he hurt you. And it wasn't my fault either. Pete had problems, and those problems weren't because of me and they weren't because of you."

The Cricket reaches out with his finger and touches the scar on Ronnie's wrist. He pulls his finger away and looks at me. He leans in very close to me, puts his mouth up to my ear. He speaks so softly that I can barely hear him.

"Not because of me?" he whispers.

"Not because of you," I answer. I hug him tightly. "And not because of me."

And then the tears come, years' worth of tears, tears like the thunderstorm that killed the fire, tears so strong I'm afraid I'll never be able to stop.

First and Last

No matter what they believe, I know that Pete was here with me this summer. But I also know that this was his last summer. He's never coming back. I should have acted earlier. I should have asked him more questions about what was going on with him. Maybe if I'd gotten him talking, it would have taken a little off his shoulders, just enough for him to keep himself alive or to ask someone for help. I'll be asking "what if I had . . ." for the rest of my life. That question is never going to go away.

Maybe the monster from our childhood didn't get to Pete. Maybe he wasn't taken away by the thorn-studded boy who hid behind every tree, who scratched at the side of the tent just a little past midnight, who lay motionless in the deep muddy puddles waiting for an ankle to wade by. Maybe it wasn't him, but it was a bogeyman for sure that whispered in Pete's ear that January and convinced him to do what he did, convinced him to take the ax and walk off into the bitter cold by himself.

I saw the Pricker Boy a few nights ago. He came to me in a dream. He had grown older. Many of his thorns had fallen off, as if he were shedding scales. He stared at me, but I didn't fear him. He was gathering things together from the woods: bits of animal fur, a few sharp stones, a tattered baseball cap, two red-tissued packs of firecrackers, a frayed jump rope. . . . He was gathering them together and retreating into the woods. I tried to walk toward him, but he clutched his prizes tighter and skittered away. He went beyond the thorns, beyond the hill, beyond all the paths . . . he would keep going until he hit the swampy areas deep in the woods, and there he would get swallowed by the muck and the slime. I tried to call him back, to tell him that it was okay, that he could stay in these woods if he chose to, that no one would mock him or beat him or play with his trust, but he wouldn't listen. He just kept running away from me, running and coveting every toy and trea-sure we had ever left for him on the offering stone in the Hawthorn Trees.

I'm waiting now, waiting for this summer to end. When it goes, there'll be no more night breezes through the open window. No more charred hot dogs off of Dad's grill. No more baseball on the radio. No more bare feet. No more staying up late at night just to look for shooting stars. It'll all go: the frogs and the birds and the crayfish and the lightning bugs and the screaming cicadas. Sitting in the shade under the leaves. Lying back in the grass.

And my friends. They'll go too.

I'm scared of what's coming in their wake. I'm scared of the winter and the frost and the cruel ice creeping across Tanner Pond.

It's the last day of summer and I'm sitting by the edge of the pond. Boris is stretched out on the ground next to me. He's probably half-asleep, but if I were to say his name he'd leap to his feet, ready for action. My foot is propped up on one of the lawn chairs. The cast is a mash of bright colors, having been the Cricket's Magic Marker drawing pad for a few weeks now. He and I are keeping an eye on Nana as she swims. It's late August, but there's September in the air. That doesn't stop Nana. She's floating in the water and singing to the Cricket, asking him over and over to come in and swim with her. I'm surprised when I hear a splash, and I look up to see the Cricket paddling around with her, his legs kicking into the air over the surface of the water.

Emily shows up, blond hair pulled back in a ponytail, walking slowly. She is wearing shoes, which tells me that her family has finished packing and that she is coming to say goodbye. She sits down next to me, so close that I forget how to breathe.

"We're just finishing up," Emily says. "My dad is bleeding the water lines, and Mom is cleaning out the fridge. I've got everything packed."

Now that she is leaving, I can't think of anything to say. I take the gold ring from my pocket and begin moving it from finger to finger. I keep looking at that ring and my fidgeting fingers.

"I just wanted to stop over and say goodbye," she offers.

"I know." I raise my head to her.

The awkward silence that follows is one of the longest moments of my life, but it is also incredible, because she is looking right at me, and I am looking at her, and I can feel my heart thudding inside my chest. We listen to Nana and the Cricket splashing in the water. I look down toward the water just in time to see the Cricket place a hand on the top of her head. She goes under, pretending that he has dunked her. She comes up and spits water at him. "Stanley, you're just as bad as your grandfather was!" she says cheerily, gleeful about having a swimming partner.

"He's still not talking?" Emily asks me.

"He will. Eventually."

Another long silence.

"Did you notice anything strange about all those things from the offering stone in the Hawthorns?" Emily asks me. "Each one of them pointed."

"What do you mean?"

"Well, each one of them somehow related to someone else. Robin's comics were written with Ronnie. Ronnie's book had my clover in it. Vivek's baseball cards, you used them to help teach him math. Everything had to do with someone else."

"Almost everything," I say, looking down at the ring.

She reaches out with her finger and pulls my chin so that I have to look at her. She points to her neck. Her locket is dangling there. She holds her finger under the chain and lifts it. "Here, open it," she offers.

I reach out and try to get my fingers around the locket, but when they get close to Emily's body they fumble over the shiny metal. She rolls her eyes and reaches up and opens the clasp herself. "There," she says. "Now take it out."

There is a tiny piece of paper inside, folded over and over and over. It has yellowed over the years. I take it out and unfold it. Inside, written in the rounded script of a young girl, are four words: I LOVE STUCKS CUMBERLAND. I chuckle. Emily smiles. "Isn't that sweet?" she asks me.

I don't even know who leans in first. Our lips meet and hold. This is not the kiss of the schoolyard, the smack and escape that I had played as a child. This is obvious; this is intentional. This is feeling my heartbeat in my throat; this is suddenly being out of breath. We only kiss for about five seconds, then one of us laughs, and we break away. Neither of us can look at the other.

"That was, that was . . . uh, nice," I stumble. My lips are tingling, every nerve overloaded. They feel swollen, like all the blood in my body is rushing to my mouth to try to grab a little lingering piece of her.

I shake my head. "No, that's not what I want to say." I

wait until she can look at me. "I mean that was my first. My first real kiss."

She nods. "Me too. It was nice, don't you think?"

"Yeah."

"I've been 'interested' in kissing you for a while." She winks.

We laugh again.

The door to the back of the house opens. Robin steps out and, seeing us, mumbles an awkward sorry and turns to go back inside.

"It's okay," I say.

She turns hesitantly, looking to Emily for confirmation. At Emily's nod she comes out and sits in one of the chairs in the circle. I hear Nana singing down by the water. "Stucks and Emily, sittin' in a tree . . ." The song is interrupted when the Cricket dunks her again.

Ronnie appears, walking across from his grandparents' cottage with Vivek. They take a couple chairs, and Vivek eyes the ring in my hand. "I found a ring this summer too," he says. "It was around my bathtub." We all laugh.

"I'm still trying to remember which one of us left this out there," I say. "We all got our stuff back, but we still haven't placed this ring yet."

"I'm still wondering which one of us left that package out there in the Hawthorns," Ronnie says.

"I think it was Stucks," Robin says.

"What are you talking about?" I reply. "I told you guys—"

Emily jumps in. "We all said that we didn't do it. But one of us must have. Someone must be holding something back."

"Or forgetting. Not sure themselves," Robin says.

"Look," I say, "I know that I'm crazy. I don't even trust my own brain to tell me the truth anymore." Emily reaches over and takes my hand.

"I don't think you're crazy," Ronnie says. "I mean, I believed it, and it was my story."

"Stucks, I'm not saying you're crazy," Robin says. "But you've been walking in your sleep since we were kids. And you did wake up out there on the first morning of the summer. So who's to say that it wasn't you?"

"Because he didn't have the items to place in the package," Emily says. "The answer to the mystery is figuring out who would have been brave enough, even as a kid, to go back there alone and collect those items after they'd been placed out there. I think it was Vivek."

Ronnie chimes in. "He always made jokes. He never took it seriously."

"But I'm a big, fat, fraidy-scared coward!" he replies.

"And you were the one who first 'discovered' the package," Ronnie adds.

"It might have been Robin," Emily says.

"Me?"

"Yes. More than any of us, you hate going home at the end of the summer. Sometimes you've had to leave early, and I know you always worry about what you might miss—or that we won't miss you, which is ridiculous. And you're sentimental. You're the one most likely to collect mementos. To hold on to the summer, even if just for a little bit."

"And you, Ronnie," Vivek says. "You always knew that the story was . . . shall we say 'invented'? You could have been hiding in the bushes"—I start to laugh at the image, and Ronnie does too—"just waiting for the widow's walk to end so you could scramble out there and grab every little treat."

"And me?" Emily asks.

"Oh, that's easy," Robin says. "You're a girl. I can't believe that you'd give up that locket for good."

"And you're fearless," Ronnie says. I detect a note of envy in his voice.

"I suppose," I say, "that even Pete could have done it. He could have gone out there before he . . . before he . . ."

"Before he left," Robin says.

We sit staring from one to the other without anybody saying another word. I can hear Nana and the Cricket splashing to the edge of the water, and then Nana's voice as she talks to the Cricket and dries him off.

"So no one's going to admit to it?" Vivek begs. "This is damned disappointing."

"I'd rather not know." Ronnie smiles. "More of a mystery that way."

"Not me," Vivek whines. "I want to know. This sucks."

We all laugh at that. Then Vivek leans over and hands

me a piece of folded paper. I open it. On the inside are four phone numbers, each one written by a different hand. Below them Vivek has written, YOU NEED US, YOU CALL.

I swallow and nod, not looking up at any of them. I stuff the piece of paper into my pocket. I stare at my ring for a moment, and then I look away, down at the water. Nana is using a cane to steady herself as she navigates the roots. It's the cane that Mr. Milkes gave me so that I could get around better with my leg in the cast. She stole it from me earlier in the day.

"Nana, Mr. Milkes is going to want that cane back," I say.

"Let him come and get it," she says, and shakes the cane in the air toward the Milkeses' house. "That old man is a pain in the . . ."

She stops. Slowly she turns back toward me. She walks over quickly and leans over me. Water from her bathing cap drips onto my head. "Where did you get that?" she asks, her voice almost a whisper.

"What?" I reply, more than a little alarmed at the fear in her eyes.

She reaches down and clutches my hand, closing my fingers and hers around the gold ring. "Put it back!" she cries. "Stucks! Please put it back!"

"Nana, what's the matter?" I ask her. I take my foot down from the lawn chair and she sits in it, but she doesn't let go of my hand.

"Your grandfather's wedding ring! You have to put it back, Stucks! You have to!"

I don't know what to say. No one does. My mouth falls open. All this time I've had my grandfather's wedding ring in my pocket. The Cricket was only an infant when he died. I barely remember him myself, but all summer long I've been holding the ring that he wore for four decades while he was married to Nana.

The Cricket sits on the ground next to me, watching us all intently. He rubs Boris's belly and the old dog groans.

"Promise me you'll put it back!" Nana cries.

"This is Grandpa's ring?" I croak.

"Of course it is," Nana says. "I don't know how you got hold of it, Stucks. I took it to the woods years ago. It has to go back!" Desperate tears begin to swell in her eyes.

"I'll take it back. But why did you leave it out there?"

She draws a breath, relieved by my promise. "Because just before Grandpa died, he said, 'You watch after those boys for me.' After he was cremated, they gave me his ring. So I took it up to the Hawthorn Trees and left it on the stone there. To protect you boys. To protect all of you. From the things in the woods."

"What things, Nana?" Robin asks.

"Just things, woodland things!" Nana says. "I knew that when you got older, you'd be off playing in those woods. If I left it there, right in the middle of those three thorny witches, they'd have to protect you. I knew you'd always

271

come home safe from the woods. No matter what happened out there, you'd always come home safe. And you always have. All of you. Even poor Peter was safe when he was in the woods." She squeezes my hand even tighter, and I'm amazed at how strong an elderly woman's grip can be, especially a woman who is missing a finger. "You promise you'll take it back?" she asks me again.

"We'll all take it up there. We'll take it back there right now if you want." I don't know if she understands that the woods have burned, but I suppose it doesn't matter all that much.

She releases my hand, patting the back of it. "You're a good boy, Stucks."

The Cricket helps Nana into the house and then returns. He grabs my hand and pulls.

"Now?" I say.

He continues to pull.

Vivek and Robin have to help me—in fact, they almost have to carry me—up through the woods to the offering stone.

The ground is black for hundreds of yards around the Hawthorns. Beyond that the brush has been gnarled by the heat. The thorns are gone, burned back into the blistered ground.

Though their thorns have been burned away, the trunks of the Hawthorns are still there, reaching like skeletons toward the sky. But they're odd, stubborn old women. I believe next year they'll sprout again.

I lay the ring on the offering stone. It'll sit there all day and through the night, and maybe in the morning it'll still be there. Maybe it won't.

Everyone is staring at me, even the Cricket. He is absolutely calm, as if all of this is perfectly natural, as if placing Grandpa's ring in the middle of the Hawthorns is the most logical thing in the world for us to do. "Wanna know something?" he asks us.

Vivek's eyes shoot open wide. Robin, of course, is immediately ready to cry, and why shouldn't she? Even Emily is stunned. Ronnie leans in as if he needs to hear the Cricket speak again before he'll believe that it actually happened.

I just smile.

"Wanna know?" the Cricket repeats.

"What's that?" I ask him.

The Cricket beams. "Sometimes . . . I can fly."

"Now that's something that I'd like to see," I say.

The Cricket jumps up, throws his arms out in front of him like Superman, and makes a buzzing motor sound out of the side of his cheek. He runs around us and the offering stone in a huge circle, around and around and around and around. I reach out and tap his hand every time he passes by me, and with each tap I feel another old ghost flit away.

And for the moment anyway, as long as he continues circling us, this summer of loss will be suspended, and our friends will stay with us, safe from both the fire and the ice.

Acknowledgments

I began working on this book seven years ago, and it would be impossible to acknowledge all of the people who have contributed along the way. I apologize in advance for any names that should be, but are not, listed here.

First and foremost, I would like to thank my wife, Beth, who was silly enough to marry me, and who read this manuscript more times than I can count. Thanks also to Derek May for his research and boundless enthusiasm, and to Jack Harrison, the best critic that the early manuscript saw.

The following people have offered their assistance, friendship, and encouragement for many years: Julia Johnson; my fellow writers at the Buzzards Bay Writing Project, especially Kit Dunlap and Heidi Lane; Carol Malaquias; my brother, Ryan; my sister-in-law, Sandra; Ken Jenks; Terry Holman; and Pat Adler.

Cunningham's Encyclopedia of Magical Herbs by Scott Cunningham was an invaluable resource.

This book would not have been published without the

support of my agent, Kirsten Wolf, who not only chose to represent me but also pushed me to improve the manuscript when I felt I had given it all I could. And to Nick Eliopulos I offer my apologies about those nightmares.

And last but not least, thanks to Rachel, who is not only a great sister but, it appears, a fairy godmother as well. I love you, you little JT. Say hi to the koalas and kangaroos.

About the Author

As a child, READE SCOTT WHINNEM spent his summers in the earthquake-ridden, ghost-infested woods of East Haddam, Connecticut. From an early age his father instilled in him a love of *Star Trek,* comic books, and monster movies, thereby condemning him to a life of incurable geekiness. In addition to being a writer, he is an avid gardener, cook, and photographer. Both he and his wife are proud public school teachers. They live on Cape Cod, where they dig clams, correct essays, and, when necessary, reassure their overweight cat that she is a devastatingly attractive feline.